ANNE BOOTH

Anne Booth has had all sorts of jobs, including washing-up in a restaurant, working as a tour guide in a haunted almshouse, bookselling, lecturing at a university and being a long-term carer for her elderly parents. She has published 25 children's books and *Small Miracles* is her first novel for adults. Throughout her youth she wanted to be a nun, and although she has ended up happily married with four children, she still feels inspired by the many nuns and religious Sisters she has met.

ANNE BOOTH

Small Miracles

VINTAGE

3 5 7 9 10 8 6 4 2

Vintage is part of the Penguin Random House group of companies
whose addresses can be found at global.penguinrandomhouse.com

Penguin
Random House
UK

First published in Vintage in 2023
First published in hardback by Harvill Secker in 2022

penguin.co.uk/vintage

Typeset in 11.76/14.7pt Garamond MT Std by Jouve (UK), Milton Keynes
Printed and bound in Great Britain by Clays Ltd, Elcograf S.p.A.

The authorised representative in the EEA is Penguin Random House Ireland,
Morrison Chambers, 32 Nassau Street, Dublin D02 YH68

A CIP catalogue record for this book is available from the British Library

ISBN 9781529114874

Penguin Random House is committed to a sustainable future
for our business, our readers and our planet. This book is made
from Forest Stewardship Council® certified paper.

MIX
Paper | Supporting
responsible forestry
FSC® C018179

For Graeme, Joanna, Michael, Laura and Christina.
Thank you for being my miracles x

Prologue

And now she was flying, soaring, held in an almost unbearable tenderness. Green leaves and sunshine, birdsong and blue sky, up and up, the feeling filled her until she felt she would burst with love, that she could bear no more. And then the embrace relaxed, and the joy remained.

One

'Bother! What did Sister Basil think she was doing, Lord?' Sister Margaret looked with despair at the pile of unpaid bills and scribbled notes on her desk in St Philomena's Convent, Fairbridge.

The ledger, which for years had been neatly filled by Sister Basil, as the convent bursar, with columns of numbers under 'Income' and 'Outgoings', was an ink-stained mess, and she appeared to have given up completely in the last months, lodging a number of bills behind a small plastic statue of Our Lady of Lourdes on the window sill, and more in a plastic bag at the bottom of an old filing desk.

'What did she think would happen? That Our Lady would deal with them?' Margaret said to herself irritably, but then recovered. 'I'm sorry, Lord. May Sister Basil rest in peace. Thank you at least that the accounts haven't been going wrong for too long.' Margaret felt guilty that the last months of Sister Basil's life had clearly been so beset with anxiety. 'I'm sorry I didn't notice, Lord. But you know the accounts were never my job, and I've had my own problems. This last year wasn't exactly the easiest one you sent us. These last years, to be honest . . .' But before Margaret could launch into listing exactly what else had gone wrong for the Sisters of St Philomena, there was a very loud 'pop' from the kitchen followed by a wail of distress, and she found herself tearing out of the office and down the corridor, putting on a turn of speed that would have been impressive even in a much younger and slimmer nun.

She threw open the kitchen door, her heart pounding, to find Sister Bridget looking down miserably at some blackened, charred items on a plate.

'What's happened?' Margaret panted.

'I heard the Bishop particularly likes pavlovas. With the oven broken, I was cooking the meringues in the microwave,' Sister Bridget said. 'But there was a bang and some smoke, and now they are ruined.'

Margaret leant against the side, puffing a little. 'Thank God! Honestly, Sister Bridget. You gave me such a fright. I thought something terrible had happened.'

'It *is* terrible!' said Sister Bridget, indignant that the tragedy was being dismissed so quickly. 'I needed an especially nice dessert for the Bishop's meal tonight. Father Hugh is going to ask for some money to fix the leak in the church roof, and for a curate, too. I need those meringues.'

Lord, give me patience. Did she need to scream? Honestly, if I started to scream about the accounts, I would never stop, and then where would we be?

'Can't you do the rest of the cooking over at the presbytery?' said Margaret, more calmly than she felt, years of teaching coming to her aid.

'I'm already using the oven there for the roast tonight,' wailed Bridget, in uncharacteristic despair. 'I wanted this to be perfect. We have to soften up the Bishop.'

4

'Is there anything else you can make?' said Margaret.

'They're like gold dust in this diocese,' continued Bridget, not really listening, 'and we know that Monsignor Wilson wants a curate at St Anne's, and he has been playing golf with the Bishop. Father Hugh can't play golf at all, God love him. These meringues could cost him a curate. And he's worried sick about the leak in the roof. There's no money, Margaret,' said Bridget, her Irish blue eyes full of concern.

I know. Father Hugh isn't the only one. I know all about there being no money.

'If we replace the meringues, can you still make a dessert? Mr Abidi might sell some in Londis?' Margaret persisted.

'Yes, I can,' said Bridget, a little woefully. 'It's just I wanted to have made it all. It's such a special meal. I hate serving shop-bought things. I wish I had made a cake now.'

She sounded so disappointed that it twisted Margaret's heart. Bridget was a very good housekeeper to Father Hugh, and so many things in the parish would grind to a halt without her happy involvement.

'The Bishop won't know,' said Margaret. 'Come on, Bridget, let's see if we can get some from the shop.' She gave Bridget a quick hug.

They walked as fast as they could down the long drive leading from the large Victorian house. A blackbird flew up, crying an alarm. Without mentioning the problem, they both tried to simultaneously avoid and yet ignore the awful potholes and cracks in the tarmac and the overgrown vegetation all along the edges. No, Margaret agreed with herself, it wasn't working. The garden and grounds had definitely become too difficult to keep on top of, and so had the house. Upstairs in the convent, there were too many cold, empty bedrooms with heavy wooden furniture covered in dust sheets; downstairs more rooms than they could find uses for. It was all too much. The convent of St Philomena had, over the years, held twelve Sisters and a regular number of young women trying out their vocation, many of whom had left, some of whom, like Margaret herself, had stayed. Even with new recruits, however, the years had taken their toll, new crosses had appeared in the cemetery, and their overall number had dwindled to six. Then, in the space of a year, this last, awful year, with the deaths of Helen, Frances and Basil, there were only three – Margaret, Bridget and Cecilia – and Margaret, for want of anyone else, found herself reluctantly in charge as both Superior and Bursar combined.

They turned right on to the London Road, past other large houses of a similar age, now mainly split up into flats or student residences for the university, and down to Mr Abidi's Londis. There they found Sister Cecilia, the remaining member of the Order, who was already prayerfully queuing, as she did every Friday, for her lottery ticket. From the moment it had started the previous November, Sister Cecilia had been sure that God would use it to help them, and five months of winning absolutely nothing had not dented her belief. They found her standing behind Thomas Amis, who was himself second in the queue behind a student. Kind Thomas, recently retired postman and friend of the Sisters of St Philomena, had started coming over to the convent regularly, and was doing his best to bring the grounds back into shape this year, but as hard as he worked, it was not a job for one man, and large parts of the garden which had kept so many Sisters busy over the years, had now run wild.

'Hello, Thomas, thanks a million again for the work today,' said Sister Bridget. 'The microwave has broken and I'm buying meringues for the Bishop's dessert,' she explained to Sister

Cecilia, who, to be honest, wasn't that interested, and would rather not have had her prayers interrupted at this vital point in the queue.

'I'm so sorry, Sister,' said Mr Abidi, who had overheard, 'we don't have any meringues, but I could get some in for you?'

'Thank you, Mr Abidi. It's for tonight, I'm afraid,' said Sister Bridget.

Mr Abidi took the student's money and checked it, frowning slightly. The student waited. Mr Abidi was not someone you argued with.

'I don't understand. Why not buy a couple of yogurts?' said Cecilia, who had resigned herself to the fact that there was now no chance of fitting in another Hail Mary before she got to the front of the queue. She had prayed so hard all week, she had to trust that it would be enough.

Margaret winced in spite of herself as an outraged Bridget, hackles risen, radiating indignation, opened her mouth to answer. Just then, as the student's money was accepted and his bag handed over so that he could leave, Thomas Amis turned around in the queue and quickly interrupted, in his soft Geordie accent, before Sister Bridget could reply.

'I do have the chocolate cake you gave me this morning, Sister Bridget. It's a lovely cake. I'm sure it's good enough for the Bishop . . . ?' He turned to Sister Cecilia. 'Sister – would you like to go ahead? I'm in no hurry.'

Sister Cecilia nodded gratefully, glad to escape a cake conversation, and took out her list of numbers, solemnly dictating them to Mr Abidi, who respected her age and would not have dreamt of asking her to go away and fill out her own ticket first. He admired and liked the nuns, and did not question this little ritual every week. If he had had the power, he would certainly have arranged for the Sisters to win. Thanks to Sister Helen admitting his daughters to St Philomena's all those years ago, and his wife and him working in the shop all the hours God gave them to give their children all the opportunities and support they could, his girls had studied hard, gone to the best universities and were respectively now a pharmacist, a doctor and a lawyer. As far as Mr Abidi was concerned, the Sisters could do no wrong.

As far as the Sisters were concerned, especially Sister Bridget, Mr Abidi could do no wrong either. He worked so hard, up early sorting out the newspapers, staying until late, strict with difficult customers and teenage shop assistants, firm but kind to the rest, however tired he was. He was always open to a chat with Sister Bridget, who popped in regularly, determined to support him against the competing big supermarkets, who had greedily started opening on Sundays too, making life that much harder for the corner shop. Mr Abidi had never been to Ireland, Sister Bridget had never been to Pakistan, but they regularly and sincerely, if unrealistically, promised each other they would visit each other's countries of birth one day, and never failed to be delighted for each other and to send good wishes to their respective families when one or the other announced an imminent, precious trip back. After an interesting discussion about hard-to-get food, Mr Abidi, never one to run from a challenge, had even performed a minor miracle and tracked down some Kimberley biscuits from Ireland for Sister Bridget, which he then started regularly stocking as a small, profitable line that was very popular with his elderly Irish customers, who could not get them in any other supermarket. Sister Bridget was working on him to stock Tayto crisps, but they were proving slightly harder to source.

It was not Irish biscuits or crisps that were occupying Sister Bridget at the moment, however, but the Bishop's dessert, and this time Thomas Amis was the miracle worker.

'Oh, thank God! Thomas, that would be so kind!' said Bridget, clapping her hands in relief. 'Of course it will be good enough for the Bishop,' she said. 'I made the best cake I could, to thank you for all you do for us! I'll make another one for you. I still can't make it in the convent because the oven isn't working, but I'll bake another one, in the presbytery kitchen on Sunday afternoon.'

'Well, don't worry about that now,' said Thomas, calm as ever. 'As Rose always said, one thing at a time. Just you concentrate on the Bishop's dinner. I think getting a curate for St Philomena's gets priority. We can't have Father Hugh going under. I'll pop back home after this and get the cake, and drop it in at the presbytery. I might have a look at the oven too, if you like.'

'Thanks a million, Thomas!' said a beaming Bridget. 'We've still got a chance with the Bishop. I know he has a very sweet tooth.'

'I can't think of anything better than one of your cakes,' Thomas said as, courteous as ever, he gestured for a young woman to take his place in the queue rather than bring the conversation to an end too abruptly.

'Thank you very much, Thomas,' said Margaret fervently. 'It would be so helpful if you could look at the oven.' She didn't care that much about the Bishop's pudding, and like Sister Cecilia she was of the opinion that he could cope with a yogurt as well as the next man, but as the reluctant Superior of St Philomena's Convent, sad possessor of only three members, she did care about averting an almighty row between two of them. She was finding Bridget and Cecilia hard enough

9

to control already. And she dreaded to think how much a new oven might cost.

Thomas watched the three Sisters leave as the young woman in front bought her lottery ticket. The convent, and the school next to it, had been such an important part of Catholic life in Fairbridge. It was sad what had happened. He and Rose had been so happy and proud when their daughter Linda had got into the school, and then years later when Linda's daughter Sophie had gone in her turn. Things had to change, he knew, but it seemed a shame that there were no more nuns teaching there any longer Sister Helen had been outstanding, and he didn't think they had left Sister Margaret in long enough to give her a chance as head. Still, they were all getting older, like himself.

Sister Helen had thought the world of Linda, even after what had happened. And Sophie, of course, had done so well when she went to the convent school. She hadn't made her mother's mistakes, and had gone to university before settling down.

He wished he had Rose to advise him. She would have known what to do. Maybe he would ask Sister Bridget when he was next over helping at the convent or at the priest's house. She and Rose, two Irish girls working in Fairbridge House in the 1950s, had been like sisters. He was sure Rose would have confided in Bridget. Yes, that's what he would do. He didn't have a clue otherwise. Linda was shutting everyone out and nobody, not even Sophie, could get through to her. It would take a miracle to sort things out. Maybe Sister Bridget could smooth things over. He felt much better having decided on that.

'Thank you so much!' beamed the young woman to

Thomas, as she left the counter. She unexpectedly and proudly showed him a small engagement ring on her hand. 'I'm hoping my numbers come up. I'm getting married soon and it would be a big help.'

'Weddings are expensive, I know,' agreed Thomas.

'If I win, I'd like to surprise my fiancé and book somewhere amazing for our honeymoon, like Italy,' confided the young woman. 'I know he is worried we can't afford to go abroad. But I don't mind really. I just want to be married to him, that's the main thing.'

'Congratulations!' said Thomas, smiling at her. This time he knew exactly what to say. He loved to see an engagement ring. She had the same disarming openness and warmth as his Rose when she was young. Whoever she was marrying would be a lucky man. He certainly had been.

Thomas put his basket on the counter.

'Good morning, Mr Abidi,' he said.

'Good morning, Mr Amis,' replied Mr Abidi, who knew all his regular customers by name, and started to check out the shopping.

'You're Sophie's grandad, aren't you?' the friendly girl suddenly said, turning back to Thomas. 'I used to work with Sophie years ago at the Miller's Arms. I remember when you had your anniversary party there. How is Sophie?'

'I am. Thank you,' said Thomas. 'Sophie's fine. She's married, with a baby, and very happy.'

'Can you give her my love? Tell her Emily from the Miller's Arms says hello,' said the girl.

'I will. I'm sure she'd love to hear from you. Would you like her telephone number?'

Emily got out a little address book from her pocket and wrote down Sophie's new number.

'I'll definitely get back in touch after the wedding,' she promised.

'Good luck then!' Thomas said, as she left clutching her ticket, full of hope.

'Sorry to keep you waiting,' he said to Mr Abidi, who nodded. Thomas took out the bag, ready to load the shopping in it. It had been Rose's bag, given to her by the girls for Christmas one year because it had roses all over it, and he liked to use it. He hoped she would be pleased with how he was managing things in general. It was two years now since Rose had gone. She had lived to see Sophie married to Ben, a GP, and had held her newborn great-grandson James in her arms in the hospice a week before she died. Thomas swallowed, the familiar pain rising as he remembered her face, lit with love for the great-grandchild she would never see grow up. *Oh, Rose.* It still felt like only yesterday, and coming home without her smile to welcome him was still hard. It hurt him that Linda was so closed off, so private. Their daughter either worked late or stayed in her room these days. They just didn't communicate any more. Linda was acting more like a moody teenager than a forty-one-year-old woman. He was glad that at least he was a handyman and gardener and could help out Father Hugh and the Sisters. It was nice to go out and be useful to someone.

Later that night, the three Sisters gathered in the sitting room, having a fortifying cup of cocoa together. Sister Bridget was looking radiant. Her meal for the Bishop had gone extremely well, and he had even eaten two slices of her chocolate cake and asked to bring the rest home. Apparently, his own cook couldn't make cakes like that. Bridget knew that pride was a sin, but it was still nice to know, and she was well adjusted enough to know that recognising your own gifts was a good not a bad thing. Sister Frances, 'May she rest in peace,' Bridget added automatically, as she thought about her with love and gratitude, had taught her that. Back in 1968, when Sister Frances had been an energetic sixty-year-old Superior, inspired by the huge changes brought about in the Roman Catholic Church by the Second Vatican Council, the old divisions of 'lay' and 'choir' Sisters in the Order of St Philomena had been abolished. Sister Frances had recognised Sister Bridget's potential and encouraged her with her gifts: after sixteen years as a 'lay' Sister, cheerfully working in the laundry and on house duties whilst only the more educated 'choir' Sisters taught in the school, Sister Bridget, who had had to leave school in Ireland at fourteen and had always done domestic work before and after joining the Order, was suddenly allowed to do further training.

Thanks to Sister Frances, the Order had paid for Bridget to go to cookery college, where, as a mature student, she had blossomed, impressing everyone with her bright quickness and her ability to cook, especially her way of baking heart-liftingly delicious cakes; she had then gone on to be the convent cook and a popular part-time domestic science teacher at the school, until she'd retired at sixty to become the parish Sister and cook. Bridget knew, deep down, that kind Father Hugh, God bless him, didn't really understand just how good she was, but he ate up everything she gave him, and thanked her.

At least her parish bingo players understood: they were all determined to win the first prize of a cake made and donated each week by Sister Bridget, and they were just as important to Sister Bridget as any bishop. She made every cake as well as she could, which was why she knew that the one she had given

Thomas would have been good enough for the Pope, and she thanked God she had done her best, because she had had her reward today. She knew that religious life was not about fancy cooking – and that a retired postman had the same status in the eyes of God as a bishop – but it was still a pretty good day when a highly cultured man like the Bishop appreciated and praised your cooking.

Margaret looked at Sister Bridget. It had been hard for Bridget these last weeks without an oven. Thomas had come over to the convent that evening, diagnosed the problem as a short circuit in the element at the back of the oven, removed it, and fixed the blown fuse (Margaret had made a mental note to learn to do that herself as soon as possible – Sister Helen had always been the go-to person for such repairs). Thomas said that he would try to find a replacement element for them, so even if they still didn't have a working oven, microwave or standard, they did now have four working hobs for Sister Bridget to cook on, and to boil a kettle for a celebratory pot of tea.

'You know we can't rely on Thomas to fix everything?' Margaret said, reluctantly broaching the subject that nobody, including her, wanted to talk about. 'I've asked him to teach me some basic DIY, but the truth is that the problem is too big for one person. Thomas says the whole house needs rewiring and that will cost thousands. I am still waiting for the report from the builders about the damp and the cracks. Sooner or later, we are going to have to sell the convent.'

'We can't,' said Sister Cecilia, firmly. 'This house was given to us by Edward Mortimer so that we could attend to the spiritual needs of the people of Fairbridge.'

'But we've been through this already. That was back in

1920, Cecilia,' said Margaret, trying to keep the irritation out of her voice. 'Seventy-five years ago. When there were more of us. When people in Fairbridge needed us.'

'The Order was founded . . .' began Sister Cecilia, but Margaret interrupted, rather rudely, it has to be said.

'I don't need a lecture on the foundation of the Order, Sister Cecilia. As deputy head and then as head I gave the same speech to the girls every Foundation Day.' Margaret stood up and recited from memory:

'The Order of the Sisters of St Philomena was founded by eight Belgian nuns who had fled to England during the First World War and were given rooms, by Catholic Lord and Lady Mortimer, in a wing of Fairbridge House on the outskirts of Fairbridge, which at that time was mostly given over to the care of injured troops. The nuns volunteered themselves to the family as nurses, and when the First World War ended, after prayer, and in gratitude for their welcome, the nuns decided not to return to Belgium but, with the support of the Bishop, were allowed to settle in England and start a new religious order, dedicated to the moral health and education of the people of Fairbridge. The Sisters of St Philomena took their name from the parish, and in 1920 the new Order moved out of Fairbridge House, settling into the present convent, a house given to the Order by Edward Mortimer, eldest son, in gratitude for surviving the war. This secondary school was built on the land next to it, and has been run by the Sisters of St Philomena up to this day.'

Margaret sat down again. 'Except that we don't. We don't run the secondary school, and we aren't needed any more.'

'They still need us, Margaret,' said Bridget, shocked.

'They need us more than ever,' agreed Sister Cecilia. 'In this day and age.'

Margaret sat and looked at them looking back at her.

It would be hard to think of two more different characters for Margaret to look at. Bridget, seventy years old, cook extraordinaire, small, round, pretty, with sparkling Irish eyes and a warm Irish accent, was the sort of person everyone talks to at bus stops. She wore the habit of the Order – a black veil with a white trim, and a simple blue belted dress with a white collar – with such happiness that it was impossible not to feel cheered just looking at her. She was the convent cook but also the cook for the priests of St Philomena's Church, which for some years had meant only Father Hugh. She ran the bingo and the toddlers' group, visited the sick, helped on the soup run. She naturally attracted affection to her and had an uncanny habit of winning raffles. Father Hugh claimed that the parish would grind to a halt without her. He was probably right.

And then there was Cecilia, or Sister Cecilia as she expected everyone – fellow Sister or not – to call her, thin, with ivory-coloured skin, hair firmly hidden under her veil, who naturally exuded disapproval from every pore and remained as haughtily aristocratic and stand-offish now, aged ninety, as she had when she first joined the convent as a twenty-year-old. She had taken her vows of Poverty, Chastity and Obedience, and for seventy years she had had no real trouble keeping them. She listened to her Superiors as the voice of God in her life, she was commendably uninterested in money or possessions, and Margaret could not imagine that men had ever loomed large in her life, nor asking Cecilia if they had. Cecilia had had a long career as a feared but fair teacher at the convent school and had spent the thirty years since her retirement sternly helping out in the school when needed until it had closed, meanwhile also building up a reputation as a local researcher of

Catholic history and writing articles for the parish magazine. Nobody talked to Sister Cecilia at bus stops. She strode around Fairbridge in her sensible flat shoes, blue overcoat and nun's veil, as determined and strong-minded as she had ever been, if a little slower in her pace.

And lastly came Margaret herself, at fifty-eight the youngest, reluctantly newly retired as head of St Philomena's Roman Catholic Convent School for Girls (now amalgamated into the big co-educational Catholic comprehensive, with its going-somewhere glass and metal extension) and reluctantly appointed Superior of St Philomena's Convent. Cecilia, by the rules of the congregation, was too old to be made the Superior, and it was obvious Bridget was too busy, so Margaret had taken on the role and was not, it had to be said, enjoying it. Dealing with teenage girls was a doddle compared to being in charge of Bridget and Cecilia. Like the others, Margaret still wore a habit, and even though she could imagine choosing to wear ordinary clothes one day, like many other religious sisters were choosing to do, there was a comfort in wearing what the other Sisters wore and had worn more or less (the veil used to be much heavier) since the Order had been founded. Besides, there was no money for clothes shopping, and they had plenty of spare habits, collars and veils to get through, and at least there was no worrying about what to wear each day. Margaret had more than enough decisions to make already.

'Well, let's pray,' said Margaret.

They opened the side door, which connected to the old part of the school, where the chapel was. The polished wooden floors echoed as they walked along the corridor, past the familiar painted statue of Jesus pointing to his heart, past a carved wooden Madonna holding her own Baby Jesus, past the display case of cups and shields won by various school teams over the years, past the black-and-white whole-school photos and photos of drama productions and school trips. There was one of a school pilgrimage to Rome, the last one Sister Helen had been on before she died, and a lovely photo of Sister Helen, Sister Margaret and all the girls at the Keats–Shelley House in Rome with an old girl of the school, Katy Bradshaw, who had been working there for the summer after graduating from university. It had delighted Helen and Margaret, and made them so proud, to bump into a former pupil working in a famous literary museum in Rome. That had been a lovely trip. Then there was the last whole-school photo, with Sister Helen and Sister Margaret sitting in the middle of staff and students. There were so many school photos with Helen and Margaret sitting next to each other in the front, smiling, relaxed, proud.

'We were a good team,' thought Margaret, bleakly. 'For twenty years, we were such a good team, Helen and I.'

There was only one school photo with Margaret as the head. She looked strained, anxious, in a way she hadn't when she was deputy. Her new deputy, appointed by on high after Helen's death, looked serious. Maybe even then he already knew the plans of the diocese to amalgamate the boys' and girls' schools. Maybe he already knew he would be the head. She had never liked him.

'I did my best,' she thought defensively, and was annoyed to find tears springing to her eyes.

She pushed open the door to the chapel, felt for and switched on the lights and checked the porch as they went through. She had a mean moment of satisfaction when she saw all the Mass sheets piled untidily from the day before. When it was just girls, the whole school could just about fit in the convent chapel, but the new, bigger comprehensive had whole-school Masses at St Philomena's Church. They still wanted to use the chapel, however, and Father Hugh had arranged that he would come and celebrate Masses for individual year groups there. The leaflets had been in a mess since yesterday's service, but she had ignored them. It was none of her business any more.

'We would never have left them in such a state,' she muttered, but this time she straightened them up anyway and put them away in the cupboard as Sister Cecilia and Sister Bridget blessed themselves and went on ahead.

The chapel itself was still and silent, the familiar lingering smell of incense from Mass mixed with the scent of flowers and candles. The tea light in the red tabernacle lamp on the wall flickered. As Margaret entered, she almost imagined for a moment that Helen was sitting in what had been her usual place, that she turned around and smiled at her in the way she always had, shifting along the polished wooden pew to make room. Margaret blinked, and shook her head. The pews were empty apart from Cecilia and Bridget. It was just the three of them.

'Well, not just the three of us – you are here too, of course, Lord,' she corrected herself in her head as she genuflected and took her place.

Sister Margaret sat alone after Night Prayer. Sister Cecilia and Sister Bridget, still clearly elated after the Bishop's dinner triumph, had just left to go to bed, but Margaret had stayed behind for a private moan.

'I know this is petty, Lord,' Margaret prayed, 'and I am not proud of this, but I need to talk to you about Sister Cecilia's false teeth. It's the way they whistle when she prays, Lord. I feel like I cannot stand one more hour of it. It made praying tonight absolutely impossible.' She paused as she looked up at the simple cross on the altar and became aware, in the quiet, that perhaps she had not been entirely honest.

'I suppose prayer wasn't actually impossible,' she conceded. 'To be honest, it's not so much the teeth – it's her. It's really because you know, and I know, that whilst her teeth are whistling, she is praying about the numbers for her blessed lottery ticket, and I don't agree with it. I can't believe you do either.

'Please don't let her win tomorrow. I know she will be disappointed again. I don't like to see her miserable every Saturday. But she just won't give up, that's the problem. She just won't listen to me. I should have nipped it in the bud right at the start, but with everything going on I wasn't on top of it. She claims you inspire her to carry on in spite of everything, and it doesn't help that Sister Bridget calls the parish bingo, and wins every raffle she enters. As a church, we're hardly consistent about gambling, after all. I know that. But I really do think you should have a word. Put her right.'

The red light in front of the tabernacle flickered, the little wooden Madonna at the side cuddled her baby, and in the absence of any direct revelation, Sister Margaret felt obliged to continue.

'It's not really about the lottery either. It's just that it irritates me that just because Cecilia chooses the numbers from saints' days, she seems to think that there isn't a religious problem. But the point is, it isn't actually up to her to decide that. Some people think it is a sin to gamble. She should have asked me if I agreed, Lord. Since Helen died I am the Superior, not that I wanted to be. And if you have made me Superior you should at least inspire Cecilia to listen to me. Sorry – but as I am trying to be honest, I think you should know that. Not that you don't already. You know everything. I know you do. But it helps me to say it. Not that I have a clear position on gambling anyway, but . . . that's not the point. You understand. It's about authority.'

Emboldened by the albeit rather one-sided conversation, Margaret continued.

'And what's all this about our furniture, Lord? She's got a bee in her bonnet about that, too. She is sure that one of our chairs or tables will come up on *Antiques Roadshow* and be worth a fortune and save the convent. She claims it was you who told her. It's driving me to distraction. Even if we do manage to sell some chairs or desks, they will hardly raise the money we need.'

The chapel remained silent, and Margaret felt no nearer to a decision.

'What am I to say to her, Lord?' she asked. 'How can I convince her that she should stop praying for some miracle? How can I convince her that the money just isn't going to come and that we should sell the house? That it's time to admit there are only three of us left, that the Order of St Philomena is finished, and to see if we can join another Order? How can I tell her that you haven't been giving her hope, that it's all just wishful thinking?'

Her prayers petered out to a defeated end.

'It would help, Lord, if you gave me a more direct answer to prayer sometimes,' she said.

No angelic voices, no vision, nothing. Not that Sister Margaret had ever had them before in her religious life. But then, until these past few years, she had never felt quite so abandoned and lost before, so much in need of a sign.

'Maybe I just need to bless her,' she thought. 'That's what Father Hugh said in his sermon last week. Bless your enemies. Not that Cecilia is my enemy, of course. But we should certainly bless each other. Perhaps that's what you want me to do, instead of complaining about her and her teeth. I'm sorry I am complaining so much. I should count my – our – blessings. I suppose I should at least thank you that you haven't let her win the lottery.'

Sister Margaret knelt.

'Please bless Cecilia this coming week,' she prayed. 'Please may she feel happy about the future, welcome new directions – be enthusiastic, even. I know that is asking for a miracle, Lord, but after all,' she said with some exasperation, 'miracles are what you do.'

Two

Around the corner from the Victorian church of St Philomena and the slightly shabby but still grand Georgian presbytery lived in by Father Hugh, and while Sister Bridget was inside bribing the Bishop with a delectable meal, George Sanders and Dr Matthew Woodburn were having a drink in the Swan on Market Street. As members of Fairbridge Choir, they were having their usual Friday-night drink after rehearsal, though as the others they normally went with had unexpectedly had other things to do (papers to mark, babies to bath, birthday parties to attend), they were on their own.

'Are you not rushing off?' said George (bass, small, forty, very handsome, dark eyes, dark hair, adventurous, poetic, musical, untidy, talkative, funny in groups, stressed travel agent, carer to an elderly mother and incredibly, howlingly lonely), trying not to sound too desperate to Matthew (tenor, tall, thirty-eight, neat, bespectacled, fair, university lecturer in art history, quiet in groups but with a wide social circle, calm, modest, musical, cautious, and loving to a fault).

'No, no. No one is home. Sarah is meeting friends. I'm in

no rush,' said Matthew, whose shy heart had lifted when he saw that it would be just him and George. Such evenings were rare. He would not tell Sarah. He did not want his twin sister putting two and two together and making five.

They discussed music, and the choir and concerts they had recently seen, and George made Matthew laugh, as he always could, and as he delighted in doing. There was something about the way Matthew's serious face lit up when he was amused – his laugh was so joyful that George always wanted to provoke it. As the evening wore on, and with just the two of them in the quiet corner of the noisy pub, George told Matthew funny stories about his life teaching English in Spain after university, and then, after more drinks than normal, how he had had a partner who had died two years earlier, and how, because of his elderly mother's needs, he had come back to England. He had bought a travel agency with a flat above it, had adopted a cat, and was trying to keep a close eye on his mother, but caring for her, as well as running a business full-time, was wearing him out.

And Matthew had listened for hours, his heart aching for this lovable, hurting man. George had even cried. He was always careful, however, to keep the name of his dead partner hidden; even grief had to be censored, and nobody in his family or English circle knew. Matthew, when George did not mention a name, did not ask for one.

Back in the presbytery, the evening had ended and prayer was taking place. Father Hugh, having waved off the Bishop after the roast-lamb dinner Sister Bridget had cooked for them, and ignoring his ever-expanding waistline – he had also helped himself to an unnecessary but mouth-watering biscuit (why had God made Sister Bridget so talented?) – had decided on an early bedtime, if only to get away from the biscuit tin. He had sat and said the official Night Prayer, gone upstairs, changed into the large blue comfortable drawstring pyjamas his sister had sent him for Christmas, and knelt stiffly down by the bed, and now was humbly praying extra, and very particular, prayers for help.

'I love her meals, dear Lord, but there's only one of me. She needs to be cooking for so many more. I want to ask her to stop making treats for me to eat, but I am afraid of hurting her feelings. She keeps saying I need building up, but you and I both know that I really, really don't.

'I know I'm weak. You know that too. I couldn't turn down the second helping, and I didn't need that biscuit. I'll never be able to judge another for giving in to temptation, and I suppose that's a blessing. But I'll die of a heart attack before that dear woman stops, and surely you don't want that? We haven't enough priests to go round as it is.

'And please may the Bishop send the curate to us, not St Anne's. He seemed very happy with Sister Bridget's cake tonight, God bless her. Thank you. I just don't want her to bake another for me, just yet, and I don't know how to stop her. It nearly killed her when I gave up sweet things for Lent, but it's nearly killing me now we're back to normal. Please help.'

Father Hugh got painfully off his knees and climbed into bed. All he needed was a week off, and time to rehearse what he was going to say. Every night he would plan to talk to her the next day and ask her for lighter meals, no more sweet treats, but somehow, by the time he saw Sister Bridget she always had a new cake or some freshly made biscuits, and she was so enthusiastic he couldn't bear to disappoint her, or, for that matter, himself.

'I just don't know what to do about her, Lord,' he said, as he switched off the light. 'I need a miracle.'

'What about you, Matthew?' George was saying in the Swan, in the haze of more alcohol than normal, noticing how blue and kind Matthew's eyes were. 'Have you always found love easy?'

'No,' said Matthew. 'Relationships . . . are not easy. Friend-ships, yes. My family. I love them . . . but—'

'You're lucky,' interrupted George, bitterly, self-pityingly. 'My mother looks at me . . . she looks at me, Matthew, and she sees . . . she sees a failure. That's what I am, Matthew.'

'I'm sure you're not,' said Matthew, gently.

'She is so disappointed, Matthew,' continued George, slightly slurring his words. 'I bet you don't disappoint your mother. I'm not an academic, like you. You have that house on the London Road, your Sarah to go home to – I've got a little flat and a travel agency, a cat, but no nice wife. She thinks . . . she thinks I'm a failure. And maybe I am.'

And Matthew looked at him and sighed, and wished a wild wish that George – witty, sensitive, clever, neurotic, exasper-ating, funny and oh so lovable George, with his wild curly hair and his big brown eyes and ridiculous ongoing jokes about his height and weight – could see himself through Matthew's eyes, and wondered . . . but he was too shy.

The bell for last orders came and went.

'Come on, George,' Matthew said. 'You are not a failure. It's late. We'd better go.'

George's flat above the travel agency was just around the corner and on Matthew's way home.

'I'm sorry for going on and on,' said George, throwing his arms around a surprised Matthew as they got to George's door. He slurred his words again and stepped back. 'You and the choir . . . and you, Matthew, mean everything to me.'

'Thank you,' said Matthew, and waited patiently as George fumbled with his key and let himself in. He did not follow.

'Goodnight, George,' he said.

Matthew stood outside and looked up until he saw the light come on in the flat upstairs. He sighed, then wandered home.

'It looks like a lovely day for it, thank God,' said Sister Bridget happily over breakfast in the kitchen the next day. Through the open window the birds could be heard thoroughly celebrating spring, and Sister Bridget was just as chirpy. She had a little pile of post next to her, including a brown paper parcel covered in Irish stamps, as she chatted. 'The weather forecast says there might be showers in the morning, but by the afternoon it will be sunny.'

'Day for what?' asked Margaret distractedly, her heart sinking as she opened her own letter. She had asked a builder to give a quote for all the repairs, and she didn't really want to see the final number in black and white.

'Sister Frances's first anniversary, of course!' said Sister Bridget, a little shocked. 'Father Hugh says he will be over at three to bless the grave, so we have plenty of time to get the flowers ready. Monica Wells was going to save some lovely blooms from the church arrangements and we can pick them up after Mass. I was wondering, as we haven't yet got the headstones for Sister Helen and Sister Basil, if we could put little bouquets on their graves too? I know it isn't in the Order's Constitution as such, but until they have their own markers, they look a little neglected.'

'Nobody in that graveyard is neglected,' said Sister Cecilia, firmly. 'There are no weeds on any of the Sisters' graves.'

'Of course, Sister,' Bridget rushed to reassure her. 'I know you and Thomas are keeping it spick and span. I just meant that they don't have the gravestones the others have. The little wooden crosses are lovely, of course, but it would be nice to see their names. Sister Margaret, do we know when we can start organising the headstones?'

Margaret was looking with horror at the number on the sheet in front of her. She knew they were in trouble, but this was beyond her worst estimates. All this work had to be done just to keep the fabric of the house intact, but it was over £2,000. Where in heaven's name would they ever get an amount like that? *Lord, help us.*

'I don't know, Sister Bridget,' she said, and got up to pour herself a glass of water and collect her thoughts. Gazing out of the window, Sister Margaret could see that the blossom had come out again in the orchard down in front of the convent graveyard, as it came each spring. Sister Bridget, who, to be honest, rather annoyingly at times, could always find something to praise in any season, had already been enthusing about how beautiful it was, but this year Sister Margaret found absolutely no desire to walk down and pray underneath it, even though she and Sister Helen had done so every spring for years. Sister Cecilia was still religiously keeping the statue of Our Lady free of weeds, but without anyone saying anything, Sister Margaret hadn't joined Sisters Bridget and Cecilia last week when, encouraged by a beautifully sunny spring day, they had sat and happily prayed the rosary on the bench in front of her. The blue forget-me-nots around the statue, now opening again, were welcome patches of colour, and still lovely to look at, but even they reminded her of how much more beautiful the garden had been. When she had ventured out in it last week to call Thomas in for a cup of tea, the out-of-control rose bushes, dense and prickly, and not yet in flower, had caught at her habit as she passed. She had not been out again.

'Well, anyway, today is a lovely day. Will you be reading the Anniversary Prayer?' said Sister Bridget, cutting into her thoughts. 'Shall I get all that organised?'

'I . . . yes. Thank you, Sister.'

'I said I would help with the flower arrangements after Mass. It seems only fair when we are getting the bouquets free for Sister Frances and the others,' continued Sister Bridget. 'Then I am going to make Father Hugh's lunch, so I am going to leave some soup ready on the hob, and some bread on the side, so that you won't have to wait. I'll have a proper meal ready tonight. Is that all right for you both?'

'I will be going to the library after Mass to do some research on Edward Mortimer,' said Sister Cecilia, 'so that will be very convenient. Thank you.'

'Thank you. I can take it on a tray in the office,' said Margaret.

'Oh, Sister, you need to have a break from the office,' said Sister Bridget. 'Sit and eat in the kitchen. Oh, now, that's grand,' she exclaimed, as the package was revealed. 'My sister has sent me some back copies of the *Sacred Heart Messenger*, and I know Bridie Kenny is desperate for some. She has some old *Ireland's Own*s she can pass on to me, and I'll pass them on to Nora Brennan, God help her, in the hospital next week. She's suffering terribly with her heart.'

Margaret felt an ache in hers. Nine months since Sister Basil's death, and six months since Sister Helen had died, and nothing had been done about their headstones. Where was the money going to come from, on top of everything needed to fix the house? Thomas had made some simple crosses, and in some monasteries she knew that all the nuns or monks were commemorated like that, but the Sisters of St Philomena had always had gravestones with the date of birth, the date of final vows and the date of death for each Sister.

'She went to Rome and she saw the Pope!' exclaimed Bridget, as she read her sister's accompanying letter. 'Oh, I would have loved to have been there.'

There was a longing tone in Bridget's voice that Margaret had never heard before, and it gave her a shock. Bridget never normally complained, was never envious or dissatisfied.

'I'm so sorry, Sister. I'm sorry we did not have the money for you to go.'

'Oh, don't be silly, Sister,' said Bridget, her usual cheerfulness reasserting itself. 'You let me go to Ireland to help the family in February. If I had been meant to go to Rome too, we would have had the money, I'm sure of it. I'm delighted that Mary got there. After the cancer scare and the family worries they have had, it will have done her good.' She smiled at Margaret, and finished her egg.

'It would have done you good, too,' thought Margaret. 'This is ridiculous, Lord. We don't even have the money for a pilgrimage for Bridget. I've got to sort this out. Other Orders send the nuns on courses and retreats. I've got to clear the debt on this house.'

This week she would stay in her office for as long as it took to sort out the administration that Sister Basil had left in an unholy mess before she died. She would sort it, and then she would have to ring the trustees and the Bishop and arrange a meeting in a week. She would know exactly how bad it all was by then. Resolving that made her feel better.

'And what have you got there, Sister Cecilia?' said Sister Bridget as she ripped off the stamps from her envelope to put them aside for the parish Brownies. They were collecting them for Guide Dogs for the Blind. 'That's an awfully posh sort of envelope. Is that some sort of crest?'

Sister Cecilia frowned as she opened it and read the contents. She sniffed disapprovingly.

'It's as I expected. The Mayor invited me some months back to the opening of an exhibition of Jack Mortimer's paintings at the university next Saturday and this is the official invitation. Apparently, as a renowned local historian and expert on the Mortimers, I will be interested in celebrating the immoral life of Edward Mortimer's younger brother.'

'Surely they didn't say that?' said Sister Bridget, shocked. 'How could they ask a Sister to celebrate an immoral life?'

'Oh, they say it is to celebrate his paintings, but the work and the man cannot be separated, to my mind. I do not understand why the wicked must always prosper,' said Sister Cecilia, vehemently.

'To be fair, he is hardly prospering, Sister,' said Margaret. 'He's dead, isn't he? Didn't he disappear from the family and public life for years?'

'He lived a scandalous life and brought shame on a good Catholic family. He ran off to Paris and didn't even come home when his father died. Why he is now suddenly flavour of the month with these art critics, I do not know. And they utterly ignore his brother, Sir Edward, and all the good he did.'

'Well, they *are* art critics. I don't think Edward Mortimer was friends with Augustus John and did any paintings himself,' said Margaret.

'Of *course* he wasn't friends with Augustus John,' said Sister Cecilia, highly offended. 'He was a man of unimpeachable reputation and good works. I am certain he is a saint – I just need some evidence. I am sure I can find something from the

Mortimer archives – some letter, some diary – to prove his holiness.'

'If you can find evidence of a miracle, then that will be a good reason for the Church to investigate,' said Sister Bridget. 'Of course, it costs a bit of money. Maybe the Bishop would help.'

'Everything costs money,' thought Margaret bleakly. 'Even saints.'

She felt a desperate need to go to Mass and ask for their own miracle. Only prayer could help them now.

Breakfast over, the Sisters walked down the London Road to morning Mass at St Philomena's.

'I've been getting a lot of requests for my Victoria sponge cakes for bingo prizes recently. I think Delia Smith's recipe is particularly good,' said Sister Bridget chattily. The sky was overcast and Margaret was sure she had felt a drop of rain. Sister Cecilia was silent as they made their way along their familiar route, but neither Margaret nor Bridget was worried about this. Cecilia wasn't one for chit-chat or small talk, and she was always a bit quiet on Saturday mornings. Praying to win the lottery every Saturday, when every Saturday the answer was 'No', was an exercise in faithful perseverance. She had no doubt that her prayers would be answered one day, if she kept praying them, and like an athlete preparing to compete, Sister Cecilia felt the need to focus on the spiritual task in hand, not on the exchange of pleasantries.

The sky got darker as they neared Fairbridge city centre.

'Oh, the weather forecast said this would happen,' said Bridget, and passed them each an umbrella.

'Pathetic fallacy,' said Margaret, out loud.

'Pardon?' said Bridget.

'Sorry. It's from being an English teacher. When the weather reflects your mood,' said Margaret.

'And look – isn't the sun shining and there's a rainbow over there?' said Bridget, as they ran the last bit to the church.

A taxi driver driving past saw the rainbow and the three nuns running, and smiled, thinking of his favourite musical, *The Sound of Music*. He played the CD of the soundtrack in his cab all that day and, on a whim, bought a box of chocolates for his wife that evening because it was one of her favourite things. She liked whiskers on kittens too – maybe they should talk about getting another cat.

The full title of the church, a Victorian building in the Gothic style, was the Roman Catholic Parish Church of Our Lady and St Philomena, Fairbridge, but it was known by its priests and parishioners as St Philomena's or St Phil's. The Sisters stopped, after blessing themselves with holy water at the entrance, to check the porch.

Bridget paused briefly to look at some cards on the notice board and to pop the Irish stamps – and the others she had ripped, with permission, from Sister Cecilia's and Sister Margaret's letters – into the Brownies' envelope. It was pleasingly full already, so hopefully there would soon be another little guide-dog puppy being trained, making the world a better place. Someone was appealing for a job, so Bridget quickly prayed they would get one. An international student at the university was asking for a room for a year with a Catholic family. If things had been more settled at the convent that might have been something they would have been able to offer. She would keep an eye on that and say a prayer. Probably best not to bring it up with Sister Margaret yet. She noted with approval that there was going to be a weekend at the

Catholic cathedral for those men and women interested in religious life. *God bless them. May He send workers for the harvest.*

Father Hugh was up by the altar, checking the right pages were open for the prayers and readings for Mass. When Cuthbert Brown had arrived early to the sacristy to serve, he had asked for prayers for his sister Myrtle, ill in Jamaica, so Father Hugh wrote her name on a postcard and put it on the stand on the altar so he wouldn't forget. He had so many things on his mind these days, what with the roof and the parish debt, and so many people needing visits and help. Even with Sister Bridget, he just wasn't on top of it all. He really, really needed a curate.

He looked down at the familiar characters in the pews, or at the side, fervently lighting candles before weekday Mass. Sunday Mass and weekday Mass congregations were different in size and make-up. Although a few younger, professional people came from time to time, and even the occasional student from the university, the little regular congregation at Saturday-morning Mass was mostly elderly and retired, and apart from Thomas Amis, Cuthbert Brown and his family, Welsh David Spencer and his family and the Pritchards, it was mostly elderly, white, working-class Irish.

Gentle Father Hugh, from middle-class English stock, was very appreciative of the Irish. Even with the support of the wealthy English Mortimers at the beginning of the century, St Philomena's parish and its connected Catholic schools had for decades mostly depended on the devotion and fundraising efforts of the Irish immigrants who had regularly come and settled in the area. The church had been built partly with contributions from the Irishmen who had come to the area to work on the canals, and was kept going in the early twentieth century by the men who came over to work in the brewery and the women who came to work in service in the big houses on the Fairbridge Road. There was a new wave of Irish support in the 1950s and 1960s, as Irishmen emigrated to England, and many had turned up in Fairbridge to work on the new road system and on the contracts for the new university and hospital and council housing estates. Young Irishwomen came over to be trained as nurses in the hospital, or had their passage paid to come and work as maids at Fairbridge House itself, a finishing school for young ladies in the 1950s, Sister Bridget and Thomas's wife Rose being two of them. Sunday Mass and the local Irish Club became dating venues, and Fairbridge's Catholic schools were populated by the descendants. Father Hugh, who had had an Irish grandmother from Kerry, loved his parish, and was very glad that he had been assigned to St Philomena's and not St Anne's, but when he was tired, as he often was, he wondered sometimes how it would be to have a bigger bank balance or more influential middle-class parishioners at his back. Maybe the Bishop would respect him more then. Maybe he would be given a curate faster.

Still, it was time to get ready for Mass. No more worries about the future. Time to celebrate God in the present. Everything would be fine.

Bridie Kenny from bingo tapped Sister Bridget on the shoulder and passed her a pile of old *Ireland's Own*s. 'Here you are, Sister,' she said, in a piercing whisper.

'Thanks a million, Bridie,' said Sister Bridget. 'I have some *Sacred Heart Messengers* to give you in exchange.'

'I don't know what sort of exchange I have to give you, Lord, to sort all this out,' prayed Sister Margaret, as the bell rang for the beginning of Mass. 'I'm not sure if what I have to offer is good enough.'

*

George Sanders, owner of the modestly named Fairbridge Tours, was on a tea break in his kitchen and talking to his cat, a black rescue he had named Sebastian the Magnificent.

'Hello, gorgeous!' he said, as the animal weaved in and out of his legs.

He replaced the water in the bowl and shook out more biscuits. Sebastian, after a hard start to life, was a cat of large appetite, and it gave George pleasure to give him treats.

'Why do I let my mother get under my skin so much, Sebastian? I thought it was right to come back and keep an eye on her after she had her heart attack – I know Miguel would have told me to. But, honestly, all she ever does is complain. She has just rung to complain about the shopping I dropped in this morning. At least I can buy her different cereal. Yesterday, it was why have I not given her any grandchildren. That's not so easy to fix.'

He picked Sebastian up and put his nose to his cat's.

'I don't think she counts you. Sorry. You definitely count to me, though. I've got to go back to the agency now,' he said, putting him down and stroking him. 'Wish me luck. We've had a bit of a slow Saturday morning so far. I could do with more people booking their trips of a lifetime. I'll see you when I get back. Not that I expect you to be waiting in, but I'd appreciate it if you did.'

Sebastian pushed his head against him and purred loudly. George smiled.

'I had such a wonderful time last night, Sebastian. When I come back, I want to tell you all about a man called Matthew.'

Three

Sister Bridget was right. It was indeed a great day for a celebration at the convent cemetery. The rain and rainbows had given way to one of those beautiful April, blue-sky-white-clouds-and-birdsong spring days that lift the heart. Reluctantly leaving her office at five to three and starting down the garden path, Margaret could see Sister Bridget and Sister Cecilia and Father Hugh already waiting at the bottom of the garden. Sister Bridget was holding colourful bunches of flowers and smiling and laughing with Father Hugh. Sister Cecilia was solemnly consulting her black notebook, in which for the past few years she had been systematically writing up the lives of all the Sisters, gathering details from the archives and oral testimony. Sister Margaret, however, was aware of her regret that it wasn't bucketing down or snowy or bitterly cold, as it had been for most of the anniversaries since Sister Helen had died. For six months, all the anniversaries had been celebrated in the chapel. Today, for the first time, they were back praying amongst the graves, and there was no avoiding the reality.

Not that Sister Bridget wanted to. Sister Bridget absolutely loved being in charge of the anniversary celebrations. She knew the teaching of the Church about Purgatory, that purifying waiting room in which many souls had to suffer before they were allowed to enter Heaven, but for her, all the women whose bodies lay in the graveyard were already having the time of their lives up in Heaven, the party having begun, so to speak, the day they died. It wasn't that Sister Bridget was unrealistic about the community. She knew that of the Sisters she had personally known, some had been grumpier than others, some fussier about their food, some could have treated her better when she was a humble lay Sister and they were choir nuns, and one, years ago, had even been quite hurtfully anti-Irish to her at first and honestly hard to forgive for that, but most of them had been kind and good and, all in all, she believed they had tried their best, given the background and personality and digestion they had each been given, and had been sorry when they had sinned, which was all the good Lord asked of any of them.

'Do your best and God will do the rest,' Sister Bridget's mother had always told her, and Sister Bridget believed that, as strongly as she believed the Pope was a Catholic. If she, Sister Bridget, with all her failings, would have happily rushed to open the Pearly Gates to her fellow Sisters, with all theirs (even Sister Basil, the one who, when Sister Bridget first joined, had sneered at her Connemara accent and even once referred to her as 'bog Irish'), then surely an infinitely loving and forgiving God would have no problem overruling whatever legitimate doubts St Peter, as the holder of the keys, might have had? Now that they were dead, for Sister Bridget they were all effectively fully fledged saints, cheerleading up in Heaven for the Order down on earth, and she found that encouraging to remember.

Sister Cecilia, if she had been asked, would not necessarily have agreed with Sister Bridget on the celestial whereabouts of their fellow Sisters. Personally, she had absolutely no expectation of entering Heaven immediately the day she died – that honour, she believed, was reserved for those who were real saints of extraordinary, admirable perfection, either officially, like her namesake, or not yet recognised by the Pope, like Sir Edward Mortimer, as their benefactor had become. Sister Cecilia was fully prepared to endure the finishing school for holiness that was Purgatory, and she knew she would infinitely prefer going there than to the finishing school her parents had forced her to endure on earth before allowing her to enter the Order. She dutifully prayed every night for the Sisters who were already there, patiently suffering for their sins, learning whatever lessons they had not learnt on earth, waiting to be judged fit for Paradise. The thing to remember was that if you had managed to get to Purgatory in the first place, it was good news – you had a guaranteed spot in Heaven – and it was just a case of waiting, and suffering, and hoping for prayers of support from those still on earth to speed up the process, and the Sisters in the graveyard she tidied so assiduously had plenty of those from Sister Cecilia. In return for her supportive prayers for them, Sister Cecilia asked for their prayers for the community still living. It was a help, especially in these times, to have their intercession. She had asked for prayers about the lottery numbers, and she was sure that they, and those saints in Heaven she also involved, were aware of the urgency of the request.

The simple service began. Sister Margaret read out the standard prayer the Order's Constitution had laid down to be read on the anniversary of the death of any of the Sisters of St Philomena:

'On the anniversary of the death of our dear Sister, we give thanks for her commitment to her faith as lived out as a member of the Order of St Philomena, we ask the Lord to forgive her sins and for His angels to lead her into Paradise, and we ask her intercession for, and the Lord's blessings on, the continuation of the work of the Order on earth. Amen.'

Sisters Margaret and Bridget and Father Hugh stopped for a moment and thought of the warm, witty, wise Sister Frances they had all loved and admired. No obituary or memorial prayer – no mere words – could ever do justice to her essence.

Margaret did not let herself look at the brown, weed-free mound with its wooden cross that was Sister Helen's grave. She could see it out of the corner of her eye, but she chose to let Sister Bridget put the bouquet on Sister Helen's grave, Sister Cecilia on Sister Basil's, while she put the main one on Sister Frances's.

'Please pray for me to be as wise a Superior as you were, Sister Frances,' Sister Margaret prayed under her breath.

'What a lovely robin singing on Sister Helen's grave,' said Sister Bridget delightedly as she came back to join them. 'My mother, God rest her, used to say that a robin on a grave was a soul from Heaven checking up on us.'

Margaret quickly turned her head to look, but the grave was empty. The robin had gone.

After an afternoon spent drafting and redrafting a fundraising letter to send to the old girls of St Philomena's, Sister Margaret bumped into Sister Bridget pushing an old hostess trolley down from the kitchen to the sitting room.

'The lottery draw?' said Margaret, rolling her eyes. 'Honestly, I think this nonsense should end. We are just encouraging false hope.'

Margaret saw Bridget flinch a little and became aware of what she had said. She had been uncharacteristically irritable and, if she was honest, rude.

'I'm so sorry, Bridget,' she said. 'Please forgive me. The paperwork . . . is not in good order. I have a headache from working on it.'

'Of course,' said Bridget. 'But you're working too hard. Come on in now. A nice cup of tea should help with that headache. We'll sit down and watch the programme together, and keep Sister Cecilia company. Then we'll pray to St Anthony to find the paperwork. Tomorrow is another day, after all. Each day has enough worries of its own.' Bridget wheeled the trolley into the sitting room, where Sister Cecilia was already sitting, back straight, in her winged armchair in front of the television, holding her lottery ticket.

'And which saints did you choose this week, Sister?' asked Bridget, pouring the tea.

'I chose one for St David's feast day, sixteen for St Margaret of Scotland's, seventeen for St Patrick's, and twenty-three for St George's.'

'That's very . . . patriotic of you,' said Margaret, trying to keep her new resolution of encouragement.

'And then I added four for St Francis, and eighteen for St Joseph of Cupertino.'

'That's lovely. St Joseph of Cupertino is the patron saint of pilots and aeroplane travellers. You never know, we might be off on holiday yet, God willing,' said Bridget, beaming, then caught Margaret's warning glare.

'Anyway, thanks to Mr Abidi, we can both keep you

company tonight,' said Bridget, whipping out two more pink tickets from her habit pockets. 'Isn't that nice?'

'What are these, Sister?' said Margaret, not really wanting to believe her eyes.

'Well, Mr Abidi gave them to me this afternoon,' said Bridget, her voice losing a little confidence in the face of two such unsmiling reactions. 'You know I baked a cake for the hospice raffle? His mother-in-law died there. Anyway, people bought the tickets in the shop. It raised £100. And ... well, when I popped in earlier this afternoon to buy some sugar, he said how grateful he was for the cake, and how he hoped we would win the lottery so we wouldn't have to sell the house ... and then he suddenly insisted I took a free ticket each for you and me, Sister Margaret, to keep her company.'

Sister Cecilia was sitting a little straighter in her seat, her silence deafening. Bridget handed the unwanted ticket to Margaret, who looked down at it in disbelief.

'It's only a Lucky Dip selection,' Sister Bridget said hastily. 'It's not like *your* numbers, Sister Cecilia. You've prayed over those so devoutly. They're the ones we are relying on.'

Cecilia inclined her head in acknowledgement. The hand holding the ticket trembled a little.

Sister Margaret sent up a swift and silent prayer: 'God – I cannot believe this! I am trying so hard. Why are you making this so difficult?'

She put her ticket down on the trolley, next to the sandwiches.

'If you will excuse me, Sisters, I have just remembered something I forgot to do and I need to write it down before I forget again,' she said. 'I will be back soon.' It wasn't exactly true, unless she counted forgetting to pray even harder for patience, but it meant she could walk out of the room without screaming.

She walked to her office, grabbed a bit of paper and rapidly wrote *AARGH!* and *HELP!* and *GIVE ME PATIENCE!* on it, then dispiritedly looked through the papers on her desk and tidied them into a pile. She was too tired to do any more work. Then she sat in silence for a little, head in hands, putting off her return to the lounge. Margaret had done her best to make what had been Sister Basil's office more cheery. She had put the brightly painted fair trade wooden cross from El Salvador which Sister Helen had given her on the wall. It was a very positive cross, with a smiling, resurrected Christ, arms outstretched, in front of a selection of vibrant yellow and red flowers and white doves on a blue background. The multicoloured, recycled fair trade rug on the floor continued the cheerful theme, but even with a little electric heater to take the chill off the air, such additions weren't enough to truly brighten the office, or Margaret's mood.

Margaret looked at the clock. Surely the lottery numbers had been called by now. She heard a sort of a scream and hurried to join the Sisters.

She entered a rather emotion-filled lounge. She couldn't quite tell from the atmosphere whether something very good or very bad had happened.

'Oh, Margaret,' said Sister Bridget, waving a pink ticket. 'We have just won the lottery!'

Sister Margaret sat down with the shock.

'What do you mean?'

'It's just five numbers and the bonus ball,' said Sister Bridget. 'It won't be the jackpot . . .'

Sister Margaret felt unreasonably disappointed.

'. . . but it will still be thousands,' continued Sister Bridget. 'I don't know how many, as it depends on how many other winners there are.'

'Oh, Sister Cecilia, I can't believe it – after all your prayers!' said Sister Margaret, not quite understanding how unsmiling Sister Cecilia was.

'It was actually my Lucky Dip selection, Sister Margaret.' Sister Bridget turned anxious eyes to her. 'But I told Sister Cecilia that if this is right, and we have won money on the lottery, we have her to thank for it. Mr Abidi would never have been given the inspiration to give us extra tickets without her example.'

'We have God to thank for it,' corrected Sister Cecilia, but she looked desperately disappointed and old, and Margaret noticed how her eyes were drawn wistfully to the pink ticket in Bridget's hands.

'Take it, Sister Cecilia,' Sister Bridget said, holding it out. 'It was your idea, not mine.'

Cecilia shook her head.

'We would never have had any lottery tickets at all were it not for you, Sister,' said Margaret, taking charge in response to the pleading look in Bridget's eyes and, knowing it would matter to Sister Cecilia, taking the formal tones of the sort of Superior she really wasn't. 'Please take care of it. Sister Bridget and I have no idea how to proceed. Would you take the ticket and go with Sister Bridget and ask Mr Abidi what the next step should be? As Superior, I'll put you in charge of the arrangements, as I have no idea what they involve.'

Two little red spots of excitement showed on Sister Cecilia's cheeks.

'We'll go and ask Mr Abidi right now,' she said proudly, and Sister Bridget and Margaret exchanged relieved glances.

Bridget could not refrain from giving her old, dry friend a big hug.

'Come on, let's have a bit of a cheer!' celebrated Sister Bridget, whose consternation at the wrong nun having the winning ticket had, up to now, spoiled the win for her. Sister Margaret laughed, and Sister Cecilia at last gave a smile.

'It's wonderful!' said Margaret, taking Sister Cecilia's hands in hers. 'And it would not have happened without you. It will make a big difference.'

'But five numbers won't save the convent, will it?' said Cecilia, looking into Margaret's eyes. 'It won't secure our future?' Ironically, it was now, with a winning lottery ticket in her hands, that she was being realistic for the first time in months, and it nearly broke Margaret's heart.

'I don't know,' said Margaret honestly. 'But still, it's a huge amount of money to come out of the blue.'

'From Heaven,' said Bridget.

'And, as I said, it wouldn't have happened without you, that's for certain. So we will go now and sort things out with Mr Abidi, and then we will ask Father Hugh for advice, and we will pray about it. I am sure God wants us to use whatever it is. I just don't know how as yet,' said Margaret. *I know you are listening, God. I'm not exactly sure what is going on here. I am trying my best, but this is not making it any easier.*

'Perhaps we should say a decade of the rosary now,' suggested Sister Bridget.

'Mr Abidi closes soon – I think we should pray later,' said Sister Cecilia.

The others stared at her in disbelief.

'Sister Cecilia – I never thought I'd hear the like from you,' burst out Sister Bridget, and when she and Sister Margaret collapsed into giggles, even Sister Cecilia had to laugh.

Four

On Sunday morning, the church hall was buzzing after the nine-thirty Mass. Sister Bridget had been on the tea rota, but there was rather a logjam at the hatch as everyone dawdled there in order to hear Bridget's excited account of their lottery win of £20,000, a tale she told with Sister Cecilia as the heroine, the mastermind. Margaret had gladly taken over responsibility for the teas and released Bridget to go out into the hall with Cecilia. There, Bridget and Cecilia were surrounded by delighted parishioners as Bridget told them in detail exactly what Mr Abidi had done with their ticket when they had gone back to the corner shop: the sound the scanner had made when the ticket was presented; the amount he had informed them they had won, thanks to Sister Cecilia's faith.

Sister Margaret saw Thomas Amis in the crowd around Bridget. It was noticeable how many faces were beaming as they listened, enraptured, to Sister Bridget.

'She has so many friends in the parish,' thought Margaret. 'She really makes a difference here – people love her.'

'Congratulations, Sister Margaret!' said Father Hugh, coming behind the hatch to catch up with her.

'Oh, don't!' sighed Margaret quietly, miserably, safe in the knowledge that nobody could overhear – everyone had their tea and they were all gathered around Cecilia and Bridget. 'It's just one more complication. I mean, £20,000 is a huge amount, and it is a big relief that I can fix the wiring and pay the bills, and we want to give you £2,000 towards the church roof . . .'

'Thank you!' said Father Hugh, not mentioning that the estimate he had been given was much, *much* greater than that.

'. . . but it is just encouraging Bridget and Cecilia to hope,' continued Margaret. 'It doesn't solve our problems about what to do next. We can't afford to stay in such a big house now. Even if we could, it wouldn't be right anyway. Not just for the three of us, not when there is such a need for housing. I have even been wondering – and this is in confidence – if I should contact Brother William, the Bishop's Vicar for Religious -and ask what the process is for finding another Order to join. That's if anyone would have us, of course, but if we join an Order elsewhere, we will have to sell the house and move to wherever the other Order is based.'

'We would miss you terribly if you left the parish, you know that,' said Father Hugh.

'But would the parish really miss us?' said Margaret, looking at her old friend. In her brief spell as headmistress, Father Hugh had been her ally and support as parish priest, and had been as sad as she was when the new management had replaced her with a younger, male head teacher. 'I mean, Sister Bridget, yes, of course, the parish would grind to a halt without her, and I know how much you love her cooking. But Cecilia and I – what good are we? What have we to offer now? Two nuns past our best-before dates.'

'Sister Margaret!' protested Father Hugh. 'Don't talk like that. You're still young! Younger than Sister Bridget, and she's rushing around everywhere. I'm only a few years older than you, so less of the "old". And even at ninety, I don't see Sister Cecilia's mind or body failing just yet.'

Margaret looked at him, and suddenly found herself in tears.

'I'm so sorry,' she said, mortified.

'I think perhaps what you need first of all, Sister,' said Father Hugh gently, 'is a holiday.' He passed her some kitchen roll from the side and she blew her nose.

'God be praised for your lottery win! Twenty thousand pounds! So what will you do with all the money, Sister?' said Mrs Ryan, coming up with her drained cup.

Sister Margaret blinked. She wasn't used to such direct questions about the convent's money, but she realised they were inevitable. The problem with such a publicly shared answer to a prayer was that other people in the church would now feel they literally had a divine right to a say in how it should be spent.

'You must be delighted, Father,' Mrs Ryan went on. 'Your prayers for funding for the roof have been answered.'

'Well, now, Maura, I didn't win the lottery,' said Father Hugh hastily. 'The Sisters have their own financial needs and we are very lucky that they are kindly donating some of that money to us.'

'Yes, but we've been praying for money for the church roof for years,' said Mrs Ryan. 'The Sisters don't need £20,000. I thought they'd taken a vow of poverty.'

'Excuse me,' said Margaret, and left before she said something she regretted. She walked away to the Ladies and, washing her hands, looked at herself in the mirror.

She had a kind face, she knew that. It was not severe. Perhaps that was why people like Mrs Ryan could talk to her like that. Why she could be replaced by that ambitious young superhead. Sister Cecilia seemed to inspire respect even though she could be so grumpy and unsmiling. Rude, even. She, Margaret, was never rude.

Margaret had not even been particularly strong at discipline at school, but then again, she had not really needed it very much with the girls. She had loved St Philomena's and its students had loved her. It had been founded as a school for the children working in the Mortimers' factory, but, after the factory closed, it had then had decades of being a small private school for Catholic families, serving rather a different constituency. That was how it had been when she had first started there.

The girls she had taught had not, by and large, been difficult, but those who had, she inevitably found, had always had good reasons for being so. Even the richest families were certainly not problem-free. Those who had volunteered to work with her in the school library had been her pride and joy; nurtured by her, they had become as enthusiastic about books as she was. Margaret had loved recommending books, seeing what inspired them and introducing them to authors who would speak to them across time. In the twenty years that Helen was head, Margaret had had regular slots with every class to talk about books, and also had small groups or one-to-ones for English tutoring across the school. Over the years, she had accumulated a number of students who had known her right from kindergarten to sixth form. By the end, she really knew not only every current child, but nearly all their parents, who had also been her students in their time. It was her life. Her community. Her family.

And then Helen had died, and everything had changed. For three short months, Margaret had become acting head – never actually a 'real' one. Margaret had known she wasn't in any way as dynamic or as strong as Helen, but nevertheless she had been determined to do her best for the school. Only, her best had obviously not been good enough.

Margaret shook her head to stop her thoughts going down the wrong path, as they did so often these days. She had been standing looking in the mirror for too long now, the hot water pouring down the plughole, unheeded and unused, wasted. The students of the environmental group at school who had met in her library would not have been impressed. Not that it was her library any more.

'Sorry, girls, for wasting water,' she said, cross with herself, as she turned off the taps.

When she emerged from the Ladies, most of the people, including Mrs Ryan, had gone, as she had hoped. Sister Bridget and Sister Cecilia had finished the washing-up, and they could make their way home for a quiet afternoon after lunch, coming to terms with the win and reflecting and praying about what to do with the money once it was safely in the bank.

Except that the afternoon was anything but quiet. Father Hugh had announced to the parish at the end of midday Mass that the Sisters had had a lottery win and were donating some of it to help fix the roof, and the story had spread like wildfire. Sister Bridget was a little too chatty on the phone to the various parishioners who rang, and somehow within hours local radio, the BBC and the *Fairbridge Gazette* had all learnt about the win, and wanted a statement.

'This is getting out of hand,' said Sister Margaret, as they sat in the kitchen at teatime.

The phone rang again.

'Don't answer it,' she said, as Sister Bridget got up to take the call. 'Now, can you remember exactly what you said to the last person, and who they were?'

'Somebody from the BBC, I think. Local radio. A lovely young woman. They wanted to send someone round to take a photograph. I said I would need to talk to you. But they haven't rung back to confirm.'

'If they wanted a photograph, surely it isn't just radio?'

'Maybe it was the *Fairbridge Gazette*, then, that wanted the photograph. I remember it was a nice young man. Sorry, Margaret,' said Sister Bridget. 'I'm not used to all this.'

The doorbell rang.

'Goodness, who can that be?' said Sister Cecilia, worriedly. She looked pale and strained.

'If that is a photographer already, I am going to ask them to go away,' said Margaret firmly.

But it wasn't. It was a very apologetic Father Hugh who came into the kitchen.

'I am so sorry, Sisters,' Father Hugh said. 'I had no idea that we had so many links to the media in our parish. My phone has been ringing constantly all afternoon and I can imagine yours has too. I've rung the Bishop and he wants us all to go over to his right now and discuss doing a one-off press conference to nip things in the bud. Monsignor Wilson is going to say my evening Mass as he has a friend who can take his. I'm to take you over to the Bishop right now.'

'But we will miss *Antiques Roadshow*!' said Sister Cecilia, unexpectedly. It wasn't like her to turn down a chance to meet Bishop John. 'I saw a trailer for it. I think they might be talking about a desk, and I'm sure we have an identical one in the convent.'

'I'll go now and set the video,' promised Sister Bridget.

'Then you can watch it later at your leisure, Sister. It won't take a minute. Modern technology is marvellous.'

Margaret felt exasperated as she got in the car. The last thing she wanted was to have to talk to Bishop John about them winning the lottery. What had they even been doing with lottery tickets in the first place? It was so embarrassing. Bishop John had never been her favourite person and she had had far too much to do with him over the years. Somehow, even when she was a young nun and he a young priest, he had always seemed to pop up at the courses or day retreats she was on and had always managed to rub her up the wrong way. It did not help that he had always been disturbingly handsome, and knew it. He was unfailingly gently patronising to women, yet in spite of this, he brought out, and was aware he brought out, passionate adoration in many pious females, and he was good-looking enough for Sister Margaret to understand this, even whilst being annoyed by it.

'I am a twenty-nine-year-old woman! I can't believe I just blushed when Father John smiled at me!' she remembered saying in confidence to a fellow twenty-nine-year-old, Sister Helen, back in 1966, after a day run by the diocese on the impact of Vatican II. 'I don't even like the man!'

'Ahh, that's the stuff of a romantic novel,' Sister Helen had teased her. 'We'd have to say you were obviously madly in love with him.'

'Helen! He's a priest! And anyway, I've taken vows!' Margaret had been genuinely shocked, and Sister Helen had relented when she realised this.

'I'm sorry. Don't worry. It's just he is one of those men, priest or not, who knows how to turn on the charm. He can't help it. He instinctively knows how to press buttons and get people to like him. He'll probably go far, sadly.'

'But I *don't* like him. I don't like how he is so sure of every-thing. I hate the fact that I can tell he expects me to blush, but I do anyway.'

'That's all it is, Margaret. You're just very kind,' said Sister Helen. 'You're a natural people pleaser, and you do what is expected of you by patriarchal and spiritual authority.'

'That's just not fair, Helen,' Sister Margaret had replied, stung to tears, deeply offended and hurt by this light-hearted but casually damning assessment by her confident best friend. 'You make me sound so weak.'

'I'm sorry,' said Sister Helen, realising she had gone far too far. 'I am really sorry, Margaret. It was only meant as a joke.'

'I just feel humiliated,' Sister Margaret had continued. 'I know I try to please people, but I'm *not* a people pleaser. I can't believe you think so little of me, Helen, I really can't. I do try to listen to God and to have integrity and be brave. I know I am not as brave as you, or as confident, but I made the decision to become a Catholic and then to join the Order even when my parents weren't happy. I gave up my flat and my job. I *don't* just blindly follow authority and do what men expect me to do.'

It was the worst argument they had ever had in a calm and long friendship, and was never repeated. Nearly thirty years ago, but remembering it still stung, even though Helen, seeing how much she had upset Margaret, had apologised over and over again, told Margaret how much she valued and admired her, and said how wrong she had been and how she regretted what she had said.

'Why can't I just forgive and forget one silly argument after all these years?' Margaret thought miserably. 'It was such a throwaway remark. She didn't mean it. Why am I remember-ing this today? I suppose it is because I am frightened Helen was right. I do tend to do what is expected of me. It was a miracle, really, that I ever managed to join the Order. I just find that I really don't want to see Bishop John, Lord. Sorry. I know you must have appointed him, and I know you must have appointed me, as there was certainly nobody else, but I honestly still don't feel like the Superior of an Order. Helen would never have reacted like this. I hate this. I'm fifty-eight and I feel like a naughty girl, summoned for a telling-off. I'm so pathetic. Lord, you have got to help me with the Bishop.'

The Bishop, to Margaret's relief and gratitude, was actually surprisingly upbeat and only a little patronising.

'Sisters, welcome. Congratulations! I hear that you have won enough to fix your roof and give a donation to Father Hugh. Excellent. I understand that you are a bit overwhelmed by the press attention, so I just want to reassure you that the diocese has an excellent press office, and it is at your disposal.'

He brought them all up to his drawing room, a room as elegant as the man himself, where a beautiful small painting of the Madonna and Child in egg tempera and gold leaf by the Catholic artist Kate Wilson was positioned over the mantelpiece. On the walnut sideboard was a photograph of the Bishop in his episcopal robes being blessed by Pope John Paul II, and next to it, in the only intimation that he had ever had a life outside the priesthood, a picture of him as an Oxford rowing blue, his arms around the shoulders of two of his smiling teammates. Sister Margaret was sure she recognised at least one who was now a politician, and another a well-known television broadcaster.

The Bishop had been a very handsome student and even now, in his mid-sixties, he was still a striking man, tall and slim, with beautiful, long, well-manicured fingers and a lightly tanned, clean-shaven face. Like the Pope, he liked to spend his holidays skiing, and one of his old friends from Oxford, now a very rich businessman, had a retreat in Switzerland that the Bishop used several times a year.

'Well,' said the Bishop, after Margaret sat and let Father Hugh, Sister Bridget and Sister Cecilia explain everything and apologise profusely, 'I don't want you to worry. I propose that we arrange a press conference tomorrow, and we can have a press release written about the work of St Philomena's. It will be a good witness about religious life. We can stress that the amount you won is relatively small and is going to be divided with the parish, and how, sadly, it won't cover all the money needed by either the Order or the parish, so donations for both from parishioners and old girls would be very appreciated. This could give you a boost for your fundraising, Father Hugh – I gather it hasn't been going so well – and might be just the right angle to get more funds for your work, Sisters.'

'That's the problem,' said Sister Margaret, breaking her silence. 'I'm not sure now, with the school taken out of our hands, what our work is, exactly.' She heard her voice sounding rather petulant and resentful in spite of herself. She knew, and he knew that she knew, that this man had been fully involved with the decision to take the school out of the Sisters' hands, and yet he was behaving as smoothly as if he had totally supported the Sisters all along.

'Surely your work is the moral and spiritual welfare of the parish, as it has always been?' said the Bishop, raising his eyebrows and making Sister Margaret feel small and silly and very cross.

'Exactly, my Lord,' said Sister Cecilia, fervently.

'Bishop John, please, Sister. And how is your research on Sir Edward Mortimer coming along?'

'I am progressing,' said Sister Cecilia, delighted that the Bishop had remembered her work. 'Of course, he was a very self-effacing man, and although a philanthropist for many worthwhile causes, I have yet to find reports of his own spiritual life or, sadly, of any miracles.'

'Yes, I am afraid in this godless age, we need miracles to attract attention. And money to investigate further.'

'Why is everything always about money?' said Sister Margaret.

'Of course it isn't, Sister. We know that. The Lord will provide,' said the Bishop, smoothly. 'Faith is what it is all about, wouldn't you agree? What I am praying for, for our diocese, is a modern English saint, and a Fairbridge saint in particular, one from this century. I think that would be a tremendous boost. That is why I believe Sister Cecilia's research into Edward Mortimer is so vitally important.'

Sister Cecilia glowed.

'So, may I say again, Sisters, Father Hugh, that you are not to worry about the lottery win and talking to the press. After the press conference tomorrow, we can all move on,' said the Bishop.

'I do hope so,' Margaret prayed, as they were ushered to the door.

Father Hugh was concerned at how pale and quiet Sister Margaret was as they took their seats for the drive back. She looked so tired, really in need of a holiday.

'As you are lottery winners now, Sisters, would you ever think of going on pilgrimage yourselves? I went on a very reasonably priced one by coach to Rome and Assisi. I found it advertised at the back of *The Universe*. There are some great Catholic pilgrimage companies.'

'It would be lovely, but we can't really afford it,' said Sister Margaret. 'We need to fix the convent.'

'But surely you could use a little bit of your lottery win? I am sure you could all do with a break.'

'Let me out of this car, Lord, before I say anything I regret,' Margaret prayed silently, but she didn't wait for the help.

'I'd like to remind everyone that we did not win a fortune. We won enough to fix the house so that we can sell it and move on.'

'Where to, Margaret?' asked Sister Bridget, startled.

'I don't know, but we are three Sisters rattling around in a house which is too big for us. We haven't had any new recruits for years. Whatever the cause, the Order of St Philomena is not attracting novices. Maybe it's time to call it a day.'

'Call it a day?' said Sister Bridget, puzzled, glancing across at Sister Cecilia.

'What on earth do you mean, Sister Margaret?' said Sister Cecilia. 'We were founded by Sir Edward Mortimer to help the people of Fairbridge. They still need us. Bishop John has the highest regard for us.'

That was too much for Sister Margaret to bear.

'Can I remind you, Sister Cecilia, that partly thanks to Bishop John, we have nothing to do with the school any more? I am Superior of an Order with *three* members. *Three* members. We have no school. We need to join an Order – we need to ask to join another Order.'

'Sister Margaret!' said Sister Cecilia.

'Another Order?' said Bridget from the back. 'What Order?'

'Yes. I don't know – Orders like the Sisters of St Joseph of Peace, the Franciscans. Sisters who make a difference – who do God's work. They work with drug addicts or the homeless, or campaign. They save the environment. They go to prison.'

'To prison?' repeated Sister Bridget, shocked.

'Yes, yes. They get arrested for . . .' Margaret was a bit vague on this point, but waved her hands to make up for it. 'They get arrested for doing things, for protesting against nuclear weapons. They help the outcast, they do God's work. They make a difference.'

'But Edward Mortimer—' began Cecilia.

'For goodness' sake,' said Margaret. 'Have you not listened to a word I have said? Don't you understand? Things have to change. You *idolise* this convent, and Edward Mortimer, Sister Cecilia, and as your Superior, I can tell you that *idolatry* is a sin.'

'How is it a sin to want to carry out the work God has given us?' said Sister Cecilia, refusing to be cowed. 'How is it a sin to pray for a miracle? And to recognise it when it happens? We may have our own Fairbridge saint in Sir Edward Mortimer. The Bishop himself thinks so. This parish could become a place of pilgrimage.'

'Oh, that's so lovely,' said Bridget. 'Like Knock, do you mean? It has a lovely basilica, and an airport, of course.'

'What are you talking about?' Margaret twisted round in her seat and looked back at the two of them. 'What are you talking about? Airports, basilicas? Even with the boiler fixed, we can't afford to heat all the rooms in our house. If we are still here in winter, we will freeze to death. We are utterly broke and you are proposing we make Fairbridge some sort of Lourdes? Honestly, you have both gone mad!' She saw the Sisters recoil in their seats.

The car came to a halt and Father Hugh gave a nervous cough.

'Well, um, here we are, Sisters.'

Margaret, previously lifted by anger and hurt, suddenly fell down to earth. 'Thank you, Father Hugh. I'm, um, I'm going to pray in the chapel,' she said, and undoing her seatbelt and fumbling with the door, she left the car and rushed into the convent before she burst into tears.

Five

Father Hugh parked up outside the presbytery. What an upsetting end to the evening. He hated to see those three good women in such difficulties. He had never seen Sister Margaret so despairing and irritable, and he had never witnessed them having an argument before. He understood money worries, and he could see that Sister Margaret felt lost, but he was sure she was wrong to want to leave. He could not imagine St Philomena's without them. He must pray for them. He felt sad, and low in himself, too. Spending time with Bishop John always made him feel a little low anyway. They had been at seminary together, although you would never have thought so by the way they related now. Father Hugh was very much the poor parish priest, going cap in hand to the brilliant man in authority. He was 'B'-list to the Bishop's 'A'.

Suddenly, Father Hugh didn't want to go back to his empty home. He got out of the car, locked it and went for a drink in the Swan. He hoped Thomas would be there, as he sometimes was. It would be nice to see a friendly face.

*

The convent chapel was in darkness except for the sanctuary lamp and Margaret had no desire to switch on the light. She plonked herself on the first seat and knelt, her face in her hands. Tears ran down her cheeks and made her fingers wet. Her nose was running, too, and she was sniffing. She felt in her pocket for a tissue, and there weren't any.

'I was head of a girls' school and now I can't even organise myself to blow my nose,' she cried. In the dark chapel she peered towards the altar and the silhouette of the cross.

'It isn't fair,' she prayed. 'This wasn't what I joined up for. I gave my life to you, and there were so many of us doing the same. It was wonderful. Well, not always wonderful, Lord, but it felt right. Even when we were novices under Mother Veronica, we could smile at each other. Nobody was alone. We prayed for each other, and she died, and things got better. That sounds awful. You know what I mean, Lord. I know you loved – I know you love – Mother Veronica too. I know we are all equally precious in your eyes. I am sure you understand why she was so mean, and that she is with you now and fully loved, and much nicer because of it. But you also know I am very grateful you took her when you did. Thank you. And left the ones who remained – Helen, but not just Helen, all of them. They were my sisters. We were so happy. We did such good work together. We had such fun. You gave us joy. It was such a vibrant, happy school. We mattered to the girls, we really did.'

She sat back on the seat.

'I want to matter again, Lord. I want us to matter the way Helen believed that we did. She believed enough for everyone. I thought you made us for a purpose. Someone has to be the Superior, but I never thought it would end up being me. And what am I Superior of? A community of three in a huge house? We have no money to do anything. Nothing worthwhile. What on earth do you want the three of us to do?'

The candle in the red holder flickered in the gloom.

'What on earth do you want *me* to do?'

Again, silence, and Margaret remembered Cecilia's shocked face.

She sighed.

'I'm so sorry I was horrible to Cecilia,' she spoke out loud in the empty chapel. 'I just find her so difficult, Lord. She is not the warmest of people, and sometimes I get a bit worn down by her. I am so sorry I said those cruel things. Please help us. Please guide us.'

She sat for a while, feeling peace slowly creep in and curl up beside the misery. Things were still bad, but not quite as bad.

There was a cough, and at the same moment the light was switched on.

'Oh, sorry, Margaret,' said Sister Bridget at the door as Margaret blinked in the light flooding the chapel.

The cough came again, and Sister Cecilia got up from her kneeling position on the other side of the room.

'How long has she been here, Lord?' Margaret sent up a silent, panicked prayer. 'How many of my prayers has she heard? Which ones were out loud?' She felt herself go red.

'I thought it might be time to do Night Prayer,' said Sister Bridget, a little tentatively.

'Good . . . good idea,' said Margaret, taking the breviary Bridget handed her, and the even more welcome tissue.

She turned away and blew her nose.

'I just want to say . . . before we pray . . . Sister Cecilia. Sister Bridget. I am sorry. I am sorry for what I said.'

Margaret looked at Bridget, who put out her arms and gave her a quick hug. She was warm, she was soft, she smelled of

Bridget – of soap and also of cooking. There would be fresh bread for breakfast. Thank God for Bridget.

'That's all right, Margaret. You're tired. It's a terrible worry, this house. This convent. And it is very sad we have lost the school. But I have a feeling God has it all in hand.' Bridget took her seat beside Margaret, felt in her pocket and handed her another tissue. Margaret blew her nose again, gratefully. Cecilia remained at the other side of the chapel, separate.

Margaret grimaced. 'I hope so, Sister, I hope so.' She turned and looked across to the figure sitting bolt upright in her seat, gaze firmly directed at the altar.

'Cecilia. Sister Cecilia. I am truly sorry.'

There was an incline of the head as an acknowledgement, but it remained turned towards the cross, and Cecilia did not get up to join them. Margaret was shocked to find a quick bubble of rage rise inside her.

'Help!' she prayed, definitely silently this time. 'I really was sorry. Am sorry. But look. She isn't making it easy.'

Bridget caught Margaret's eye and gave her a sympathetic smile. She shook her head.

'Best leave it,' she mouthed. 'Best just say our prayers.'

'Well, I truly am sorry,' said Margaret to the chapel at large, carefully avoiding looking at Cecilia in case Cecilia wasn't looking at her. 'I had no place to say what I did. I still do not know what we are going to do, that is true.' Margaret was disconcerted to find a wobble in her voice. 'But, anyway, let us say Night Prayer and commend it all into the hands of God, who knows everything and has a plan for us, which I am sure will be revealed.'

As she found the marker for Night Prayer, she added under her breath: 'And please can you do it soon.'

*

On Monday the Bishop was as good as his word. He arranged for Father Hugh to take the Sisters to the cathedral straight after morning Mass in the parish, and they had a short press conference at the Bishop's house, where photographs were taken, much was made of the relatively small amount won, and lots was made of the need for funds for both church and convent. Sister Bridget charmed the press with her lovely Irish accent, her smiley chattiness and her unfeigned gratitude, delighting everyone by giving them, unasked, an impromptu recipe for a celebration cake she planned to bake and share at the next parish bingo. The journalists enjoyed the press conference, even if they were rather disappointed by the Bishop's emphasis on how small the lottery win was. Most of them went back to their offices armed with their notes and the press release, happy to write various short pieces on the subject. The amount wasn't enough to hit the front page of any mainstream newspaper, or any major news bulletins, but it was enough to raise a smile in 'Other News'.

The Sisters were back from the press conference by eleven. Very soon, delicious smells and the crooning voice of Bridget's favourite, Daniel O'Donnell, were stealing down the corridor and creeping under Margaret's office door. Daniel O'Donnell was cheerfully singing the blues to Sister Bridget, and Sister Margaret knew without being there, that Bridget was happily dancing along. Margaret wished she could be as consistently upbeat through all circumstances. The music changed to the contemplative sound of the St. Louis Jesuits, and Margaret glanced at the clock and saw that it was lunch time. She joined Cecilia and Bridget for potato and leek soup and, without formally organising it, they had a quiet lunch listening to hymns.

'Thank you, Sister Bridget,' said Sister Margaret at the end. 'That was just what I needed after a morning like that.'

Sadly, the lunchtime peace did not last long for Sister Margaret. She set about working out which bills and repairs could be done first, and what £20,000, minus £2,000 for Father Hugh and the church, would cover. They seemed to be back at square one really – the immediate problems were solved, but the win didn't help cover the long-term running costs of the convent, and the more accounts Margaret did, the more she realised the extent of the problem. At two she went to the kitchen for a break and to unburden herself to Sister Bridget, but Thomas Amis was there, having his own soup with Sister Bridget.

Sister Margaret took a teabag, made a cup of tea for herself and went back to the accounts.

'So, Thomas, tell me. How are things?' said Sister Bridget, clearing away Thomas's soup bowl and pouring him a freshly made mug of tea. He had, as promised, fixed the oven and spent the rest of the morning working in the garden, weeding and clearing the convent vegetable patch so they could grow more of their own.

Sister Bridget asked him the question with the same attention that Rose always had. This was someone who really wanted to know – and Thomas felt a huge relief.

'I'm worried about my Linda,' he confessed. 'I miss Rose so much. She was such a perfect mother and wife. She would know what to do.'

'What happened, Thomas?' said Sister Bridget, her eyes full of concern.

'I don't know. Linda has just got so withdrawn and low. She's still only young, whatever she says. Forty-one is no age, but the way she talks, you would think she was much older. I don't know . . . she was so busy these past years, rushing around running the estate agent's and helping Sophie look after James, I was often worried she would get worn out, but suddenly all that energy has gone. I don't know if she is ill, but when I mentioned going to the doctor's she bit my head off. Sophie says she is funny with her too. Since James started nursery, she is over there much less. Sophie says she hasn't actually been there for a week now, and she doesn't know why. They all miss her. I wish Rose was here. She'd know how to help me.'

'We'll pray,' said Sister Bridget. 'We'll pray and everything will be all right, you'll see. I invited Sophie and little James over this afternoon. Maybe we can find out a bit more then.'

At half past four, not much further through cleaning out the Augean stables, as Sister Helen would have put it, Sister Margaret went into the kitchen to make herself some more tea. Thomas was there having a break again, but this time, for some reason, his granddaughter Sophie was also there, and her toddler James was sitting on his great-grandfather Thomas's knee. There was a cake and a teapot and mugs on the table.

Margaret was wearing slippers and trod on a plastic brontosaurus that appeared to be roaming the kitchen floor. It really hurt.

'Hello, Margaret! Would you like a cuppa?' asked Sister Bridget. 'We're just about to have one.'

'No, no, that's fine,' said Margaret, unconvincingly, 'you're busy. I'll come back later,' and she turned back to the office. She noticed a leaflet on the front-door mat and tutted in irritation. Not more paper to deal with. She picked it up and was about to crumple it up when she noticed what it said.

Spread your wings and fly to a new nest! the leaflet proclaimed, with a bluebird of happiness flying over a house. *Do you want to know how much your property is worth? Bluebirds Estate Agency will come and value any house with complete confidentiality.* She knew the estate agent's was run by Thomas's daughter, Linda, had awards for customer service, and was only a phone call away.

Margaret strode into the office and picked up the phone.

Six

Margaret had just put down the phone when Sister Bridget came in with a cup of tea for her.

'Oh, thank you, Bridget,' said Margaret, taking the cup. 'By the way, we're having Bluebirds Estate Agency over for a valuation this week. Just for a valuation, not for putting it on the market – yet. Nothing is going to happen out of the blue. I am not going to do anything without your and Sister Cecilia's support. I . . . I just think it would be useful to know how much the convent might be worth.'

Sister Margaret expected more disappointment or opposition from Sister Bridget, but instead Sister Bridget looked interested.

'Bluebirds Estate Agency? Isn't that the one Thomas's Linda runs? When are they coming?'

'Wednesday. About eleven.'

'Do you know who will be doing the valuation?'

'Linda. Thomas's Linda.'

'Oh, good.'

'Why?'

'Nothing. Just it'll be nice to see her. I'll let you get on, so,' said Bridget.

'Thank you,' said Margaret, relieved to see the door close behind her.

Linda replaced the phone and wrote down: *St Philomena's Convent. Wednesday, 11.* She felt a little pang at the thought of going there and not seeing Sister Helen. Sister Helen had never given up on her. The last time she had seen Sister Helen for their regular coffee and catch-up had been seven months ago, only, it turned out, a month before Sister Helen had died, not that Linda had known how ill she was.

Linda had told Sister Helen then that Sophie had found James a full-time place at a nursery.

'That means you can apply to university at last!' Sister Helen had said, beaming. She had been Linda's favourite teacher at school, and when seventeen-year-old Linda had got pregnant and insisted that she did not know who the father was, it was Sister Helen who had suggested, amidst all the drama and shock and tears, that Linda might still, with help, be able to go to university after the baby was born. Nobody had listened to the young nun, but Linda had heard and, despite agreeing to look for work at home, had never forgotten Sister Helen's suggestion. And twenty-three years later, now the head teacher of St Philomena's, Sister Helen had never forgotten the promise of that bright young student either.

'I can't, Sister Helen,' Linda had said. 'It's too late. I'm too old.'

She remembered how surprised she had felt by the bleakness that overwhelmed her as she said that. How, safe with Sister Helen, she had allowed the tears to come into her eyes.

How she had allowed herself to feel the sadness that most of the time she kept firmly pushed down.

She remembered how Helen had taken her by the shoulders, looked into her eyes and said, furiously kind, 'Stop that now! That's just not true. It's not too late! I've watched you over the years, always putting others first. You've worked so hard. You've paid for everything for Sophie, put her through university, cared for your mother, paid for Sophie's wedding, given her and Ben a deposit for their house, for goodness' sake.'

'Well, I'm her mum. That's what I should do. She didn't ask to be born.'

'No, none of us did, to my knowledge,' said Sister Helen, drily.

'You know what I mean.'

'What? Sophie has been surrounded by love all her life. Your Sophie is fine. She is a beautiful woman, she has been to university herself – she's a graduate married to a GP, for goodness' sake. She has a lovely husband and lovely parents-in-law. You don't have to be her only source of support.'

'I wasn't there for her when she was little.'

Sister Helen had tutted.

'Yes. But you had no choice, did you? Your mother was so adamant she would look after the baby. You gave up your A levels and your university place and went straight into Blue-birds Estate Agency, and you've worked so hard. Look how well you've done. Listen, Linda.' Sister Helen made sure Linda was looking into her eyes. 'You don't owe Sophie – you don't owe anyone – anything. Stop feeling ashamed. You should be proud of yourself. You've achieved so much, but also you've given up so much. Sophie has had everything any girl could ask for—'

'Except a father—'

'Linda! Stop this! Is this what your mother said to you? Because if it is, you must stop listening to her voice in your head. There was so much wrong with people's attitudes to girls getting pregnant in the past, here and in Ireland. Your mum was wrong to shame you so much. I don't know why you couldn't or wouldn't name the father, but I trust your decision, Linda. Your mum should not have punished you.'

'Mum did everything for me, for us,' said Linda.

'She did, and in many ways Rose was a lovely woman. But she wasn't perfect – and even a lovely mother can still be wrong,' Sister Helen said gently but firmly, meeting Linda's eyes.

'But . . . I don't feel good talking about Mum like this. You didn't see how upset she was back then. And then she put her own life on hold because of my mistake, and dedicated her life to Sophie . . .'

'That was her choice. I know she brought up and loved Sophie, and I'm sorry, Linda, I know how upset she was, but I have never agreed with how she treated you when you got pregnant, not letting you go to university, insisting you found a full-time job whilst she looked after your baby. You're so worried about Sophie, Linda – but she had so much love growing up. Please stop punishing yourself. There are far, far worse things than bringing a baby into the world, believe me.'

'I did save enough to pay for Sophie's wedding and give her and Ben the deposit for their house. I looked after James so she could do her part-time PGCE,' Linda repeated, as if to convince herself.

'Exactly. And you? Why didn't you ever get your own flat?'

'I could have done it in my twenties, to be honest, but Mum and Dad were so attached to Sophie, any time I mentioned moving out with her, Mum got so upset. It didn't seem fair to them after all they had done for me, and then Mum got cancer, and I couldn't move out and leave Dad to deal with everything on his own.'

'You're such a good daughter,' Sister Helen had said.

Linda shook her head, but Sister Helen had persisted.

'Honestly, Linda. You are such a good daughter, and such a good mother, and such a good woman, whatever that voice inside is telling you. I've watched you over the years, and I bit my tongue, but I always hoped that one day you would get the chance to do what you wanted to do. You've done so well – but I want you to have that chance for yourself now. You have to live life whilst you have it. I want you to promise me.' She gazed into Linda's eyes with a fierce compassion, but with something else, a sadness, in it, which made sense now. Sister Helen must have known she did not have long to live.

'I promise.'

Sister Helen had hugged her, and that was the last time Linda had seen her. The hospital admission and then her death had come so quickly, one after the other. The one person who had really seen her had gone, and Linda found now that she could find no strength to keep her promise.

The visitors had gone. Sister Bridget dried up the dishes. 'Lord, give me the courage to change the things that I can,' she quoted to herself, reading the tea towel. It was awful to see Thomas so worried. He had fixed the oven, and he was doing such great work in the garden. He didn't deserve such worry over his family, and he was all on his own now his Rose had died. Sometimes you needed to be a woman to sort out women's problems. If Rose were here, she wouldn't stand by and let her daughter suffer, and neither would Sister Bridget.

*

Sister Cecilia never watched television in the daytime. She had waited all day to watch the recording of *Antiques Roadshow*, and after dinner, Bridget got the video and television ready for her.

'There we are, Sister. It should come on now,' said Sister Bridget. But it didn't. Instead of a smiling Hugh Scully presenting a team of experts, the television screen looked like a snowstorm, and the only sound was a hiss of white noise. Sister Bridget quickly turned it off and on again, but nothing worked.

'I'm so sorry, Sister,' she said. 'It must be the electrics or something. I mustn't have recorded it at all.'

Sister Cecilia pursed her lips and sighed.

'Never mind, Sister. It can't be helped,' she said. 'I will continue with my jigsaw.'

'I could ask at morning Mass to see if anyone else happened to record it?'

'No, leave it. It must be meant. I had an idea . . . but maybe that's not the way we should go.'

'Are you sure? I feel so bad. It's always worked before.'

'No. If God wanted me to watch that programme, I would be able to,' said Sister Cecilia firmly, going over to the side table where her thousand-piece jigsaw of St Peter's Basilica in Rome was waiting, an unwanted Christmas present passed on to the community by Father Hugh. 'I will just keep researching Edward Mortimer. That must be what I should do.'

'Wait a minute. Maybe St Clare will help . . . she is the patron saint of television,' said Sister Bridget. 'St Clare, help us,' and she switched it on again, but the disappointing blizzard returned.

'Ah well, maybe she isn't the patron saint of video recorders,' Sister Bridget conceded.

Father Hugh climbed wearily into bed. It was only Monday and already he had celebrated Mass, been to a press conference, paid a care home a visit, had a hospital visit, an afternoon school assembly and an evening meeting with a young couple about a wedding, and had sorted out those pillars of the church Maura and Bridie, who had had a big falling-out over who should replenish the candle stand in front of Our Lady's statue. He had compromised by suggesting they get another candle stand in front of St Joseph's statue and split responsibilities. After all, he had been meaning to get one for ages, as he always felt St Joseph was a bit neglected, and they could use some of the £2,000 the Sisters were giving them.

'Please, Lord, send me a curate, enough money to fix the roof, and get Sister Bridget to cut down her portions. I can't do anything about any of these. I pass it all over to you. Lord, you told us the story about the widow asking the unjust judge for help, and how in the end he gave in. You said specifically that we mustn't give up telling you what we need. So I humbly ask you again. Please help. Thank you for the good meeting with Emily and Chris tonight. Bless their wedding and their marriage and all their plans.' He got out his rosary and said a decade for peace in the world, before he fell fast asleep.

Margaret woke in the night and lay in bed for a few hours. She tried to pray, not for her own immediate concerns, but about all the national and international news. It didn't actually help. She hoped that praying more about the problems of others might bring some sense of proportion to her own worrying, but somehow, thinking about all the terrible things going on just made her feel worse, and then she felt bad for not caring enough and being self-absorbed and not having enough faith, or hope, or charity, and after all that, sleep still would not come.

In the end, she got up to make herself a cup of chamomile tea. The night-time kitchen was a very different room without Sister Bridget and her nearly constant Daniel O'Donnell soundtrack these days. It was quiet, with the moonlight shining on the sink, left, as always, sparkling clean by Sister Bridget. The tea towel on the rack was dry and Margaret picked it up to put it back on the hook, reading the words on it.

God, grant me the
Serenity
to accept the things
I cannot change, the
Courage
to change the things I can, and the
Wisdom
to know the difference.

'God, please help me get the house ready tomorrow for the valuation,' she said. 'I can't change the world, and I already don't need the wisdom to know I can't change Cecilia and Bridget, so please give me serenity and courage.'

The tea towel made her feel better, and she made her chamomile tea and took it back to bed with her, falling asleep as soon as she had finished it.

Emily lay in bed, fizzing with happiness. She might not have won the lottery on Saturday, but Father Hugh had been so comforting and encouraging. The wedding was going to be lovely. The woman he had recommended about the flowers had been so helpful – she was even going to meet Emily and take her to the market where she normally bought the flowers for the church for Sunday Mass. It would save so much money.

Emily could get her bridal bouquet and the bridesmaids' flowers there, and some flowers for her hair.

'My hair! I've got to get an appointment before the wedding!' She sat up in bed and switched on the light. Emily scribbled *HAIR* in her notebook, underlined it, then put lots of exclamation marks and a smiley face.

Thank goodness she had remembered. She knew exactly how she wanted it and it would be absolutely amazing.

She settled back and daydreamed about the wedding. She couldn't wait.

It was Tuesday morning, and Matthew Woodburn, in his office in the art history department at Fairbridge University, couldn't settle down to work. He had a reference to write for a student applying for a job, an interesting book on Augustus John and his contemporaries to review, and he wanted to read over his short speech for the opening of the exhibition. It was quite disconcerting, albeit pleasurably so, that at last Jack Mortimer, the artist whose work he had been quietly researching for years, was starting to get the attention he deserved, and modest Matthew was adjusting to the fact that, as the acknowledged expert on Jack Mortimer, he himself was also suddenly getting much more attention than ever before.

Saturday was going to be such an important day. Matthew was an experienced lecturer by now, but somehow, even without this new surge of interest in his specialist subject, he had never quite managed to conquer his stage fright before an event and, hiding his fear from his colleagues, would normally ask Sarah to listen to him read through any speeches before he gave them. Which was why it was odd that, instead of his sister, he should pick up the phone and ring George.

'Hello, Fairbridge Tours,' came the familiar voice, and Matthew's heart lifted.

'You look cheerful,' said Jenny, George's part-time assistant, as he put down the phone.

'Yes, yes, I am,' he said.

'A date?' asked Jenny, daringly. She had not been working for George for very long and wondered. He was really nice and he was gorgeous-looking, with his brown eyes and dark hair and his lovely smile. He wasn't like the boys at school. He was a real man.

'Not exactly,' he said, smiling. 'But . . .'

There were no customers in the shop, and Jenny had wandered off to the kitchen. On impulse, George picked up the phone.

'Hello? It's George again. I was wondering – before we go over your speech tonight, shall we get a bite to eat? I know a little Spanish restaurant around the corner from the pub. We could get some tapas there if you like? Yes? Wonderful. It's called El Toro, in Oak Street. See you there at seven? Great.' He hung up, smiling.

Suddenly, his face changed. 'Bother. I forgot about Mother.' He picked up the phone yet again.

'Mother, it's George. I have a meeting at seven – can I come over straight after work tonight and fix your dinner early? What meeting? It's a friend from choir who's giving a talk at the university this Saturday and wants my help. What? On art history. Why do you say that? I know quite a lot about Spanish art, if you must know. No, no, it's not on Spanish art, it's a lecture on an English painter and my friend wants to run through the talk with me. Why not? No, it's not strange at all. For goodness' sake, Mother, I'm not discussing this. All right.

I know six is earlier than you like. I'll try and rearrange. I will come over at seven and put your dinner in the oven. I have to go out again at eight. Why? To the meeting. Yes, it was at seven, but I'll rearrange it. I'll put on a nice film for you before I go. I can't keep talking, there are customers. See you at seven.' He put down the phone and glared at it.

'Coffee?' said Jenny sympathetically, standing in front of him with a freshly made cup. She was a very attentive assistant.

'I suppose it's too early for gin!' he said gratefully. 'My mother is a nightmare, Jenny. How is yours?'

'She's nice, but she thinks I'm a child,' said eighteen-year-old Jenny indignantly, standing just a little too adoringly close to him as she put down the cup.

'I'm forty and my mother still thinks that!' said George. He noted with amusement Jenny's unguarded recoil at his advanced age. *Just as well. I don't need that complication.*

When the phone rang Jenny answered it a little faster than normal, and they were soon interrupted by the door opening and some customers coming in, followed by the postman with a handful of brochures and bills.

'I'll ring Matthew again at lunchtime and rearrange the tapas,' thought George. 'We can go later, after the pub.' He felt cheered by the prospect.

Seven

Sarah Woodburn paid for parking and set off shopping. Tuesday was her day off. She would pop into the delicatessen to get her and Matthew's dinner, and buy something nutritious for Miss Taylor for her lunch whilst she was at it. Getting over-involved with patients wasn't something she agreed with, or normally did, but Miss Taylor had got under her skin: her complete aloneness, her total lack of self-pity, her gentle politeness and appreciation for anything Sarah did.

'Maybe it's because she is so kind, like Mum,' Sarah thought. 'And she is Mum's age. Or the age Mum would have been if she'd lived past fifty. I might have been looking after my own mother now.'

She didn't question why she automatically thought of herself, not her twin brother Matthew, as the caregiver. That's just how it was. That's how it had always been since the accident that had killed both their parents twenty years before, when the twins were eighteen. At least, that's how it had been after Matthew had gone from bereavement to traumatic heartbreak at Oxford and had transferred back to Fairbridge

University. It had made sense back then for her to put her own plans on hold to hold her sensitive twin together.

To be honest, she wasn't sure what alternative life plan she might have followed if Matthew hadn't come home from Oxford halfway through his first year. Maybe they would have sold the house they'd inherited, developed separate lives. But at the time it had made sense for her to live in the family home whilst she trained as a nurse and midwife in Fairbridge. She was still there twenty years later, after ten happy years as a midwife, then as a district nurse. The brilliant, hurt Matthew had joined his sister, poured his sensitivity into his art history studies at Fairbridge, completed a highly praised PhD, and become a lecturer at the university and an expert in his chosen field. They loved each other. More unusually, perhaps, they even liked each other's company. As twins they had known how to live together since before they were born. They loved their respective careers. Things were comfortable. Everything was fine.

Sarah bought a slice of quiche and some salad for Miss Taylor, but was having difficulty making up her mind about dinner. The phone box outside was empty, so she popped in to give her brother a ring, as she often did.

'It's me. I'm just next to the deli and wondered if you'd like me to buy a quiche for dinner, or if we should get fish and chips? Oh . . . you're going out tonight? OK.' She was surprised, but tried not to sound it. They were both adults and had a perfect right to their own lives, but actually, going out to dinner was such a rare thing for both of them, she thought she would have known. Matthew normally put any departmental events up on the calendar. She always put the surgery Christmas meal on it.

Matthew knew Sarah was put out, even if she was trying not to be.

'It's with a work colleague,' he lied, and immediately regretted it.

'Really? Who?'

How had he forgotten that Sarah knew everyone?

'Someone new. No one you would know.'

'I didn't know anyone had joined the department?' Sarah's voice had an edge to it now.

'No. Look – it's someone from the choir. They are helping me go over my presentation.'

'Someone from the choir? Why would you say they were from work?' She sounded hurt now.

'I'm sorry, Sarah. I just didn't want to make a big thing of it, that's all,' said Matthew. 'I didn't want you to put two and two together and make five.'

'Oh. So . . . has this person got experience with public speaking, then?' Sarah asked.

'Yes,' said Matthew. They both knew he was lying, but Sarah appreciated the thought. She didn't want to carry on this interrogation, and was grateful to let it drop.

'Hugo rang this morning,' said Matthew, trying to change the subject.

'Oh, lovely. How are Cassie and the boys?' said Sarah. She had always liked Hugo. One of Matthew's friends from his brief stint at Oxford, he had kept in touch after Matthew's breakdown and stayed close friends over the years. At least something good had come out of that terrible period.

'Very well. He's asked me to do a radio interview about Jack Mortimer for a BBC arts programme he's producing. It's being recorded on Thursday evening and going out on Friday, which is useful, as I'll be able to plug the exhibition opening and study day on Saturday.'

'Shall I come with you on Thursday? It's always fun going with you to the radio station.'

'Actually, no. I've . . . I've already asked my choir friend.'

'The one with public-speaking experience?'

'Yes, that one,' said Matthew, with some relief.

'Well, that makes sense,' said Sarah, the cheery district nurse again, but her sisterly brain was making an anxious five, six, seven, eight out of it so loudly her twin could hear it in spite of her efforts, and was irritated. 'Well, see you later tonight.'

'Yes. It . . . it may be late, so don't wait up,' said Matthew, gently but firmly.

Sarah walked up the path to Miss Taylor's house. She admired, as she always did, the harlequin-patterned tiles of the path, the bay windows, the pottery flowerpots of geraniums on either side of the door. There was a key under one of them, and, as agreed with Miss Taylor, she let herself in. Miss Taylor's house was similar in size to that grumpy Mrs Sanders's, but the atmosphere was completely different. The walls were covered with full bookshelves, and framed oil and watercolour paintings. The chairs were comfortable. The little walled back garden, seen through the French windows at the back of the long, open lounge, drew the eye with its pots full of flowers, green shrubs and a small flowering cherry tree. It was obviously a garden lovingly tended by its owner in her retirement, and was full of colour and life.

Which made Miss Taylor's wanness all the more striking.

Sarah was glad she had brought her monitor with her, and took Miss Taylor's blood pressure.

'You know Dr Pritchard would love you to go into hospital for checks as soon as possible,' she said again.

'Not yet, Nurse,' Miss Taylor repeated, firmly and politely. 'I have a commitment. A promise. Someone depending on me I cannot let down.'

'Do you have any relatives who could help with this commitment?' asked Sarah. 'Anyone you could ask?'

'No, I'm afraid not.'

She didn't appear deluded, just quietly determined, and her implacable opposition to Sarah had absolutely no aggression or nastiness or self-pity, just impeccable politeness, as usual. No wonder she was Sarah's favourite patient.

'Try to get her confidence, Sarah,' Dr Pritchard had said. 'She really needs to go in for those tests. We need to get to the bottom of why she is refusing them, and she won't even tell me.'

Sarah rummaged in her bag. 'I wondered if you might like to share lunch with me, if you haven't cooked already.'

Both of them knew that Miss Taylor did not feel well enough to cook anything.

'No, I haven't cooked yet. That would be very nice.'

'It's a quiche and some salad. We could have it in the garden, if you like. I could make us some tea and bring it out.'

'Thank you. You're very kind. Just to say that if you could, please, not look in the broom cupboard, I would be grateful.'

Hmm. What was that about?

'Of course.'

It was good to get Miss Taylor out sitting in the sun. The cherry tree was in blossom and tulips and daffodils were still colourful and bright in the beds and pots. But there were signs the gentle gardener was neglecting her work, and there were weeds growing up in the beds and between the paving stones. Sarah wondered if it would be overstepping any boundaries to offer to garden as well.

Dutifully ignoring the broom cupboard, Sarah laid out the lunch on plates and put everything on a tray. She brought it out and poured the tea. They sat in peaceful, companionable silence, listening to the birdsong, but she was concerned to see how little and how slowly Miss Taylor ate. Then Sarah delved into the bag and brought out some biscuits, along with a newspaper she had bought from Mr Abidi on the way.

'Have you heard the news about the nuns?' she said, showing the photo on the paper's front page.

'I know them!' said Miss Taylor, with more energy than Sarah had seen for a while. 'In fact, Sister Margaret was a very good colleague of mine for many years when I was teaching.' Her face lit up with pleasure.

Sarah chose her words carefully.

'I know you feel you cannot go into hospital because you have a responsibility, and you cannot tell me what this is. But we both know you need the tests. If I could contact her, would you feel able to talk to this Sister Margaret in confidence about this?'

'Yes, yes. I would like that.'

It was a miracle.

Lunch over, Sarah helped Miss Taylor back into the house, looked up the convent in Yellow Pages, and phoned Sister Margaret.

'Hello, am I speaking to Sister Margaret? My name is Sarah Woodburn, district nurse, and one of my patients, a Miss Taylor, would like to speak to you.'

'Hello, Sister Margaret. I'm so sorry to bother you. It's Antoinette here.'

Half an hour later, Sister Margaret walked up the path to Miss Taylor's house. Sarah opened the door.

'Thank you for coming,' she said, instinctively warming to Sister Margaret. 'We urgently need Miss Taylor to agree to go into hospital for tests, but something is bothering her. I'm so relieved she has agreed to speak to you about it.'

The moment Miss Taylor saw Sister Margaret walk into the sitting room, her shoulders visibly relaxed and she looked as though a weight had lifted off her.

'She has complete faith in this woman,' thought Sarah, her instinctive positive feeling towards Sister Margaret further reinforced.

'Hello, Antoinette!' said Margaret, noting how unwell her old colleague looked. 'I came as quickly as I could. How can I help you?'

'Could you go to the broom cupboard in the kitchen?' Miss Taylor said. 'Both of you. And look inside.'

Margaret and Sarah glanced at each other in puzzlement, went into the kitchen, opened the half-shut door and looked inside.

Curled up on a towel at the bottom of the cupboard, looking up at them, was a very pretty and very pregnant white cat.

Margaret gently closed the door, leaving a little gap again.

'I didn't know you had a cat, Miss Taylor!' said Sarah.

'She's not mine as such. She's a friend. A dear friend. She's been popping in to see me over the last few months. I let her come and go, and I tried not to feed her in case someone was missing her and worrying about her, but she looked so thin and frail recently, I felt she needed looking after, so I took her to the vet and asked him to do some tests.'

Sarah and Margaret exchanged glances. Miss Taylor seemed unaware of the irony of the situation.

'He confirmed she was pregnant, and she decided to move

into the broom cupboard, and there we are. So you see, I cannot possibly go into hospital until she has safely delivered the kittens, poor thing.'

'But, Antoinette, there are rescue centres for cats—' began Sister Margaret.

'*No!*' said Miss Taylor very loudly. Margaret took a step back, Sarah a step forward, but Miss Taylor waved her away. 'I'm sorry for shouting like that, but I just cannot do it. I feared this would be the response. I have to tell you here and now that I am not abandoning her in her hour of need. I cannot let her down. I have promised her I will find good homes for her babies – her kittens – and I will. I just don't know how. Please, please can you help?' She stopped, deflated after her uncharacteristic outburst, and looked at the two concerned women in front of her.

'Maybe the Bishop would like a kitten?' said Sister Bridget at dinner that evening. 'Father Hugh could have one too – it would be company for him if he doesn't get the curate.'

Margaret had a sudden vision of a cat in a clerical dog collar, and a very disappointed Father Hugh.

'Sister Bridget, please, let's leave it for this evening,' said Margaret. 'It's not our responsibility. They haven't even been born yet and we don't know how many there will be. Sarah, the district nurse, is taking care of things. She said she will look in on Antoinette and the cat every day, and I am going to ring her, and visit her too, and keep Sarah informed. But we are not a cat rehoming centre.'

'Sure, you are both very good. But she'll still need help with finding homes for the kittens when they come. I was thinking, we could even have one?' continued Sister Bridget, oblivious to the atmosphere. 'An old house like ours attracts mice . . . It would be nice to have a little cat around the place. If it was a little white cat we could call it Pangur Bán, like the poem we learnt at school. I loved that. The little white cat hunting mice, the monk studying. Yes, a little white kitten would be nice. I'd love a cat.'

'But I keep telling you, Sister Bridget, we don't even know if we are staying here . . .' began Margaret in exasperation, but Sister Cecilia had already started clearing the table and bringing the plates over to the sink, and Bridget had already started filling the kettle for tea and didn't hear her above the sound of the water, so she was speaking to herself. The subject was, for the time being, dropped.

'Wish me luck, Sebastian,' said George, changing his shirt for the third time that evening as his cat lay on the bed and regarded him. He looked at himself in the mirror. 'I'm going for casual, but irresistibly attractive. What do you think?'

Sebastian yawned. 'That's not very supportive,' said George, unbuttoning the latest shirt and throwing it down on the bed; it was a little too near for comfort for the cat, who got up in protest and went to jump off the bed.

'No, don't go, I need your advice!' said George, picking him up and stroking him. 'I like this man, Sebastian. But I don't know if he likes me. And he lives with someone called Sarah, and I don't know what their relationship is. I've got to ask somehow. For all I know this could just be a nice straight man in need of a friend.'

Sebastian purred.

'I know. Friendship is good. I really, really like this man. I know I would be lucky to be his friend. But I think . . . I think I want more. I just don't know if he's the right one, or if he feels the same.'

As George left, he picked up a framed picture from the side and kissed it.

'You told me to keep loving. Goodnight, my darling. I hope you are happy with all your saints and angels. Say a little prayer for me. I'd love this man to be the one.'

'Why are you all dressed up like that to go to a meeting?' asked his mother sourly, as George served pasta carbonara for her evening meal. She had suddenly decided when he arrived that, even more than eating at seven, she wanted to sit up at a properly set table with a tablecloth and candles. Apparently, even though George had never known her mark the date before, it was the anniversary of George's father first asking her out, and she was feeling very sad. So George had laid the table with fine white linen and cooked the meal as well, and it was all slowing him down.

'Your aftershave is a bit strong.'

George started to count to ten, but lost it at five.

'I think that's rather rude, Mother, and it isn't true. This is very expensive and subtle.'

'So why are you wearing it to a meeting? Why not save it?'

'Why not? Why not splash out once in a while, live a little?'

His mother shrugged. 'My life is over, anyway.'

'Don't say that!'

'Well, what is there to look forward to?' she complained. 'Your father is dead, you have no time for me, I have no grandchildren.'

'I will not rise to it,' George repeated silently to himself. 'I will not let her ruin my evening.'

'Have some wine, Mother,' he said. 'Then I'll set up the video for your film.'

'I haven't had my dessert yet, and you know I don't like watching films on my own.'

'Well, I'll watch it with you tomorrow, then, but now I really must go.'

'Put it on then,' said his mother long-sufferingly. 'I suppose I can have my dessert in front of the television for tonight. What is it?'

'It's ice cream, Mother,' said George.

'I thought you might have made something nice. We had a very nice meal the first time your father and I went out.'

'I'm sure you did, Mother, but I've been busy at work, and I can assure you this is extremely expensive ice cream from the delicatessen in town.'

His mother twisted her mouth in the way that George hated, but allowed him to settle her into her chair and bring the ice cream on a tray. He set up the video.

'What am I watching?' she said.

'It's Doris Day. *Calamity Jane*. You know you love it.'

'I don't really feel like a musical,' she said.

'What do you want, Mother – a horror film?' muttered George under his breath.

'Pardon?'

'Nothing. Look, I have to go. My friend has an extremely important lecture to give and I promised I would help.'

'Will you be coming back tonight?'

'I don't think so. I may go to a restaurant afterwards.'

'Which restaurant? It's a long time since I've been out to a restaurant.'

'I'll take you one day. The Spanish one.'

'Oh, no. I don't like Spanish food. I've never liked Spanish food, and I've never understood why you do,' said his mother with vehemence.

'Well, it's a good thing then that I'm going tonight and not you. Right, well, that's fine. I'll see you tomorrow then,' said George, kissing her. 'Enjoy the film!' He pressed 'Play', passed the control to his mother, and left quickly before he said anything he would regret.

Eight

It was Wednesday. Linda walked up the convent drive, noting, with her professional eye, the weeds and general air of neglect. She knew her father was working on the garden behind, but if the Sisters really wanted to sell the convent, the front needed attention. It was all about kerbside appeal, although it wasn't clear exactly who the potential buyers would be. The size of the house, whilst fine for a wealthy Victorian businessman with a large family and servants, was too much now for a family home. It could be turned into an attractive hotel, or a student residence. The window frames, though needing fresh paint, appeared to be in good repair. The heavy front door was original. She rang the bell to the side and it was opened almost immediately.

'Linda!' said Sister Margaret, smiling. 'Welcome. Would you like tea?'

'Thank you, Sister,' Linda replied. 'Maybe when we have done the tour, if there's time. I've got to be somewhere else later. I've brought a tape measure and I can take some photos now if you like. That way we can get some idea of what we'll be marketing and what we might need to work on to get the best price.'

She was so professional. Margaret immediately felt she was in the presence of someone who knew exactly what she was doing. By the end of the hour she would have a good idea how much this convent was worth – in pounds sterling, anyway. The trouble was, after all she had said to Bridget and Cecilia, Margaret suddenly wasn't sure if she was ready to know.

Linda and Margaret did their tour of the convent, including the kitchen and garden.

'Come back when you have finished and say goodbye before you go,' said Sister Bridget when they visited the kitchen. She was busy washing up, and there was a smell of baking already coming from the newly repaired oven, but she seemed uncharacteristically disinclined to linger and chat. Thomas waved at his daughter from where he was very busy weeding and preparing the old vegetable patch, but he didn't come over.

'There's a lot of land,' said Linda. 'I don't think I'd realised. I like the orchards. This must have been lovely when it was busy and up and running. Of course, at school we didn't get a chance to see behind the walls, but we always wondered.'

'It was wonderful,' agreed Margaret, in her mind's eye seeing her fellow Sisters working in the garden. She suddenly remembered Sister Martha speeding on the sit-on mower, and that very hot day back in 1976 when Sister Frances, who was watering lettuces, suddenly had a wild moment and sprayed water on a group of novices as they were walking past. They had laughed so much.

'We used to play football there – and frisbee,' said Margaret, pointing out an overgrown lawn.

'Seriously?' laughed Linda, her professional façade crumbling. 'I bet Sister Helen played football. She was great at coaching the girls' team.'

'Yes – she was brilliant at scoring goals.'

'Who did you play against?'

'Well, when there were enough of us, we played five-a-side. Mainly it was just a bit of fun and exercise, but once we had a visit from some Loreto Sisters and we had a proper match.'

'How did you do?'

'We won, of course. Sister Helen scored five. I was goalie and let in two, but, really, they didn't have a chance.'

They both smiled and immediately sighed.

'I miss her very much,' said Linda suddenly, annoyed to hear her voice wobble.

Tears came to Margaret's eyes.

'We all do,' she said.

They walked in thoughtful silence back to the office. 'I can send you an estimate later this week,' said Linda.

'Could you give me some sort of rough idea now?' said Margaret. 'I'm keen to work out our future, and it will help me think of options.'

Linda took out a spiral-bound notebook and a calculator and did some sums, then scribbled down some notes.

'Well, obviously I'll do this in a much more detailed way when I'm back in the office, and any offer will be subject to survey – that may uncover things which will push the price down – but even taking into account the fact that this will need a complete rewire and other cosmetic work, I think you should still be able to get a good price for the house and land. At a conservative estimate, this is what I think we should market it at.'

Linda wrote a figure on a notebook page, ripped it out and

gave it to Sister Margaret, who nearly dropped it when she read the amount.

'That much?'

'Yes. It's a very beautiful house, and with it being so near to the university and city centre, I think it might become a hotel or even student accommodation. But even if someone demolished it and sold the land, they'd still be getting a bargain, to be honest.'

'Would you happen to know how much a rewire would cost?'

'I'm not sure it would be worth you doing it, to be honest, if you're selling quickly. Maybe I shouldn't say this, as obviously I want to be the one who sells it, if you are going to sell, but I'm sorry. I can't imagine Fairbridge without the convent, though I do understand things have changed.'

'They certainly have. Too much. Well, I know you have another appointment. Come and say goodbye to Sister Bridget,' said Margaret. 'Even if you don't have time for tea, she won't forgive me if I let you go without saying goodbye.'

'Of course,' said Linda. 'It's been really nice seeing you again, Sister, even if it's for a sad reason.'

'It's been lovely for me, too, Linda.'

They walked down to the kitchen, and Margaret opened the door. She felt Linda recoil at the scene. The kitchen was busy, with a teapot on the table and a big coffee and walnut cake taking centre stage. Thomas, Sister Bridget, Sophie and little James were all there, and Margaret could see the table had two more places set.

'Banma!' said a delighted toddler, trying to wiggle off his mother's knee.

'Join us for tea!' said Sister Bridget, gesturing towards the empty seats.

'No – sorry. I can't. I have an appointment,' Linda said, 'I have to go. Bye-bye, James, darling,' and she turned tail.

Margaret closed the door, but not before she heard James's heartbroken cries for 'Banma'.

Margaret caught up with Linda, who was crying.

'Linda, what's the matter?'

'I'm so sorry. I had no idea they would be there. It's not their fault but . . . I can't quite cope with them at the moment, you see. Family. It's hard to explain. I love them, but . . .'

'No, don't apologise. I do understand. Sometimes we just need a little space. Even from people we love.'

'Yes,' Linda said gratefully. 'Sorry. I don't know what has come over me really. I'll be all right in a minute.' She blew her nose.

'If there's anything I can do . . . ?' asked Margaret.

'No, there's nothing. Thanks, Sister. I have to go. I'll send you the official letter with my estimate,' said Linda. 'Goodbye, Sister.' And Margaret watched Linda rush as fast as she could without actually running, down the drive, away from the convent.

Margaret did not go into the kitchen straight away. For a moment, a little voice inside suggested she went to the chapel, but she ignored it and went back to the office to tidy up, relieving her feelings by ripping up old papers and envelopes and filling a bin. She didn't know exactly why, but Linda's tears had made her feel so angry and upset, as well as sad. She left her door open, and as soon as she heard voices calling out 'Goodbye' and the front door close, she went down to the kitchen, where Sister Bridget was clearing the table.

'Bridget – Linda was terribly upset when she left. What was that all about?'

'I don't know really. Thomas has been so worried about Linda being low and withdrawing from the family – she has been avoiding everyone, even little James. I thought that it might cheer her up to see everyone. A little surprise.'

'But it's obvious that wouldn't work if you didn't warn her in advance,' said Margaret, trying to contain her exasperation in the face of Sister Bridget's obvious disappointment. 'This is not some TV programme about heart-warming family reunions.'

'I can see that now. I just didn't expect it to go so badly. I just . . . I thought that it would do them all good to have a treat, and they all said she is working too hard. I made a cake . . .'

'You shouldn't have ambushed her and taken advantage of her being here on business. She has a right to her privacy, her own personal space. This is Thomas's family, not yours, Sister Bridget. You're not Rose, you know.'

The moment the words were out, and said in such an angry tone, Margaret regretted them. She saw Bridget take a step back and grow pale, her eyes widening with shock and hurt.

'I'm not Rose, no,' said Bridget, quietly. 'I've never thought I was. Nor has Thomas.'

'Bridget . . . I'm so sorry—' started Margaret.

'I can't talk about this now,' said Sister Bridget, 'I have to cook Father Hugh's lunch,' and she left the kitchen.

Nine

Bridget came back from Father Hugh's a little later than usual, so Sister Cecilia and Sister Margaret said midday prayer together without her. Margaret stayed behind to have a little remorseful weep, and when she joined the others in the kitchen, and Sister Bridget served her and Cecilia some onion soup, Margaret rushed to apologise.

'Sister, I am so, so sorry about earlier. I know that you were only trying to help Thomas and his family, and Thomas has been a good friend to all of us. He is doing marvels with the garden. I'm so sorry,' she said, as Bridget passed her the soup.

'Well, it did shock me. You hurt me very much, Margaret, but I . . . I am sorry too,' said Bridget. 'I definitely should not have done that today. I've had a good talk to Father Hugh and have been to confession and I see what I have done. I do know I need to step back, that I shouldn't interfere, and not everything can be fixed by cake.' She gave a rueful laugh. 'And I know you are tired.' And she seemed genuinely peaceful as she said this, and smiled, although she wasn't quite the cheery Sister Bridget she normally was.

But Margaret was glad to leave it at that. She would try and go to confession too. It would be such a relief to confess all this horrible anger and despair, which felt ready to explode for the smallest of reasons. She was fed up with it, and with herself.

'I took out a book about Jack Mortimer from the library,' said Sister Cecilia, who was totally oblivious to Sister Margaret's red eyes and the unusual tension. 'It is by the academic who is giving the talk this Saturday, so I felt it necessary, but I have to say that I am not enjoying it at all. I find it extraordinary that he could be the brother of such a saint. He lived an extremely wild life in his youth, and then the distress he caused his family just by simply cutting off all contact with them is appalling.'

'Well, families are complicated, I suppose,' said Sister Margaret.

'As are communities,' she thought to herself, and changed the subject.

'So, Sister Cecilia, did you enjoy *Antiques Roadshow*?' she asked.

'Didn't I tell you?' said Sister Bridget. 'Sister didn't get to see it. The video recorder doesn't work. I don't know if I even recorded it in the first place. I tried it with a different video – the one from Lourdes – and that didn't work either.'

'It can't be helped,' said Sister Cecilia, bravely.

'I don't know,' said Margaret, desperate for something to go right. 'Maybe we can try again.'

'I could ask Thomas . . .'

'No – why don't we try it again ourselves first?' said Sister Margaret. 'Come on, Sisters.'

'I don't normally watch television in the afternoon,' said Sister Cecilia, following her, betraying a touching belief, much appreciated but not, to be honest, entirely shared by Sister Margaret, that Sister Margaret could fix it.

They gathered in the sitting room and put the original

video in again. Sister Margaret switched it on. The hissing snowstorm reappeared.

'You see – it's broken,' said Sister Bridget.

'Let's see,' said Sister Margaret, and suddenly gave the machine a sharp tap. All at once the picture appeared, and they could hear Hugh Scully's voice, although this time Hugh's legs were at the top of the screen and his head at the bottom, and he sounded as if he was talking underwater.

'Well, that's . . . an improvement,' said Sister Bridget, pleased. 'So, I obviously did manage to record it at least.'

Sister Margaret was focused. 'I'm going to try it again. Say a prayer, Sisters,' she said, and gave it another tap.

All at once, everything fell into place.

'Welcome to tonight's edition of *Antiques Roadshow*,' said Hugh Scully.

'Thanks be to God!' said Sister Bridget, delighted.

'Thank you very much, Sister Margaret,' said Sister Cecilia.

'And let's have a cup of tea and watch it now,' said Sister Margaret, recklessly.

Back at the travel agency, George was singing as he popped upstairs at lunchtime to check on Sebastian, who was asleep in the armchair.

'*Once I had a secret love, which lived within the heart of me!*' he sang, and danced a little with the broom. The cat looked up. George stroked him and Sebastian purred.

'Yesterday evening was wonderful. Did I tell you? I know I did, but I am sorry, Sebastian, I am going to tell you again. I can't tell little Jenny in the agency, obviously. I can't tell Mother! So I'm sorry, you have to be my confidant. Matthew is so clever. Honestly, the lecture about Jack Mortimer is going to be fascinating. I could have listened to him all evening.

'*I could have danced all night, I could have danced all night, and still have begged for more*,' he continued singing, switching musicals. 'Not that we danced, Sebastian, but we went to the tapas bar, and he is absolutely gorgeous. And so kind, so gentle. I just want to kiss him, I just want to— Stop, George! What am I going to do? He might be married. I don't know why I just didn't ask. I wanted to say casually, "So, who is Sarah?" or straight out, "Are you married?" but I lost my nerve. I need to know, but I can't bear it if the answer isn't what I want. You know I don't go for married men. Oh, pull yourself together, George. God, you disgust me,' he said irritably as he put the broom back in its place and left the flat. Sebastian, who had said nothing, only purred, went back to sleep.

George went downstairs to the travel agency and spent the next hour in moody silence, which was in sharp contrast to a morning spent alternately breaking into songs from musicals and being exceptionally charming to Jenny and his customers. His assistant had never known him so unsettled, and it was a bit exhausting. His afternoon gloom was only broken when a phone call came from someone whom she heard George address by the name 'Matthew'.

'I'm going to a BBC radio interview tomorrow, Jenny,' he said, putting down the phone, smiling again. 'I'm going to sit in a booth and listen to my friend being interviewed. Just that. Just a friend, you know.'

'That's nice,' said Jenny.

'It *is* nice, isn't it? It is very nice,' said George, beaming. 'Nothing wrong with that at all. Have you ever been to a radio interview with a friend, Jenny?'

'No,' she said.

'But it would be fine if you did.'

'I suppose so,' said Jenny, puzzled.

George went out and came back with two cream cakes.

'Here, my lovely Jenny,' he said. He made coffee and brought hers out to her, then insisted on clinking cups as if they were filled with champagne.

'Is it a special occasion today?' asked his assistant, a bit bemused.

'No, not really,' said George. 'I just felt happy . . . you know. I've been unhappy for such a long time, I feel a bit drunk, you know. No, you wouldn't know.'

'I would,' said Jenny, indignantly. 'I've been drunk before.'

'Of course you have. I'm so sorry, you must think this old man very strange.'

'You're not old,' said Jenny, adoringly.

'Bless you, Jenny,' said George with a dazzling smile that made Jenny's heart flip a little and forget how old he was, but then, to her disappointment, he quickly got lost in his own thoughts, smiling and humming to himself, paying her no attention at all.

Back in the convent, *Antiques Roadshow* was nearly over. Some military medals, an Edwardian watercolour, Georgian sugar tongs, a Victorian washbasin and a replica of a Fabergé egg had all been shown and discussed and their respective owners rendered variously proud, delighted, intrigued, surprised and disbelieving by the experts' valuations.

Sister Margaret could almost feel Sister Cecilia, in her high-backed chair, willing the last item to be relevant, and it was with a feeling of inevitability that she heard the last piece announced and saw what appeared on the screen.

'Now this is rather fun,' said the expert.

'I knew it!' exclaimed Sister Cecilia, with great satisfaction.

'That's your desk, Margaret!' said Bridget, excitedly.

'Financially worth very little, of course,' the expert continued. 'I'm afraid this type of heavy, squat wooden desk is just not popular at the moment.'

'But not worth anything. What a shame,' said Margaret.

'But there is just one feature which I'd like to point out,' continued the expert. 'If you press here, by the drawer' – the camera zoomed in – 'you can hear a slight click and then . . .' He peered into the drawer and, head tilted sideways, the gold rim of his scholarly half-glasses shining in the light, reached inside. As the camera did a close-up of a small coin in the palm of his hand, he remarked genially, 'Ah, what a pity, just a farthing, I'm afraid, in this hidden compartment. Your grandfather obviously had no shameful secrets.' The elderly white-haired lady owner of the desk looked a little bashful as the camera honed in on her, and a slightly apologetic expression appeared on her face. Hugh Scully, the presenter, said goodbye and looked forward to meeting viewers next week, while experts and members of the public gave farewell beams to the camera as the disappointing desk stayed in shot, its owner smiling nervously at the expert, still holding her farthing. The theme music and the credits rolled.

'Did we need that, Lord?' Margaret silently sent up a swift, appalled prayer. 'A secret compartment? Couldn't you just have left it as it was? Now what is going to happen?'

Cecilia leant forward and switched off the television.

'Yes, all right,' said Margaret, before anyone said anything. 'But there won't be anything there, I'm sure of it.'

Peering through her glasses, Sister Cecilia approached Margaret's desk, pressed the same part that the television expert had pressed, and, her blue-veiled head tilted to one side, put one long, thin hand into the back of the drawer and brought out . . . an envelope.

'A letter! How exciting!' said Bridget, clapping her hands delightedly.

'Please may it be an ancient bill,' begged Margaret, soundlessly.

Two small, pink spots of colour had appeared on Cecilia's ivory cheeks as she looked down at what the desk had yielded. Her eyes were unusually bright as she handed the envelope to Margaret, in an almost liturgical gesture.

'As the Superior, you really should open it,' she said.

As the Superior, Margaret accepted. She was going to have a *lot* to say later in Evening Prayer. Hadn't they been given enough to deal with already?

The address was handwritten with a flourish and in fountain pen. The stamps were Italian – the postmark dated the letter from 1920. It was addressed to Edward Mortimer.

Sister Bridget looked over Margaret's shoulder.

'Edward Mortimer!' she said happily. 'It must be a sign! You are right, Sister Cecilia. He *is* looking down from above, helping us again.'

Sister Cecilia looked radiant.

'How is an old letter going to help us?' said Margaret, resisting the temptation to roll her eyes, but with a rising feeling of discomfort, almost fear.

She opened the envelope and pulled out a thin piece of folded writing paper, yellowed with age. She unfolded it and read it out loud.

' "Dear Edward, I have found Ellen. She is at the convent in Cardellino. See for yourself, and then forget her." '

'There is no name or address,' said Margaret.

She looked into the envelope and brought out another

folded envelope and an old black-and-white photograph. The three Sisters stared at the image of a young, fair-skinned woman in a long nun's habit, in what seemed to be an orchard. The strange thing was that judging from the position of the edge of her robes she appeared to be floating a little above the ground as she prayed. She was with some other nuns, who were looking at her with amazed expressions, although one elderly Sister stood out incongruously because her face was rather cross. The quality of the old photograph, and the framing veil, made it hard to make out the young nun's particular features, but even with this difference of time and space, what shone out from the image, even more than the curious levitation effect, was that she was so very . . . happy. Her expression, clearly caught by the camera, was one of bliss, and as they looked at it, each woman separately became aware of a sudden ache of private, previously unacknowledged and as yet unexamined longing, so strong it seemed to escape and fill the very air of the office, although nobody said anything.

Margaret swallowed and filed the feeling away for later. Quiet prayer time was going to be busy tonight, that was for sure. She broke the silence.

'How extraordinary.' Margaret turned the photograph over. All that was written on it were the words: *Ellen – 'Sister Angelina' – Cardellino, 1920.* Margaret took out the second envelope and compared it to the first. 'This one appears to have arrived a few months after the other one – it is from Italy again, presumably the same place.' She opened it and took out a second piece of paper.

Dear Edward, it began, in careful, round, almost childlike writing, so that although the ink was faded, the words were as clear as if they had just been written. Sister Margaret read it out loud, reluctantly but clearly.

'*I write this under instruction from the Superior here and the parish priest. I ask you not to continue to try and make contact with me. It was not my wish, or that of the convent, that you should have come into possession of the photograph. If I, as an unworthy servant of the Lord, have been privileged to receive undeserved blessings within the confines of a convent chapel, it is not for the wider world to know. What we shared in our past lives in Fairbridge must be left to the mercy of God. I am happy here, happier than I have ever been, and it is the Lord's will that you should leave aside all concern for me and for my welfare and concentrate on your duties as a husband. As for me, my life here is coming to an end. I am assured of God's love for me, as He loves the sparrows that fly in the air, and in that love I take my leave, asking only as I do that absolutely no further enquiries should be made about me, and that the photograph should be shown to nobody else in our lifetimes.*

'*Yours in the Lord,*

'*Ellen.*'

'Aah, she was dying,' said Sister Bridget. 'She was saying goodbye before she died.'

'"In our lifetimes,"' quoted Sister Cecilia, thoughtfully.

'She *specifically* didn't want it followed up,' said Margaret. Her voice came out louder than she had meant it to. She felt Sister Bridget looking at her, but avoided her eyes. She focused on Cecilia instead.

'*Then* she didn't, yes. But not now, now she is dead,' said Cecilia, intensely. 'Now she is dead and a saint in Heaven, it's all completely different. Don't you see? Don't you see her levitating during prayer, her feet off the ground? It's clear she was a holy woman. A saint. Our Fairbridge saint!'

Margaret sat down and put her face in her hands for a minute. Then she looked up. 'Sisters, I am sorry, but I just can't cope with this right now, not with everything else going on. I wouldn't know where to start, to be honest. Just looking at it, I have no idea whether the picture is a fake, for example.'

'A fake? But sure, Margaret, we know saints *have* levitated,' said Sister Bridget.

'Indeed. St Catherine of Siena and St Joseph of Cupertino spring to mind,' agreed Sister Cecilia.

'St Martín de Porres too. He bilocated and levitated. Padre Pio was well known for it,' added Sister Bridget.

'But we know that things aren't always what they seem,' said Margaret. 'Photographs can be doctored.'

'This is a very old photograph, Sister Margaret. You can see from the postmark,' said Sister Cecilia.

'Well, so were the photos of the Cottingley Fairies. They took in Sir Arthur Conan Doyle, no less,' explained Sister Margaret wearily.

She looked at the other two. She could see by their expressions that her argument was going nowhere.

'Look, I don't want to fight. I can see you want to follow this up. Is it because this Ellen was a local girl?'

'Of course! It completely ties in with what the Bishop said to us about needing new saints to catch the imagination. Imagine how the people of Fairbridge will react if they know that a local girl became a levitating saint? It could revitalise the whole town – the country!' said Sister Cecilia, fervently.

'Really? In 1995? Do you think ordinary people will be that impressed?' said Sister Margaret tiredly.

'Holiness is holiness,' said Sister Cecilia passionately. Margaret had never seen her so transfigured, her normally rather dour face positively beaming.

'But why this saint? Why wouldn't God send us more

information about Edward Mortimer himself, if he wanted to give us a Fairbridge saint?'

'I don't know, Sister, but I don't think it is our place to ask, and we can see there is a link with Edward Mortimer already. Maybe we will find there are two saints, not one.'

'And it's lovely she is a nun,' added Sister Bridget.

'Look. I promise we will talk about this later, but can we just leave it for a few days. I will . . . I will make an appointment with Bishop John. I promise. But can we just not talk about it for a few days whilst I get on top of everything else?'

'I can continue my research on Edward Mortimer?' asked Sister Cecilia.

'Of course. Just give me a bit of time. To catch my breath. First the lottery, then this – it's a lot to take in.'

'Of course,' said Sister Bridget. 'But it's very exciting, isn't it?' And she went off singing.

The next day, Thursday, was, on the surface, quiet for the Sisters of St Philomena. They met as usual for breakfast and morning prayers, went to morning Mass together, and walked back together, but in spite of all the opportunities to talk about the letters, everyone was very careful to avoid the subject, although there was an air of suppressed excitement about Sisters Cecilia and Bridget that Margaret noticed, but did not comment on.

Thomas was working in the garden again, and Margaret saw him in the kitchen with Bridget having a well-deserved cup of tea, but did not go in. Nor did she mention it to Bridget, who she hoped hadn't seen her coming to the kitchen door. Bridget, who had seen her, and how she had walked away, did not mention it either.

*

Margaret said a prayer and dialled a number.

'Linda,' she said when the phone was answered, 'I was wondering if you would like to meet up? Sister Helen loved you very much, and I can't help feeling that she would be helping you if she were here. I know I'm not her, and I may not have any solutions, but it's obvious something is upsetting you very much and at least I can be a listening ear. And it would all be in confidence, of course.'

'You just don't understand,' said Linda. 'There's nothing anyone can do.' But to Margaret's relief, she reluctantly agreed to come out for mid-afternoon coffee with her on Saturday.

At the agency, George sang and hummed, and was very cheery with customers all morning, until he sold an expensive cruise to a married couple going on their ruby anniversary, which would normally have cheered him up, but for some reason, after he told Jenny how much he admired long marriages, he was plunged into gloom. Jenny didn't understand it. He was really nasty to her and snapped when she asked him a question about the brochures for honeymoons, and then apologised profusely. He bought cream cakes again. Jenny was glad she had Friday off. This week had been too long already. She decided George was still very handsome, but her crush was over. Older men were just too difficult to read.

Matthew picked George up at six, after work, and they drove to the BBC studio. They were put in a booth by a smiling young male producer and were both given headphones. The young producer sorted George's headphones so he could listen in but not speak, which was just as well as George was a bit high on excitement. The producer was very helpful and seemed enchanted by George's enthusiasm. Hugo, the host, said a few words to Matthew before the interview, and then the light went green, and the interview began.

'The international art world has been intrigued by the growing popularity at auction for paintings by the relatively unknown British painter Jack Mortimer,' Hugo said. 'And here at *Painting the Past* we have an exclusive interview with Britain's foremost expert on Jack Mortimer's work, Dr Matthew Woodburn. So, Dr Woodburn – can you fill us in on the work of this artist and his contemporaries . . . ?'

Matthew described the work to be shown at the exhibition, and gave a little background to Jack Mortimer's time in the trenches at the end of the First World War, and his friendship with Augustus John. He was clear and informative and confident, and George found it thrilling.

'So, you are saying that it looks like Jack stopped painting when he left England?' said Hugo.

'Well, occasionally a painting set in what looks like Italy would be released via a very discreet London gallery, which always absolutely refused to give any information about the artist, who, they said, demanded all personal information to be withheld. There were surprisingly few paintings over the years, but we have a small collection of them at the university, bought by the Department of Art History, because he was an artist from Fairbridge and I have been researching him for years. I teach a module on him and Augustus and Gwen John and their contemporaries. We were able to buy them, of course, when Jack Mortimer paintings were out of fashion and so much cheaper.'

'A very wise move, then, considering there are so few of them.'

'Yes. But it does seems strange to me that there are so few, because we know the paintings we do have were produced in a very short time, and his style remained very consistent with that, so he would seem to have been a painter who naturally worked fast. We would have expected him to have produced a great deal more work.'

'Perhaps he needed to paint as a reaction to the First World War, but then his life changed in some way and he didn't feel the same need?' said Hugo.

'Maybe, but I would have thought someone with the artistic passion of Jack Mortimer would always need to paint.'

'Well, a mystery for our times,' said Hugo. 'If he did paint more, where are they? Maybe, considering the prices they are fetching now, listeners should check in their attics to find a spare Jack Mortimer painting? So, we have come to the end of *Painting the Past* for this week, and all that's left for me to do is to thank Dr Woodburn for a fascinating insight into our overlooked British artist Jack Mortimer, and to urge those listeners who live in England to go to Fairbridge University tomorrow to the exhibition and study afternoon.'

The programme's closing music played.

'Thanks, Matthew. That was as good as ever. Hopefully, it will get you a few more people at the exhibition opening on Saturday. It must be good news for you at the university that Jack Mortimer is finally getting well-deserved, if belated, recognition?'

Matthew grimaced. 'Well, it's actually turned out to be rather awkward for us that his paintings are selling for quite so much, because now the university is leaning on the art history department to sell the small collection of paintings we do have, to raise funds.'

'Seriously? Surely that's terrifically short-sighted?'

'Well, of course I think so, but they are arguing that if we sold them now it would benefit the university as a whole. I'd like the opposite to happen. I think we should keep what we have and, if possible, buy more Jack Mortimer paintings to create a dedicated Jack Mortimer gallery. He is a Fairbridge artist, after all. But, realistically, the prices his paintings are selling at now make that impossible.'

'You need some philanthropic donor to help you,' said Hugo.

Matthew sighed and pulled a rueful face. 'I wish!' he said, and George, who had been desperate to interrupt but was keeping himself in check, found himself longing to have a million so he could buy Matthew all the Jack Mortimer paintings he could desire.

'That went very well,' George said enthusiastically to Matthew as they left the studio.

'Thank you,' said Matthew, smiling back.

'That young man who helped us was very sweet, wasn't he?' said George. 'I've never been in a recording studio before.'

'Yes, he seemed to like you very much,' said Matthew. *Of course he did. Who wouldn't love gorgeous George? He is out of your league, Matthew. Don't make a fool of yourself. Again.*

'And you were wonderful! Would you like a drink to celebrate your triumph?' said George, nonchalantly.

'I'd better not,' said Matthew, opening the car door and missing George's crestfallen face. 'I think Sarah was a bit disappointed I didn't ask her to come to the recording today, and I was out late last night. I'd better get back.'

'Oh, of course. I'm so sorry,' said George. 'Poor Sarah. Of course you should go home.'

'No, don't be sorry. Thank you. You've been a great help this week. So . . . I will see you at choir tomorrow?'

'Yes. Well, I think so,' said George. *I don't know if I can bear to see you, knowing I cannot have you. But I don't know if I can bear not to see you either.*

The two men said goodbye. Neither slept very well that night.

It was Friday, and there was no Amis to be seen mid-morning in the convent kitchen. Thomas, after a very busy week, was taking a day off.

Margaret was grateful just to sit with Bridget on her own. Bridget poured Margaret's tea into her own precious Pope John Paul II mug, normally kept safely on the kitchen window sill, a gesture that twisted Margaret's heart.

'My mother, God rest her soul, always said, "Do your best and let God do the rest," and I think she was right,' said Bridget, passing the tea.

Margaret held the mug in her hands. It was good to be in the warm kitchen. She had done her best to decorate the office, but however bright and beautiful it was, her office was cold, and every day her fingers were frozen.

'I think I've paid all the outstanding bills now,' she said.

'Thanks be to God!' said Sister Bridget, delightedly. 'Have you told Sister Cecilia?'

'No, I will at lunch. We haven't seen much of her these last few days.'

'I think her mind is on her research on Edward Mortimer,' said Bridget, privately thinking Cecilia was actually probably researching the photograph of the levitating nun, but not wanting to upset Sister Margaret by mentioning it.

'Oh, yes,' said Sister Margaret, who also thought that Sister Cecilia's mind was on the photograph, was sure Sister Bridget thought the same, but was grateful to Sister Bridget for her tact in not saying it out loud.

Sister Bridget gave her a hug. 'Have patience, Sister

Margaret. The main thing we know is that we have paid our debts and we have enough money now to fix all the things that need fixing, thank God. And . . .' Sister Bridget could not quite resist temptation and mentioned it anyway '. . . we have that letter to look at next week, when you have had a rest. Let's count our blessings,' she said hurriedly, not quite looking at Margaret. 'And have another cup of tea and a biscuit?'

'Where will we be this time next year?' prayed Margaret, after Night Prayer that evening. 'And Cecilia. What will happen to her, Lord? Even if another Order wants me and Bridget, they will hardly want to look after a ninety-year-old. I know some convents have dedicated homes for their older Sisters, and some Sisters go to local nursing homes, but somehow . . . I just can't see Cecilia fitting in. She isn't one for community sing-songs or creative crafts. Although, on the other hand, to be fair, I sometimes think she has more energy than someone twenty years younger. Or even more than thirty, if I'm honest.'

Margaret sighed.

'Please bless Cecilia and Bridget. And me. Please bless us and help us and guide us.'

Cecilia, on the other side of the chapel, took out her rosary beads and blessed herself, the way that her old nanny had first taught her as a child.

She said the rosary in thanksgiving.

'Thank you, Lord, for the letter and the photograph of the levitating nun. Grant us, I beseech you, a new saint for Fair-bridge so that our work on earth can continue,' she prayed. 'I promise solemnly to dedicate my life to this.'

Ten

'So, I am just off with Cecilia to the university, to the art exhibition of Jack Mortimer's paintings,' prayed Margaret in her room the next morning. She had gone to look for her gloves and, thanks to a quick response from St Anthony, had found them, so had a spare few minutes to sit on her bed for a chat.

'I'd just like to ask, Lord, that it all goes well. I know that Cecilia isn't a great fan of Jack Mortimer because she considers him an immoral artist, but I hope that she enjoys it. She seemed almost cheerful at breakfast.

'And please can you help with the coffee with Linda this afternoon? I invited her to meet me at the exhibition – we had the ticket for Sister Bridget, but she didn't want to go. It felt like the right thing to do, but to be honest, I am tired. I could do without getting involved in some family row. But I know there is something wrong there, and I know Sister Helen would have wanted Linda to be helped. So I will try. But you have to help, as I can't do it by myself.

'I am sorry about all my complaints recently. I *am* trying to be grateful. To count my blessings. To trust. It's just . . . it's just a little difficult. I'm very tired and, to be honest, a bit baffled by everything. I must say that the letter and photograph haven't helped . . .' She could hear herself tailing off. She had meant to be positive, but it was hard to sustain. She could feel desolation creeping up on her in spite of all her good intentions and, sitting on her bed, she closed her eyes.

'Sorry. I think I need a bit of help here, Lord,' she said. Cecilia was waiting for her downstairs. Margaret just had to find the energy from somewhere to get on with things. Then, suddenly, outside her window, a bird began to sing. A blackbird. It was an extraordinarily beautiful, ordinary sound. Numinous. Margaret gave herself up to listening to it, and the pure wordless incantation of Joy, of life, flooded her soul, her senses, for three eternity-crossed minutes.

'Thank you,' said Margaret, as the blackbird's song ended. 'That definitely helped.'

They left Sister Bridget happily cooking in the kitchen. Daniel O'Donnell was imploring her cheerfully to stand beside him, a request he would not, in reality, need to make twice.

The walk to Fairbridge University campus was not long, and the day was sunny. Buses and cars and vans passed back and forth on one side, but the trees alongside the main road were full of green leaves and encouraging birdsong. Cecilia walked with purpose and an energy Margaret admired but could not copy. It was obvious that the disappointment about the lottery was long gone. Sister Cecilia just wanted this Jack Mortimer event over and done with, so that she could get back to researching the Mortimer brother she was interested in, and the fascinating photograph he had been sent, which she was sure was *not* a fake, but of a real, levitating saint.

When they arrived at the campus and the art history building, Margaret was pleased to see that Linda had accepted her invitation to take up Sister Bridget's ticket after all and was waiting shyly there.

'Thank you, God,' Sister Margaret said under her breath.

'Good morning, Sisters!' beamed the Mayor, who was standing at the entrance of the small university gallery with a group of people. 'I'm just about to open the exhibition. It's a wonderful thing for Fairbridge. Please, do come in.'

The gallery was heaving with people, but, guided by the Mayor, Cecilia and Margaret and Linda somehow managed to get a good position at the front, next to Matthew's sister, Sarah, to whom the Mayor introduced them. Linda and Sarah recognised and smiled at each other, and managed a quick hello before the Mayor introduced the event.

'I'm delighted to begin this art history study day by opening a small permanent exhibition of Jack Mortimer's paintings here in Fairbridge University Library. Jack Mortimer is, I think we would all agree, Fairbridge's most illustrious son, and we are lucky enough, at a time when interest is suddenly increasing in his work after years of neglect, to have our own Dr Matthew Woodburn researching him at this moment.' He gestured towards a tall, fair, bespectacled academic in his late thirties, with a fair beard and a handsome, strikingly kind face.

Margaret felt Sister Cecilia tense beside her, and didn't need to look to know that Cecilia's lips would be pursed at this upgrading of the bohemian Jack Mortimer. *'Most illustrious son',* *indeed!*

The Mayor had no idea of the deep offence he had caused, and continued blithely on. 'I am also absolutely delighted to welcome a local expert on the Mortimer family, Sister Cecilia of St Philomena's convent, which was originally, of course, Jack and Sir Edward Mortimer's family home before Jack's brother Sir Edward gave it to the nuns.'

Eyes turned to Cecilia, who inclined her head, somewhat mollified by the mention of Edward's name at last.

'So, without further ado, I declare this exhibition open. I suggest we have an hour or so here, and then we can reassemble in AH1, the first seminar room in the corridor next to the gallery, at 11.30 for the first open seminar with Dr Woodburn.'

Margaret, Cecilia, Linda and Sarah joined the crowd and began to look at the small collection of paintings. Margaret found herself cheered by the colourful bohemian scenes, the happy faces, the dancing, kissing, laughing figures – adults and children in green countryside. There were lots of outdoor campfires and Romany wagons. It all seemed very relaxed, very free. Very sunny. Uplifting.

Sister Cecilia tutted next to her. 'Immoral,' she said, a little too loudly. Some people close by turned to look, a little startled by such vehemence in a gallery.

'It's the way things were,' said Margaret, hurriedly, relieved to find Linda and Sarah had drifted away out of earshot. 'Augustus John, famous painters – they all lived like that. Jack was in their circle.'

'That doesn't make it right,' retorted Sister Cecilia. 'Sin is sin, whoever you are, and whenever and wherever it happens.'

The Mayor hurried over with Dr Woodburn, the researcher. 'Sisters,' said the Mayor, 'it is so lovely to see you. May I introduce you to Dr Woodburn?'

Dr Woodburn smiled, a shy smile that reached his eyes, and put out his hand. Margaret shook it. His handshake was good – firm enough to be sincere, but not too forceful or too tight – a courteous handshake from a gentle man.

Sad to say, Cecilia's curt nod and failure to extend her hand could not be described as courteous. It was an offended nod, and it was clear from the confusion on the men's faces that they did not know what they had done.

'Honestly, Lord, Cecilia can be so embarrassing,' Margaret prayed silently, and gave her best smile to the two men.

'Sister Cecilia may well be able to help you with family information about the Mortimers,' continued the Mayor to the academic. He felt a little unsettled by the glare Cecilia was giving him, but battled on nevertheless. He tried to engage both Sister Cecilia and Sister Margaret as he went on. 'Dr Woodburn here has been telling me that even though there has been this sudden interest in his work, there is frustratingly little known about Jack Mortimer after about 1920. He appears to have left the country, and we know he kept painting because he was still selling pictures from a London gallery up until 1939, but we cannot find any more information. The gallery was very discreet, and then it was bombed in the war, so any paperwork which might have helped was destroyed.'

'I know nothing about Jack Mortimer apart from the fact that there was a rift between him and his brother, Edward,' said Cecilia, firmly. 'Edward Mortimer was a very moral man, of course. Jack, as we know, and can clearly see here, was not, and I have not the slightest interest in him.'

'Oh dear,' said the Mayor ruefully to Sister Margaret, as Cecilia coolly walked away from them without so much as a goodbye, only to stand, back straight, radiating disapproval, in front of an early Jack Mortimer – a very bacchanalian scene involving laughing women with very little on, sitting round a campfire.

'I'm so sorry,' said Sister Margaret quietly to Dr Woodburn and the Mayor. 'I'm afraid she takes anything to do with the

Mortimers very personally, and she sees the emphasis on Jack Mortimer as a slight to Edward and his morality.'

'Don't . . . don't worry at all,' said Dr Woodburn, stammering slightly in his shyness and desire to reassure.

'What a lovely, good man,' thought Margaret, caught up in the kindness of his blue eyes.

'I do . . . I do understand. My grandmother would agree totally. Indeed, many contemporaries of Jack Mortimer would have felt the same about his bohemian life. I am sure there was some argument about morality which led to the estrangement. It's just rather frustrating and puzzling because we simply don't know where he ended up after he left the country. He covered his tracks very well. It's rather a mystery.'

'Well, I hope you solve it,' said Margaret, smiling at him.

'It would certainly be very exciting if I did!' he replied.

They walked over to Cecilia.

'Sister, Jack Mortimer also painted this breathtakingly lovely Madonna we have in the exhibition,' said Dr Woodburn. 'It is the only example of religious art we have by him, sold by the London gallery in 1922.' He gently steered Cecilia away from the painting she found so offensive towards a very beautiful painting of the Madonna and the Child Jesus as a toddler. Linda and Sarah were already standing in front of it.

'It's so lovely,' Linda said to Sister Margaret and Sister Cecilia as they joined her.

'It's exquisite, isn't it?' Matthew said, smiling in appreciation. 'We don't know if he painted any more religious work, or why he did it.'

'Well, Doctor, it seems to me as if Jack Mortimer had some sort of conversion back to the faith, then?' said Sister Cecilia, her frosty manner melting slightly. 'Some reformation? I imagine his brother Edward would have been praying for him. He was a very holy man.'

Dr Woodburn coughed. 'I am afraid we don't know anything about Jack Mortimer's later life, Sister. He is frustratingly enigmatic and demanded complete privacy when dealing with his gallery. He was a complete recluse. We don't even know where he lived, only that he dealt with a London gallery. If you mean he concentrated solely on explicitly religious themes at the end of his life, I am afraid I can't quite put your mind at rest. After he left Fairbridge he did continue to paint, and have exhibited, work which would be perhaps less to your taste, but we don't know of any specifically religious pictures other than this one at all. Um . . .' Dr Woodburn could see from the unimpressed expression on Sister Cecilia's face that his honesty had not gone down well. 'I do think you might appreciate these rather beautiful Italian landscapes we have by him, however,' he continued, indicating some delicate watercolours of an Italian church and piazza. 'I will be mentioning them in my lecture later on.'

'Poor man, Lord. Cecilia is not making it easy,' prayed Margaret silently. She shook her head with the right degree of polite reluctance in order to make up for Cecilia's immediate and audible 'tut' and offended and vigorous shake.

'Thank you so much,' Margaret replied, smiling at Dr Woodburn. 'I am sorry we won't be able to stay for lunch or for the study session. We are off to midday Mass and then Sister Cecilia has some research to do in the library and I . . . have some errands, some financial things to attend to . . .'

'Of course, of course,' said Dr Woodburn, not able wholly to hide his relief. 'Well, Sisters, thank you so much for coming. I do hope you're not too offended by some of the paintings . . .'

'Goodness, no!' said Margaret, a little too enthusiastically, and blushed. Dr Woodburn's grave face lit up with a quick, amused smile, which he immediately and politely hid.

'Well, I believe the *Gazette* is interested in taking a photograph, and so I have to go, but, again, thank you so much for joining us.'

'Yes, yes, of course,' said Margaret, and to everyone's mutual satisfaction, Dr Woodburn crossed the room to join a photographer.

'Thank you so much for the invitation, Sister,' said Linda to Margaret. 'I love these paintings. I am going to stay and go to the open lecture by Dr Woodburn.'

'I'm so glad,' said Sister Margaret. 'And you seem to have met his sister already?'

'Yes. Sarah and I went to Brownies and Guides together years ago when we were children, and then I used to see her when Mum was ill. She was one of the nurses who came in. It was lovely to catch up today.'

'Are we still on to meet for coffee later?' said Sister Margaret. 'There's a very good little independent bookshop in Miller's Lane which has a tea shop.'

'That sounds perfect!' said Linda.

The Sisters made their escape to Mass at St Philomena's, where Bridget would be waiting for them.

'This afternoon I will return to the library and research Edward Mortimer,' said Sister Cecilia as they marched away from the university to church. 'I feel called to look more closely at his correspondence and the circumstances around that.' They each immediately thought of, but did not mention, a certain letter and a photograph. 'I have already spent more than enough time on Jack Mortimer.'

Margaret did not argue.

Sister Bridget was already sitting in the front pew when Cecilia and Margaret got there, but had twisted round to talk to Linda's daughter, Sophie, who was seated behind her, her little boy James busy with a plastic bucket full of dinosaurs he was arranging intently (and surprisingly quietly) along the pew seat. When Cecilia and Margaret arrived to join her in the pew, she turned to face the altar, but the smile she had given to James, who really was an exceptionally sweet little toddler, still lingered on her lips.

'Help me be more like Bridget,' prayed Margaret. She raised her eyes to the ceiling. The wooden rafters always reminded her of a boat. 'Noah's Ark,' she thought. 'You kept him safe from disaster. And all those animals too.' She felt something sharp poke her in the back, and turned to find James exercising a Tyrannosaurus rex along the hymn-book shelf of the pew behind.

'Sorry, Sister Margaret,' whispered Sophie, whisking the child and the dinosaur back to their place. Probably the same blooming dinosaur she had stepped on in the kitchen was in that plastic bucket.

'Are we religious Sisters just dinosaurs?' Margaret suddenly prayed in anguish. 'Do you need nuns any more? Is there a place in the Ark for us? But you killed off all the dinosaurs,' she thought bleakly, if a little confusedly. The bell for the beginning of Mass rang, breaking her thoughts, bringing her back from mixed metaphors of prehistoric times to the present day, to a kind priest and beautiful flowers and the colours and candles, and her Sisters, and good people praying around her, and the Mass. Somehow, even if only for forty minutes or so, the readings at Mass, the beautiful words of the liturgy, Communion itself, all lifted her out of her worries and did her good.

'From age to age, you gather a people to yourself,' she repeated. Maybe it wasn't about dinosaurs, it was about generations of people muddling along, trying to love each other, making mistakes, asking God for help. Things did work out. She glanced to each side at Sister Bridget and Sister Cecilia and felt a rush of love for them and for their faith, when hers felt so weak.

Father Hugh was available after Mass and Margaret asked the others to go on home whilst she went to confession about being so horrible to Sister Bridget. It was a relief. Father Hugh was always so kind.

'Thank God for a good confession. Say three Hail Marys and try to be especially nice to her today, to make up for it,' he counselled. 'But forgive yourself too, as the good Lord forgives you. He knows you are under great strain.'

After lunch at the convent, Margaret walked back into town and met Linda, as arranged, at the higgledy-piggledy little bookshop.

They queued up for coffees and brought them over to a table for two.

'I am so glad you enjoyed the lecture today. I do want to apologise again for upsetting you so much the other day, with your family being sprung on you,' said Margaret, choosing her words carefully and praying for inspiration. 'I can't leave it at that. I know Sister Helen was very fond of you, and I am worried about you.'

Linda stirred her coffee, even though she had put no sugar in it, and bit her lip, looking down so Margaret couldn't see her tears.

'I want to understand. Please let me help,' said Margaret. 'I know Sister Helen would want me to.'

'I don't know. When I am at work, I feel fine, but as soon as I am home, I am so tired. I am so tired, Sister Margaret. I do actually feel a lot better this afternoon – that exhibition and lecture were fascinating – but I'm scared that when I get home, I will just feel so exhausted again.'

'And have you been to the doctor?'

'No, because what sort of illness means that I am fine at work, but tired at home?'

'And do you feel tired when you go to see Sophie and James? Toddlers can be very tiring . . .'

'I don't know. James is at nursery full days now, so Sophie doesn't need me so much during the week any more. I used to work my hours around them, working early or late to look after James and give her a break during the day, but Sophie has gone back to teaching part-time and I think at the weekends they should have some family time because Ben works hard too. I don't feel I should intrude.'

'I'm sure they don't feel like that, Linda,' said Margaret. 'I'm sure they would love to see you. James seemed very excited to see you the other day. Why would visiting them be intruding? I think they miss you, Linda.'

Linda gave a little sob. 'I'm sorry. I miss them all so much too, but I feel so needy and useless. I just feel as if I am a bottomless pit of need and misery, and I don't want to impose that on them. That's not what a grandmother should be like. I'm awful company, Sister.'

'You don't seem awful company to me at all,' said Margaret.

'I just . . . when I'm at work, I am the manager. I'm good at my job. I know what I am doing. But when I'm not at work . . . In the past, all my free time was being James's grandmother, helping Sophie. Before that I was caring for Mum. I've had years of caring for people. Dad is such a happy and busy person. He's always over at the convent, gardening – he doesn't even need me to cook for him, as Sister Bridget gives him his lunch, and he says it's his main meal. I don't know what to do with all this free time. I don't know who I am any more.'

'Oh, Linda, this is not surprising. You have spent all your life looking after others – Sophie, caring for your mum, helping with James. But you are more than the people you care for. You can have dreams, too, now. What would you like to do? What makes you happy?'

Linda shrugged. 'Work does, but at the same time I feel a bit stuck. I've been at Bluebirds since I was eighteen, and I'd like a change, I suppose. Management isn't what I want to do with the rest of my life.'

'Well, what is it about work you like? What brings you joy?'

'I suppose my favourite thing is visiting the houses themselves. I loved looking round the convent, actually. I know it went wrong at the end, but actually looking around the building was so interesting. I loved that. There are so many beautiful houses out there, so much fascinating history about the architecture.'

'And you liked the lecture today? You said you didn't feel tired looking at the paintings, or listening to the lecture.'

'No, it was brilliant. I loved Jack Mortimer's paintings, and in the lecture I learnt so much about him and his use of colour, and the influence of Augustus John on his work. Dr Woodburn was so interesting about the background of the Great War too.'

'I think you should think about what makes you happy, Linda, what brings you joy and energy. You didn't come across as tired then at all, talking about architecture and Jack Mortimer.'

'No, you are right.'

'Did you ever think about going to university? I know you were going to go when you were young.'

'I couldn't leave Fairbridge and Dad and Sophie and James and Ben.'

'You wouldn't have to – Dr Woodburn and the Department of Art and Architectural History at Fairbridge have a very good reputation. You could go to university. You have been working since you were eighteen – do you have savings?'

'I was putting money aside for Sophie.'

'Sophie can cope. She has a good degree, a lovely husband and parents-in-law. You've done enough.'

'I don't know,' said Linda, hesitantly.

'Linda, please promise me you will think about this, and really listen to what gives you energy. Read some books about art history and architecture. I am sure Dr Woodburn would talk to you about what you would need to apply. Don't worry – everything will fall into place.'

Margaret got up and hugged Linda, and for both women it felt as though Helen was very near.

'Thank you,' said Linda. 'I feel hope now. You're so good to talk to. I wish I had talked to you before.'

'So do I,' said Margaret. 'But now we have started, we mustn't stop!'

Eleven

The next evening, the Bishop welcomed them to his home again. He poured a glass of sherry for all the Sisters, even abstemious Sister Cecilia, but not for Father Hugh, who had offered to drive again.

'Well,' said the Bishop, after Margaret sat and let Father Hugh and Sister Bridget and Sister Cecilia explain everything, 'how satisfying this all is! It can't be a coincidence that the lottery win and the story of the Flying Nun have all happened within a week. This seems meant.'

Margaret wished she could share in everyone else's enthusiasm. She had the odd feeling of being disconnected, an onlooker.

'I have also uncovered some very interesting documents in the library today, My Lord,' said Sister Cecilia.

'Bishop John, please,' the Bishop corrected Sister Cecilia jovially. This evening was an absolute answer to his prayer. Only that very morning, praying in the cathedral, he had been tempted to despair about the lack of faith in today's society, the crisis in the Catholic Church, the lack of reverence for the holy. He had thought about his upcoming meeting in May with Cardinal Hume, longing to have something impressive to tell him about the diocese, and he had asked for faith, and then this wonderful little Flying Nun had appeared out of nowhere. 'And what would these be?'

'It was in the Edward Mortimer archive. When he died, as such an important person in the town all his personal papers were passed to the library. I have been working through them for my history of Fairbridge, but I confess that I was concentrating on papers related to England. This was a letter from Italy I had not yet looked at, but I thought that because of our discovery the other day, I should take a look, and I believe in the letter we have the final answer to our puzzle. I copied it out. It's from a Monsignor Lawrence, based in Rome, written to Edward in 1925.'

'Fascinating!' said the Bishop.

'If I may read it out, Bishop John?' said Cecilia.

'Please do,' he said.

Cecilia fumbled in her handbag and brought out a black notebook. Her hands trembled slightly as she opened it and read from her own meticulous notes.

' "Dear Edward, Your little parlourmaid appears to have become something of a local saint. I have uncovered a report, which I enclose, from some five years ago, of an English nun in the convent in a town in Italy who was seen to be levitating during Divine Office." '

'He goes on to say: "As you mentioned a convent in Cardellino in your letter of enquiry, I presume this to be the same young woman with whom you were concerned. So," ' Sister Cecilia continued, ' "I took it upon myself to make enquiries about the present whereabouts of this same religious. I am sorry to relate that it appears that the young religious Sister, your family's former employee, has gone to meet Our Lord and His Blessed Mother."'

'She died, you see,' interrupted Sister Bridget unhelpfully. Sister Cecilia ignored her and continued.

'"I am reliably informed by a fellow priest that Cardellino has started to have somewhat of a reputation. Apparently your Ellen Kerr, or Sister Angelina, as she is referred to in the newspaper cuttings describing her when she was alive, is, in death, interceding for childless couples and obtaining for them the gift of a child."'

'Well, that certainly is most interesting,' said the Bishop. 'I must say that I have never heard of this Ellen Kerr. So, she was a local Fairbridge girl, the Mortimers' parlourmaid?'

'That's not the end of the letter. Why don't you continue, Sister?' prompted Sister Bridget.

'Oh, yes. Well, the letter finishes with the Monsignor saying – now, let me see – ah, yes, here it is. He says, "I must confess to an eagerness to find out more about this saintly Englishwoman. I feel that God may have prompted you, through your scruples as to the eventual fate of your former servant, to contact me, and through me to give England, Our Lady's Dowry, another saint to be proud of. I intend to travel next month to Cardellino, with a view to seeing if we can open proceedings to have Ellen Kerr, or Sister Angelina, be officially recognised as a saint."'

'Good heavens. That would have made her a local celebrity here. Why have we never heard of her? Did the Monsignor never go through with it?'

Sister Cecilia sat up proudly. 'Well, I can't be sure as to what happened exactly, but I made some enquiries to an archivist I know who has done a lot of research on Catholic clergy in Rome. She discovered that this Monsignor Lawrence died in Rome the same month this letter was written.'

'So that is perhaps why nobody has followed up this Sister Angelina's cause,' said Father Hugh, looking over at the Bishop.

'Surely her community in Italy would have done so?' mused Sister Margaret.

'I have made enquiries and there is nothing listed. There appear to be no pending investigations for Sister Angelina of Cardellino, as far as I can tell,' said Sister Cecilia. 'I have found no books, no articles, no pamphlets about her. Nothing. It is a mystery.'

'Perhaps it was a question of resources,' suggested the Bishop. 'Regrettably, the canonisation process requires quite a lot of research, and that means time and money.'

'I've always thought there was something wrong about paying to get a saint made,' said Margaret, surprising herself and everyone else. 'What about St Francis – I thought he was poor? Or St Patrick – or St Bridget, or Margaret or Cecilia, for that matter. Who paid for them?'

'Well, of course, it isn't the older saints we are talking about,' said Sister Cecilia, looking over at the Bishop in embarrassment. 'Nowadays we know there have to be a lot of investigations, detective work and so forth. We know they have to employ a devil's advocate to make sure that there aren't any skeletons in cupboards, so to speak. The Church has to be sure. It doesn't do to involve the Church in scandal.'

'Well, still,' Margaret said rebelliously, 'don't you think it's terrible to pay for a saint?'

Cecilia was looking at her, appalled, as if Margaret had taken leave of her senses.

'Maybe I have,' thought Margaret.

'"Pay for a saint",' the Bishop repeated thoughtfully. 'I am sure that if you find enough information in Italy, God will make sure that any necessary funds are found to go through the process. There are some influential Catholic donors who would, I am sure, be interested.'

'Would these donors be interested in paying for the repairs to the church roof?' asked Father Hugh, but they could tell from the tone of his voice he had no expectation of a positive response. And he was right.

'Ah, I'm afraid there we expect the parish to come up with the funds,' said the Bishop smoothly. 'I am afraid if we start approaching the donors I have in mind to pay for all the church roofs with holes in them, we would quickly overwhelm them! The generous donation from the Sisters must have helped, surely?'

Father Hugh nodded, though he should have shaken his head. The Bishop had that sort of effect on him.

'So,' continued the Bishop, 'you most emphatically do have my blessing for this fact-finding pilgrimage.' He paused for a moment.

'You will need some time to prepare. I think a week is rea-sonable. Yes,' he nodded approvingly, agreeing with himself. The time was now. He wanted as much good news as possible ready for his upcoming meeting with the Cardinal. 'A week is right. I suggest you go to Fairbridge Travel Agency and buy three tickets for a flight to Rome for next Sunday and book a taxi and rooms in a hotel in this Cardellino for . . . three nights should be enough.'

'Next Sunday?' said Margaret, startled. 'A week today?'

'Yes, Sunday,' said the Bishop, in a tone that did not invite further discussion. 'You have passports?'

'Yes, we have passports. Sister Helen got them all renewed two years ago, when we thought we were going to Lourdes for Sister Basil's jubilee, before we knew about the money problems we had. Then Sister Helen got ill and everything changed and it all got postponed. But, I . . . I'm not sure if the lottery money will have come through in time,' said Margaret, stuttering a little in disbelief at the speed of it all.

The Bishop opened a drawer and took out a chequebook. Then, taking out a very fine fountain pen, he wrote a cheque for £2,000, signed it and gave it to Sister Margaret.

Father Hugh tried not to feel a pang that the Bishop had never done anything like that for him.

'You can pay me back when the lottery money comes through. Then, I do not want you to worry – I will be speaking to the Cardinal and I am sure we can find more money for investigations into the canonisation process et cetera. The important thing, I feel, is for you to go as soon as possible to find out about this story. I have a feeling, Sisters, that directly approaching the nuns yourselves would be better than writing a letter.'

'But we don't speak Italian,' said Sister Margaret.

'Hopefully they will speak English, most people do,' said the Bishop, rather airily Sister Margaret felt. 'If there *is* any problem, contact me and I should be able to find someone in Rome who can join you. But I have a feeling, given all that has happened for you so far with this, that it will all fall into place, and, to be honest, I'm hesitant to tell too many people at this stage. It's delicate. You will need to be discreet. Technically, this will be a matter for the Italian Church. There will be local bishops, local church interest in Italy, and we don't want to step on any ecclesiastical toes or start any gossip. But I know I can trust your judgement on this. For the time being, you are merely going on pilgrimage to Rome. Cardellino and the little Flying Nun will remain our secret.'

'Thank you so much,' said Margaret, looking at the cheque in bemusement.

'Isn't it exciting!' said Sister Bridget. 'I feel like we're in some holy spy film. Thank you so much! But what about your meals, Father Hugh?'

'Ah, don't you worry about me,' said Father Hugh, who, with Sister Bridget going away, was cheered at the thought of so much culinary temptation being removed. It would be nice to have some relief from the constant feasting. A little bit of fasting could be a treat.

'I don't want you to worry about a thing, Sisters,' said the Bishop. 'From now on I want you to concentrate on getting ready for this exciting pilgrimage. Now, if you bow your heads, I will give you all a blessing before you go to buy your tickets and pack.'

Margaret got ready for bed. She unpinned her veil and placed it on the side. She put on her long blue nightie, so warmly necessary in their cold Fairbridge home, full of unwanted spaces and gaps for unwanted draughts. She placed her neat navy suit on a hanger and knelt down beside her bed for a last prayer before sleep.

A vision of the young nun so filled with God's spirit that she levitated filled her mind, and Sister Margaret found herself longing for the fervour and enthusiasm – the sheer energy – of her youth.

'Where has my oomph gone, Lord?' she prayed. 'Please give me purpose.' Margaret was surprised to feel a tear trickling down her cheek. 'Oh for goodness' sake,' she thought angrily. She prayed again, as she had at Evening and Night Prayer, for self-effacing Miss Taylor, and that extraordinarily kind nurse, and even for the patient pregnant cat. She thought of the young nun, her sister in religion, albeit from another time, and prayed for her intercession for the community. 'Sister, if you are truly a saint, help us and pray for us. Intercede for us to be filled with the Holy Spirit. Intercede for us' – she fell back on the imagery of the psalms – 'to be lifted on eagles' wings in God's love.' She smiled to herself at her uncharacteristic floweriness, and she found herself suddenly, and unexpectedly, touched by Joy. She had knelt down, weary and depressed and troubled by aches in her bones. She got up from her knees with the feeling of a burden being lifted and got into bed to sleep the soundest sleep she'd had for months.

Twelve

On Tuesday morning, George made his way down the stairs to his travel agency and winced at the memory of the day before. He had sat alone and drunk too much, recovering from such a disappointing weekend, thanks to Mother. He had suggested taking Matthew out for a drink on Saturday night to celebrate the study day, and had been so happy when Matthew had agreed – but then Mother had decided to have a dizzy turn in the late afternoon and had fallen and cut her leg. He had ended up closing the agency an hour early, taking her to A & E and spending all Saturday night with her. Sunday lunch was an obligation he could not miss, and he couldn't leave her alone on Sunday night, and so the whole weekend had passed, not to anyone's happiness. Monday was his day off, so he was already there and had the delight of watching her be embarrassingly rude to the nice district nurse who was dressing her wound. He had apologised to the nurse on the doorstep when she left, then went back in and stayed as long as he could bear, making his mother lunch and dinner, even though she was perfectly capable of doing that herself. He had then gone home and wasted the rest of the evening drinking Rioja and watching his video collection of murder mysteries back to back. Now it was Tuesday morning, he was exhausted and hungover, and already it felt as though the week ahead was too long.

'I'm a disappointment to my mother, and I'm swiftly becoming a disappointment to myself,' he said, walking into the shop. Jenny had rung in sick, but he wasn't expecting a busy day. He switched on the computer and turned the door sign from Closed to Open, and was surprised to see two customers waiting outside.

'Hello!' said a young woman, pushing the door open and rushing in so eagerly that George had to step out of the way in order not to get struck.

'Ooh – sorry!' said the girl. 'We're just so excited, you see.' She was in her early twenties, with dark curls and an open, friendly face, prettily made-up, wearing an inexpensive, fashionable high-street dress and jacket, diamanté studs and high heels. She was holding on to the arm of a tall, fit-looking young man around the same age who was wearing jeans and a blue checked shirt and cotton jacket, not once disentangling her arm from his, and on the hand on his sleeve glittered a small diamond engagement ring. The man was looking down on her with such love that George felt a pang of self-pity.

'Yes?' he said, but then was actually a bit shocked by how unfriendly he sounded. Miguel would have been so disappointed. Miguel's sister Anna even looked a little like this girl, and they had had such good times with her. But this wasn't Anna. And Miguel wasn't here. Still. This wasn't good for business. 'How can I help you?' George continued, trying to sound more enthusiastic. This would not be a luxury tour or a safari, that was for sure. Neither of these people looked well off.

'Well,' confided the girl. 'We're getting married, you see.'

George envied the way she could so easily announce her love, stroking her fiancé's jacketed arm and smiling up at him without a care in the world.

'And you are hoping to go when?'

'Well, this is the exciting bit,' said the girl. 'We're getting married this coming Saturday morning, but it's all been a bit awful because there are buckets all over the church.'

George frowned.

'Sorry – buckets?'

'Yes, buckets. There's a leak, you see, and I cried. Because, you know, going up the aisle and the buckets. It just wasn't my idea of a wedding. Of course, it might not rain. Chris says it won't.' And she looked up at Chris adoringly as he smiled and nodded.

'Oh, so handsome Chris is a weather forecaster,' thought George.

'Anyway, Chris says that after we have our night in the hotel in Fairbridge on Saturday – my mum and dad have paid for that – instead of going to the Lakes on Sunday, to my auntie's caravan – which is really nice, and it is really kind of her to offer – he wants to make up for the buckets and take me to *Rome*! So that's what we want.'

'You want a holiday in Rome? For when?'

'This Sunday,' said the girl, trustingly. 'Until Wednesday. Chris has just sold his motorbike,' and she went on tiptoes to kiss her fiancé. 'He's so wonderful.'

Chris, who had let her do all the talking, looked down at her and smiled.

And George was undone by this. He looked across at the

couple, then looked down to hide sudden tears. This was real love.

Sod Mother and her mean summing-up of people. He had thought that Miguel had changed that trait in him, made him a better person. But inherited pettiness and envy obviously weren't that far below the surface. *You are a self-pitying snob, George, and that's not good enough.*

'Sit down, and we will see what we can do,' he said out loud. 'So, how much are you thinking of spending?'

'Chris won't tell me,' said the girl, squeezing her beloved's hand and beaming at him.

The young man reached into his pocket and got out a folded piece of paper, pushing it across the table to George. The two men's eyes met. Chris's brown eyes were pleading.

George opened the paper and understood why. Even if they were staying for just a few nights, this amount would cover the plane flights but very little else. The accommodation would be hostel standard. If buckets in the church had made the girl cry, it would be nothing compared to the honeymoon.

'It may be that there just won't be anything at this short notice,' George started to explain. He saw the look of raw disappointment in the girl's eyes, but how she quickly covered it up.

'I don't mind, Chris. I really don't. We can go another time. It was a lovely thought. And you're right, I'm sure it won't rain. I don't mind where we go, as long as we are together.'

George felt torn between anger and pity. Why was he being put in this position? He wasn't some sort of honeymoon fairy godmother.

'Could you . . . could you look a bit more and let me know if you find anything?' said the young man, and gave George a card.

Ah. He's a gardener. No money growing on trees for him, poor lad. It will take a miracle to find them an amazing honeymoon in Rome for the amount he has, at this short notice.

'I'll get back to you. I can't promise anything. I'm afraid I don't think there is much hope, but I'll do my best,' said George.

'Thank you for trying,' said the girl and Chris at the same time, and they left the shop hand in hand. George saw them kiss quickly on the street before they went off in opposite directions, and he saw how they smiled at each other, but how their faces fell when they thought the other couldn't see.

'They love each other, Miguel,' said George out loud. 'Like we did. I miss you so much.' He grabbed a tissue and blew his nose. 'Yes, yes, I know you find them adorable. I know you aren't jealous of them for getting married or being on honeymoon. For both being alive. Jealousy just wasn't part of you. If you *are* listening, if you *are* up in Heaven with your precious saints, as you believed, Miguel, then maybe *you* can help them get their honeymoon. And whilst you're listening – *if* you are listening, Miguel, you darling man – please, please help me. How about praying for me? Because I can't do it. I can't do this on my own. I can't do anything on my own any more.'

And at that point three nuns came in.

George wasn't an expert on nuns. He had seen *Sister Act*, 1 and 2, with Miguel, who had adored them, but he didn't know any nuns himself, so he was a little startled by meeting three all at once in his agency. They were not dressed in long habits, but all had veils and crosses, and the little one, with her big smile, was particularly engaging. He knew she would have been Miguel's favourite.

'How can I help you, Sisters?' he said.

'We've come to book tickets to Rome,' she said excitedly, in a broad Irish accent. Yes, Miguel would have adored her. 'For this Sunday.'

'What is it with Rome and this Sunday?' he thought.

'I see. Very good. And you will be coming back . . . when?'

'Actually, I think we will need three return tickets and initially to come back on Wednesday, but perhaps we need them to be open returns, as we are not quite sure how long we will be there,' said the youngest of the nuns, aged in her late fifties. Her voice was educated, clear, English. She seemed resigned rather than excited, which was interesting. George would have thought all nuns wanted to go to Rome.

'We're not really staying in Rome, you see. We're going to a little place an hour or so away called Cardellino,' said the Irish nun, chattily. 'Do you know it?'

'I know *cardellino* means "goldfinch" in Italian,' said George, 'but I don't know any place as such.'

The oldest nun looked a little agitated, and glared at the Irish one as if she didn't want her to say any more, but her companion appeared not to notice and carried on.

'Isn't it wonderful that you know Italian? We're going on a pilgrimage to Cardellino, but none of us know a word.'

'We're going on a pilgrimage to *Rome*,' corrected the youngest of the nuns, who seemed aware of the oldest nun's agitation. 'We're just visiting Cardellino.'

'Oh! Yes, yes, of course. We're only visiting Cardellino. Of course. Just visiting,' said the Irish nun, looking very guilty.

What is going on? It's a bit like a detective story. What are they hiding? Are they even nuns? George made himself laugh inside at the ridiculous question – these were obviously the real thing – but he kept his composure.

'So, you would like tickets to Rome. No accommodation there?'

'No, not this time,' said the youngest nun. 'We'd like to spend the day there, hopefully get Mass at St Peter's, and then on to Cardellino in the evening. I believe it is about a forty-five-minute drive there. I don't know if you can order a taxi at all? I don't feel confident about driving.'

'I do have a contact, yes. So you would like me to book return flights to Rome and find transport to Cardellino and three nights' accommodation there, but none in Rome?' said George.

'Yes, please,' said the youngest nun, who seemed to be in charge.

'And I presume you would like early-morning tickets to Rome so that you can spend a full day there?'

'Yes, yes, thank you,' she said, almost as an afterthought, although George noticed how delighted the other two were. So the pilgrimage to Rome wasn't as important as this visit to Cardellino, wherever it was. Jessica Fletcher from *Murder, She Wrote* would have had a field day. Miss Marple would have got it out of them in no time, he was sure.

The nuns gave him their passports and George, having ascertained their budget, looked things up whilst they waited. The Irish nun could not sit still, deciding instead to walk around, looking at the posters on the walls and beaming. She was enjoying being in the travel agency like nobody George had ever met. Miguel had been an enthusiast too – he was the only person George could have imagined looking at posters with quite such relish. George noticed out of the corner of his eye that she was trying to interest the oldest nun in a brochure, but the oldest nun was sitting down with her eyes shut and appeared to be praying with her beads. It was probably the first time anyone had prayed in his agency. George suddenly remembered the look in the young man's eyes as he had passed him that piece of paper. Maybe technically that wasn't a prayer, but it had certainly had the desperation of a heartfelt wish.

'Right, so I have found the hotel. There seems to be only one in Cardellino. I need to ring them now.'

George picked up the phone and very soon was speaking fluent Italian. He nodded and frowned, looking over at the Sisters, but then, in response to what he heard on the other end of the phone, a surprised smile came over his face.

'Sisters – they are asking, are you from St Philomena's Convent in Fairbridge,' he said.

'Yes, yes, we are,' said Sister Cecilia, proudly.

He replied, and carried on talking, looking down at the various figures he had written on the paper beside him, nodding his head more and more as he did so. He said something and then paused, turning to Sister Margaret.

'Well, I'm not quite sure what is happening, as it seems that the hotel has been closed for refurbishment, but when I mentioned you were nuns coming from Fairbridge, they have decided to open up especially for those three nights, and they have even offered to send a car to collect you and bring you to the hotel. They have quoted a very good price. They said they can take you back to the airport for your return flight on the Wednesday too. They must have a soft spot for nuns!'

'It's meant!' said Sister Bridget, excitedly. 'They heard we were from Fairbridge. They must know about—'

'Well, thank you very much,' Sister Margaret interrupted. 'And the tickets to Rome?'

'I'm afraid I can't get all three seats together going out, so one of you will have to sit in a separate row, but you are very close. It's very nearly full. Is that acceptable?'

The Sisters all nodded and agreed that it was.

'So,' said George. 'I will go ahead and book with the hotel, then. They really have given you an amazingly good deal.'

'Could you just quickly ask them if anyone speaks English there?' said Sister Margaret, suddenly. 'We might need an interpreter to help us with something.'

'Oh, what a wonderful idea!' said Sister Bridget.

George spoke in Italian, and then smiled and continued in English. 'I will tell the Sisters this.' He turned and did a thumbs-up, mouthing 'no problem' to the Sisters, then continuing on the phone. 'This is excellent news. So, if we could book, as we discussed . . .'

'The Bishop was right!' whispered Sister Bridget loudly and enthusiastically.

'It seems so,' said Margaret. It all seemed unstoppable.

'That's fine, then. Three returns to Rome Fiumicino Airport, leaving early Sunday morning, so that should give you a full day in Rome,' George said, passing over an itemised bill. Margaret wrote out a cheque, and George printed out the tickets.

'Margaret Lewis?' he read out.

'Here, thank you,' said Sister Margaret.

'The car will pick you up outside the English College in Rome. It's easy to find, and not far from St Peter's. I have put a map in each envelope.'

'Thank you,' said Margaret, with more resignation than excitement in her voice.

'Jean McKenzie?' he said next.

'That's you, Sister Cecilia,' said Sister Bridget, unnecessarily.

Sister Cecilia received the passport and tickets reverently.

'May I ask why the name is different?' said George.

'Well, you see, in the old days we were given names when we joined, but then later, in the sixties, after Vatican II – that's the second big council of all the bishops in the Roman Catholic Church – we had the chance to choose to go back to our baptismal names,' Sister Bridget answered, unasked, for Sister Cecilia, much to Cecilia's and Margaret's relief. Cecilia was not the best at explaining religious life and its more unusual twists. 'I liked being Bridget more than Sister Paul, as St Bridget is very important to me, so I changed back, but Sister Cecilia liked being Sister Cecilia better than Jean, so she kept it. What were you, Margaret?'

'I was Sister Aloysius, and I changed back too,' said Sister Margaret, 'but I'm sure Mr . . .'

'Sanders. George Sanders,' offered George.

'. . . I'm sure Mr Sanders doesn't want a potted history of religious life,' said Margaret.

'Not at all, I honestly think it is fascinating,' said George. 'I don't think I have ever talked to nuns before. So these, then, for Bridget O'Sullivan, are yours, Sister Bridget?' and he passed the envelope to her.

Bridget O'Sullivan nodded and clutched it like a prize, beaming with joy.

'What a wonderful vocation you have!' she exclaimed to George, looking him in the eyes.

'Pardon?'

'You must bring so much joy to so many people in your work,' she explained, her eyes full of approval and kindness. 'So many people needing well-needed breaks, adventures, honeymoons, too, I imagine? How wonderful to make people's dreams come true!'

George was completely undone by this, and to his utter surprise burst into tears. The nuns all exclaimed with concern – Sister Cecilia taking one step back, Sisters Margaret and Bridget stepping forward.

'I'm so sorry. It just took me by surprise. My mother thinks I am a failure – a huge disappointment. My . . . a dear friend died just two years ago . . . I don't know why it is hitting me so hard today. Maybe it is because he loved nuns. My mother isn't being very easy. Sorry. I'm just a little emotional. I'm so sorry,' he babbled.

'We'll go,' said Sister Cecilia.

'Are you all right?' asked Sister Margaret, kindly.

George sobbed a bit more.

'You poor man! Could you take Sister Cecilia home, Sister Margaret? I'll stay,' said Sister Bridget.

George heard the ping of the bell as the door shut and then, somehow, he was in Bridget's care. He found himself being given a big hug and was handed a huge wad of tissues that he proceeded to howl his way through. The shop sign was turned to Closed, and Sister Bridget bustled him out to the back kitchen, where she gave him a cup of tea and a biscuit in what seemed a miraculously short time.

'You haven't many biscuits left,' she said, sitting down for a cup of tea with him and looking in the nearly empty tin. 'I'll come back with a nice cake later. And look at this – a lovely little fellow popping through the cat flap to keep you company. Isn't he a dote?'

Sebastian the Magnificent jumped up onto George's lap and pushed his head against his chest, purring loudly.

'Well, he obviously loves you *very* much!' said Sister Bridget, approvingly. 'Isn't this a lovely set-up you have? A top-class travel agency and this lovely little back kitchen and storeroom here, and I see a pretty little enclosed garden for him to sunbathe in, out the back. And would your flat be upstairs – I see a fire escape in the garden? I suppose the little fellow can go up and down without coming into the agency?'

George nodded, not quite sure why the comings and goings of his cat should be of such interest.

'I thought so,' nodded Sister Bridget. 'Very thoughtful of you. He has a lovely safe garden to enjoy himself in whilst you are working, and he can come and go as he pleases.'

George felt ridiculously cheered by this praise. He had no idea he was doing so much right. People didn't normally praise forty-year-old men so thoroughly, and certainly not for cat care. She was talking to him as if he were five, but, surprisingly, he didn't mind at all.

'And this back kitchen is *immaculate*. I wish I could teach Father Hugh to clean up after himself. You always know when he has made himself a cup of tea. Well, I have to say, this whole enterprise is beautifully arranged. I don't know what your mother is disappointed in. Is she ill, do you think?' said Bridget conversationally, as if only an ill mother could disapprove of a son owning such a wonderful travel agency.

George gave a watery smile. 'She had a heart attack a year or so ago, not long after my friend died. I moved back from Spain to keep an eye on her. She lives on the London Road. But she isn't easy to please. I'm finding it rather . . . difficult.'

'She's probably lonely,' diagnosed Sister Bridget. 'A widow?' George nodded.

'So you lost your father, God rest him, too?'

'Yes – but fifteen years ago.'

'That's very hard. Any brothers or sisters?'

'No.'

'Well, that's a terrible pressure on you. You should bring her to bingo. I call the numbers every week. St Philomena's church hall, just round the corner. Is she able to walk?'

'She is, yes. She is fine now. Just . . . unhappy, really.'

'Well, then, tell her to come this Thursday. If you bring her yourself, you can leave her with me and go back to work. I'll introduce her to some nice friends.'

'I just don't think she would come, Sister. She has never played bingo.'

'She'll adore it!' predicted Bridget, confidently and utterly inaccurately. George couldn't think of anything his mother would like less. Sister Bridget saw the expression on his face and tilted her head to one side, considering. 'Would it help if I popped round? I live on the London Road myself. The big convent next to the school. What number?'

'Seventy-four. But I warn you, Sister, I really don't think Mother will come.'

Bridget patted him on the shoulder. 'Don't you worry about a thing. Leave it up to me.'

It was Sarah's day off and she was going to the hairdresser's before meeting an old friend for lunch. She knew she shouldn't be worrying about Antoinette Taylor on her day off, but she also planned to pop round to her later with a cake, and to check on the cat. She could bring her a slice of her favourite quiche, too, and a salad. In case she hadn't eaten lunch. Sarah was confident the cat would get fed, but not so sure about the woman.

She looked around at their shared space: their full book-shelves, still with many of her parents' books, her pot plants, Matthew's piano, the paintings their parents had chosen on the wall, the chairs and tables and sofa they had grown up with. It was a nice house. They liked each other's company. Things were comfortable, safe. They had good mutual friends, and friends of their own from work. They enjoyed walking holidays together, films, concerts. Separately, Matthew went to choir, she went to painting classes. Sometimes they played chess together. Matthew was an excellent cook. She gardened and friends who came over always said what a peaceful atmosphere there was. They both worked hard and were busy. There was nothing wrong with their lives.

But Sarah had a feeling things were going to change. Something in Matthew seemed different. He had never been so dedicated to the choir, so preoccupied. There was a spring in his step, a hopefulness, a vulnerability about him that she hadn't seen for years. He seemed . . . younger somehow. There was this mysterious friend who had helped him with his speech, who had gone to the radio station instead of her. It made her happy to see him happy again, but it made her feel scared for him too.

And it made her feel older than her twin. And that wasn't right.

She knew she had been snappy with Matthew recently, and she knew that it wasn't fair. It made her miserable to be mean to him.

They were thirty-eight. Life wasn't fixed. And Matthew being happy was a good thing. It was what she wanted for him, even if seeing him quite so happy and not knowing why, even if she suspected the reason, was . . . unsettling.

She checked her reflection in the hall mirror before she left the house. Her long blonde hair, tied back in a ponytail, even on her day off, bored her. She didn't want to be sensible Sarah any more.

Yes, it was time for a change.

Thirteen

Francesco watched his wife Maria clear the table after breakfast. He thought she was even more beautiful at fifty than when they had first met thirty years before, and he had never met a more beautiful twenty-year-old. Unselfconsciously, she pushed a strand of hair behind her ear, and he was filled with desire.

They shouldn't still be here in Cardellino. They should have been travelling by now, drinking wine, rising at dawn to watch the sunrise and going for long, moonlit beach walks, holding hands by the sea somewhere. It had been their promise to each other all those years ago when they had first agreed to come back to help. They would help run the hotel in the summer, and then they would travel.

'If we can travel every winter, I can cope,' Maria had said, twenty years before. She had gone for a long walk on her own to think it over when the idea of returning to Italy had first arisen, and she had come back to their flat in Paris prepared to give up her satisfying job and go back to Cardellino with him. When she decided something, she stuck to it. Even back then he had known she was truthful to a fault, but he had still wanted to check. He knew that she had given up so much when they realised they would never be able to have children. They had already changed their lives completely, and were happy, with good careers, good friends. To ask her to give it all up a second time seemed too much.

'Are you sure? It was never in our plans to run my grandmother's hotel,' Francesco had said.

'Let's change our plans then!' said Maria, laughing. She had looked into his eyes and hugged him. 'We've had to change much bigger plans before, and look, my love, after everything, it has worked out well. Let's have another adventure! That's what we are good at, you and me!'

And so they had come back to Cardellino, and for the next fifteen years, through all the springs and summers, they had run the hotel as Francesco's grandmother and great-uncle grew too old to do so. They worked so well as a team, and together made it a place of hospitality and fun and love. They made sure that everyone around their table felt welcome, and few noticed how skilled their hosts were, how hard they had worked to make strangers feel like friends, to keep the chat effortlessly lively whilst steering the table away from argument. The hotel was filled with laughter. Guests went to bed happy, even when they had unknowingly exhausted their hosts, and people booked year after year, counting down the months before they could see Maria's beautiful smile again, tell them both their news, get wise advice, laugh as Francesco told jokes and replenished their glasses with wine and served them wonderful meals. The children they had wanted might not have arrived, but they knew that everyone they met felt part of their family, and they had been happy. They worked hard every season and took long winter breaks, travelling, catching up with friends, old and new, cleaning and opening up the hotel again in the spring, refreshed, full of life and love. Life may not have been how they had planned it, but it had been good. It had been very good.

But these last five years had been too hard, thought Francesco. His great-uncle had died, and they were all grieving for him, but Nonna was on a different level. She was stuck, refusing to let go of anything belonging to him, refusing to move on, refusing to talk about the future. She refused to move, and in her increasing frailty could not be left alone. Francesco and Maria had cancelled their plans, and their treasured winter breaks, and were stuck in this limbo with her. And then Maria had been diagnosed with, and treated for, cancer.

This was not right, Francesco thought savagely. He couldn't bear that he was feeling so much anger towards his beloved Nonna, but he was. Maria didn't ask for much, but after all she had been through – the scare, the operation, the chemo – she deserved not to have this burden of the hotel any more. He wanted her to be delighted by new sights, to make new friends, to catch up with those she loved. And she loved so many, and so many loved her. The doctors said they had caught it in time, that there was no more sign of cancer, that she would just need yearly check-ups, but now he had come so close to losing her, he didn't want to waste a single day of their lives together. This was the first spring they had not opened. They had closed the hotel 'for refurbishment'. It was time for them to travel while they could. But then there was Nonna. She had had her life – why was she not letting them have theirs? Why would she not let go of the hotel and all her memories?

Maria looked over, caught his eye and smiled, and his heart flipped again. How had he ended up with such a beautiful woman?

'Come here, *carissima*,' he said, and pulled her into his arms.

'Are you worrying?' she asked, lovingly. 'Don't. Things are going to change. I can sense them changing already. I know it. The subject of that radio programme. Wasn't that a miracle?'

'A small miracle,' Francesco conceded. 'But knowing how much things are worth doesn't seem to make Nonna any keener on giving them up, to move on. To let us move on.'

'You have to be patient, my love. And now suddenly we have the nuns coming from Fairbridge. How can that not be a miracle too? That can't be a coincidence, not coming straight after the programme. Something is going to happen. Nonna wants to see them. This is exciting, Francesco. Something good is in the air, I feel it.'

'Something very good is in my arms,' said Francesco, smiling. 'That's all I am interested in feeling right now,' and he kissed her.

From the moment Sarah arrived at the hairdresser's and smelled its familiar mixture of hair products and fresh coffee, she knew she had made the right decision. It was a kind place. The receptionist took her sensible jacket as if it were a precious garment, and hung it up with care.

'Hi, Sarah! What can we do for you today?' asked Nick, the owner.

'I don't know,' said Sarah. 'I just need a change. I feel a bit stuck.'

Nick considered her.

'A big change?'

'Well, something that won't startle my patients too much,' said Sarah. 'But, yes, something different.'

'Hmm,' Nick said thoughtfully, weighing her hair in his hands and looking at it with the eyes of an artist, as if he were holding precious cloth or silk. 'Your hair is gorgeous and thick, and so long, and I love the colour, but maybe, if you tie it back normally anyway, let's take some length off, unleash that curl. I feel it's so long that it's weighing you down. Yes, yes, I can see what we could do. Would you be happy if I make quite a radical change?'

'Yes. Why not?'

Her hair was washed carefully by a young apprentice who conscientiously checked if the water was too hot or too cold, massaging her scalp and rubbing shampoo and conditioner into and then rinsing them out of her wet hair. Sarah closed her eyes, relaxed and enjoyed the attention.

Before she could fall asleep, the girl was putting a new towel around her shoulders, and ushering her to her seat.

The careful apprentice came with coffee and a newspaper. Nick glanced down at it as he cut her hair and the golden locks fell to the floor.

'Oh, the lottery nuns! Do you think they cheated and got a bit of divine help?'

'I met one of them last week, actually,' said Sarah. 'The younger-looking one, on the left.'

'Really, what was she like?'

'Kind. She used to work with one of my patients and she came over to help. We're trying to help her together.'

'That's so good to hear,' said Nick, combing her hair and snipping at the ends, assessing and measuring by eye, looking at her in the mirror as he did so. 'You do great work, Sarah. I really admire you. You and old Dr Pritchard were great with my nan. I won't forget that.'

'Thank you. Nick – I don't suppose you want a kitten, do you?'

'A kitten? Why, is your cat expecting?' asked Nick, stepping back and narrowing his eyes, scrutinising his work.

'I don't have a cat. It's the patient I was telling you about. A pregnant stray moved in with her, and the old lady won't agree to go into hospital until they all have homes.'

Nick resumed cutting and combing again with the concentration and confidence of an expert, turning the chair slightly to and fro as he did so.

'It's funny you should mention kittens. My wife's mad about cats, and she's been hinting about us getting one for ages. Her birthday's next month . . .'

'That would be perfect! Honestly, I have to get these kittens spoken for or she just won't agree to going in for the tests.'

'I'll take one. And I'm sure I can persuade one or two of my regulars too. Give me a ring when the kittens arrive and you see how many need homes, and I'll see what I can do.'

More locks fell to the floor, and Nick kept cutting. 'No going back now,' thought Sarah. Then he squirted sweet-smelling hair mousse into his hands and ran it through her wet hair, looking at her in the mirror. He got the hairdryer and the brush and blow-dried it.

'Now – what do you think?'

Sarah, still beaming about Nick's offer, looked up and was taken aback by her reflection.

'It's so good, thank you!' she said.

'I'm very pleased,' said Nick, with the dispassionate judgement of the artist. 'You look beautiful. It takes years off you.'

'I wish!' said Sarah, but suddenly, irrationally, she felt it was true. At least, she felt there was so much more life in front of her than before.

*

'And that's what happened today,' said George later that evening to Matthew, as they sat drinking in a quiet corner of the Swan. It was because of Sister Bridget. She had only left him on condition that he wouldn't have an evening on his own.

'Now, have you got a nice friend you could ring so you won't be on your own tonight? Probably better not to go and see your mother. You can ring her. You said she had plenty of food in, so I am sure she will be fine. But I think you need some company.'

So George had rung Mother and, fortified by Sister Bridget's understanding, had ignored the inevitable grumbles and guilt trips, saying he had a headache and wasn't up to coming round for dinner, and had then looked up Dr Matthew Woodburn in the phonebook and rung his university number to ask if he would like to go for a drink that evening. And, marvellously, Matthew had said yes.

'She's wonderful,' enthused George, helping himself to some crisps Matthew had considerately opened and left on the table between them. It wrung Matthew's heart to think of him sobbing, and he felt very grateful to this Sister Bridget. 'She came back later with an absolutely delicious banana cake for me, and she is going to visit Mother tomorrow. I don't hold out much hope in that area, though. But I adore her, Matthew.'

Matthew gave a snort of amusement. 'It sounds like she adores you too, and I'm not surprised!' he said, smiling at George, who was still rather emotional, but the words came out a little too fervently. George looked up, startled into hope by the tone, but Matthew carefully cooled it down, chiding himself silently.

Don't be a fool. Don't risk ruining things again, scaring him away if you've got this wrong. Maybe you shouldn't even try.

'I'd like to meet this Sister Bridget,' he said. 'I've actually already met the other sisters you describe – Sister Margaret and Sister Cecilia. Sister Cecilia is quite an expert on the Mortimer family, and came to last Saturday's opening of Jack Mortimer's exhibition. She definitely doesn't approve of him, that's for sure. Far too scandalous for her tastes. I think she is personally offended that I am researching him and not his brother. I imagine she would consider the fact that his brother wasn't an artist to be absolutely no excuse!' They smiled at each other. 'Hmm. And this place, Cardellino, you say Sister Cecilia didn't want to mention. For some reason that rings a bell,' Matthew continued thoughtfully. 'But I cannot quite remember why—'

'Something she said,' interrupted George. 'Something Sister Bridget said about me making dreams come true. I've been thinking about it all afternoon. There was a young couple in earlier and they really couldn't afford to have a honeymoon in Rome, but I've been thinking. I might be able to get a discounted package if I use some contacts. I haven't been on holiday myself this year, and I have an arrangement with a hotel in Rome . . .'

'And I have a cousin studying in Rome who might be able to arrange a pass to the Vatican,' said Matthew, warm again. 'I think I could ask him to get two free tickets to the Sistine Chapel for this honeymoon couple. Do you think they would like that?'

'I do!' said George. 'It's rather wonderful to think we can make someone's dreams come true like this!'

They beamed at each other and, to his embarrassment, Matthew found himself blushing a little.

'So, what do you think the choir should tackle next?' he asked, swiftly changing the subject.

*

The next morning, Chris had just finished weeding a front border when he decided to take a break. Grumpy old Mrs Sanders had been glaring at him through her window, as usual, daring him to take time off, although he and she both knew he always did an excellent job, but he had worked for hours and needed to get away for five minutes to stretch his legs, so he walked out anyway. He kept thinking about Emily and how hopeful she had been about Italy, and how he wished he earned more money so he could give her what she dreamt of. There was no way that travel agent could have tracked down something they could afford, but he found himself in the nearby public phone box ringing him anyway. Mrs Sanders could probably see him from her window. She had nothing better to do.

Amazed, he listened to the travel agent at the other end explain that he had been going to ring him at home that very evening about the full-board package he had found for this coming Sunday, and the complimentary tickets to the Sistine Chapel. A huge smile spread over Chris's face. He confirmed all the details and that they would be coming with their passports before the end of the day, and then, ignoring his miserable old client, whose accusatory gaze he could feel even through the glass pane of the telephone box, he found more coins in his pocket and rang his fiancée.

'Emily – it's me. I've got some incredible news!'

While he was talking on the phone, a cheerfully determined nun walked past him on the street, then turned up the drive to Mrs Sanders's house.

'I've confirmed the details for the Sistine Chapel tickets with my cousin,' said Matthew, ringing George at his agency on Thursday afternoon.

'Wonderful!' said George, still glowing from Emily and Chris's joy when they had come with their passports the day before. 'I'll ring tonight and tell them. They said this honeymoon means everything to them. They're staying one night in the hotel where the wedding reception is, and then they're off to Rome on the Sunday. They're so happy, I'd almost like to go with them!'

Matthew at the other end gave an amused snort.

'So . . . um . . .' George decided to be brave and make clear that he knew where he stood. 'Is Rome where you and Sarah went on honeymoon?'

'Pardon?' said Matthew, in surprise.

'Honeymoon. Did you and Sarah go on honeymoon to Rome?' George persevered.

'No. No. Sarah is my twin sister. I . . . I'm not married. I've never had a wife,' said Matthew.

There was a moment's silence. As neither man could see the other, they both rushed to fill it.

'I'm still trying to work out where I've heard the name Cardellino before—' began Matthew.

'And another miracle – Sister Bridget took Mother to bingo today. She rang me to say she had done so, and that Mother had even won a jar of jam. I doubt if Mother is going to admit to either of these things tonight,' continued George at the same time.

'Maybe she'll make you jam roly-poly,' said Matthew. 'That will be the clue.' He winced inside at the rather lame joke.

George laughed a little too enthusiastically at this.

'Yes – that'll give the game away! Sister Bridget said that Mother took a little while to get used to it, but then she cheered up when she won the jam, and she's agreed to go again in a fortnight, when the nuns get back.'

'Sister Bridget sounds like an amazing woman,' said Matthew.

'I really think she is,' said George. 'And I'm sure your sister is too,' he heard himself adding. 'I'd like to meet her.'

'What are you blithering on about, George?' he said to himself in a panic.

'Well,' said Matthew, sounding a little surprised. 'I'd be happy to introduce you.'

'Perhaps you would like to come to dinner soon?' said George. 'You and Sarah?'

Why did I invite Sarah too?

'Yes. Well, thank you. That would be very nice,' said Matthew, a little stiffly.

'Next Sunday?' said George. 'Seven p.m.?'

'I think that should be fine. I'll ask her and ring you back to confirm,' said Matthew.

Both men sighed as they put down their respective phones. The conversation hadn't quite ended as they had hoped.

On Friday, Emily, her mum and her bridesmaids all had their hair cut at the hairdresser's. Nick, who was coming to do their hair the next day, had provided complimentary cava for the already giggly wedding party. The whole salon felt lit up with happiness, as each stylist smiled at their client in the mirror and the bridesmaids, mother of the bride and bride called across to and complimented each other and generally got excited about the big day.

'I can't wait to marry Chris!' said Emily, who, as the bride, was having her hair cut by Nick himself. 'Then we're off to Italy for the best honeymoon *ever*, and then when we get back we are going to find our own home. Then I want the lot – kids, cats, dogs.' Emily waved her glass of cava enthusiastically.

'A career, too – but I definitely want a family. We might start with a cat. I'd love a cat.'

Nick smiled, and remembered Sarah's request.

'Well, if you want a kitten when you're back, I know some that need adopting.'

'Oh, I'd love one!' said Emily, longingly. 'It's just that Chris and I will be looking for a house and I suppose that if we're renting they probably won't let us have one.' She suddenly sounded a little deflated.

'You're staying with me first, and I wouldn't mind,' said Emily's mum.

'Yes, but then if we couldn't take him with us I'd be leaving you *and* the kitten,' said Emily. 'That would make me sad.'

'Let's not talk about sad things,' said Nick. 'Let's concentrate on making you the most beautiful bride St Philomena's has ever seen!'

'She will be!' said her mum, proudly. 'And don't forget to tell us about that kitten when it arrives. They'll be living with me, so there won't be any problem giving it a home, and they'll soon find one.'

'Oh, Mum!' said Emily, beaming again.

'Well, you've got to hope. Maybe Nick can keep an ear out for a cat-friendly flat for a young couple. Miracles do happen! Look at you two going to Rome when you didn't expect it. I think you're a lucky couple, Emily, I really do.'

In Cardellino, Nonna went and sat in her beloved's room. For years he had worked there, and she had come with food and drink when he would stay late. She walked over to the window, hearing the sound of her shoes, the familiar creak of the bare wooden floorboards, remembering the sound of his footsteps as he would walk to and fro, now fast, now slow, thinking of different approaches, different angles to his work. She stretched out her hand to the wooden shutters and touched them, remembering winter nights when the wood stove would be lit, candles filling the room so he could see to work, or hot summer evenings, when the smells of the warm earth and sun-warmed garden and orchard, the sound of cicadas outside, would drift through the open window . . . Then he would suddenly declare that he had worked enough that day, and take her in his arms. So many embraces, so many memories . . .

'I know I need to move out. I know that I can't manage the winters on my own any more, and Francesco and Maria are only staying here because of me. I know that I am being selfish. But how can I leave you?' she said as she walked around, her hand shaking as she touched each precious piece of work he had left. 'How can I walk away from our life together? Francesco and Maria – they still have each other. There are so many memories here, and I am losing them from my mind. I need to see them in front of me. If I leave this building, this home, these walls I love so well, how can I leave the work within them? If I cannot see this record of our love, how will I remember it existed?'

Fourteen

The Bishop had requested Father Hugh drive the Sisters to the airport early on Sunday morning and informed him that Monsignor Wilson, whose priest friend was still staying, would be happy to cover morning Mass. Father Hugh tried not to feel taken over. After all, he was glad to take the Sisters on the first leg of their adventure. It was nice to be involved in something so hopeful, like the lovely wedding on Saturday. That had been one of the happiest he had done in a while.

He drew up outside the convent, loaded the boot with the luggage, and the Sisters got in. Sister Cecilia took her place, solemn and determined, in the back of the car, her excitement only revealed by her blinking more than usual. Sister Bridget beside her, on the other hand, was fidgety with enthusiasm, rummaging in her bag to check if she had everything and beaming at everyone.

'Now, isn't that annoying – I've left the boiled sweets. You need boiled sweets for the flight. I bought a lovely bag from Mr Abidi only yesterday, but with all the chatting I must have left them on the counter.'

'You didn't tell him about the Flying Nun, did you?' asked Margaret warily, looking back over her shoulder from the front passenger seat. She knew Bridget and her enthusiasm.

'I'm sure she did not,' said Sister Cecilia.

'Indeed I did not,' replied Bridget indignantly, pride replacing offence as she remembered just how discreet she had been. 'I told him we were off for a pilgrimage to Rome with the lottery win – it was only a little white lie.'

'It's not a lie at all, Sister,' said Father Hugh, soothingly. 'I'm sure you'll have some time today to look around Rome before you set off to Cardellino. Right, here we are, Sisters. I'll drop you off here, and God bless you all.'

They checked their luggage, and got through passport control and security. There was a small bit of excitement when Sister Cecilia set off the security alarm because she had kept her rosary in her pocket, but they finally got through and found a clean table to sit at for a cup of coffee before making their way through departures for their early-morning flight to Rome.

Margaret smiled at the other Sisters. She still wasn't exactly happy about this trip, but she had a sense of letting go. They were on this journey whether she liked it or not, and there was no turning back. Sister Bridget was quite obviously having the time of her life as she drank her cappuccino and looked around at all the steadily increasing hustle and bustle of the airport, even at such an early hour. She looked excited and very happy. Cecilia had got out the little leather purse she carried her rosary beads in, had extracted the photograph of Sister Angelina, and was looking at it.

'Cecilia looks so thrilled, Lord. Whatever happens later, getting away like this is good,' Margaret prayed in her head.

'I think we should probably be making our way. I see Gate

7 has come up on the board. Have we all got what we need?' said Sister Margaret out loud.

There were hurried checks in bags. Sister Bridget had bought another big packet of boiled sweets for them all to suck on the flight. She normally went by coach or train back to Ireland, and the pilgrimages to Lourdes she had been on involved very long train journeys, with time to say many rosaries, but the last time she had gone back to Ireland it had all been such a rush that she had caught a plane, and had suffered terribly from earache.

In an effort to be more committed than she felt, Margaret had bought a small Italian phrasebook and guide to Rome.

'*Andiamo*,' she said, consulting the page. '*Prendiamo l'aereo.*'

'Ooh! What does that mean?' asked Sister Bridget.

'"Let's fly!"'

Even though it was early, the flight to Rome was fully booked and buzzing with cheerful anticipation. There seemed to be at least two big organised pilgrimage parties, each with matching coloured holdalls, and a scattering of priests and nuns throughout the plane when they got on. People loaded bags into overhead lockers, edged past each other, made unintentional physical contact and apologised. Margaret and the Sisters found their seats and stashed their luggage away. Sister Bridget was in the middle, sitting next to a tired-looking Italian businessman in the aisle seat, with Sister Margaret sitting next to her, by the window, and Sister Cecilia directly behind him, next to a young couple who seemed slightly disconcerted by being seated next to an elderly nun in a navy blue habit.

Sister Bridget simultaneously sucked her boiled sweet and fingered her rosary beads, frowning with concentration as she peered forward, trying to follow the balletic movements of the young woman giving the safety instructions in Italian and English. She was totally absorbed by the whole flying experience. The plane taxied down the runway and then set off at an alarming speed, slowly rising into the air, tilting seats and challenging their sense of perspective. At last, as the plane righted itself, Bridget put her rosary beads back in her little purse and then back into her handbag, gave a small satisfied sigh for a job well done, and thanked God that her ears, this time, were absolutely fine.

The plane ascended, and Sister Margaret looked down over fields, gardens, houses and roads. All those lives going on, with their hidden dramas and mysteries, their hopes and dreams. It was amazing, really, this miracle of flight. What was that song again? 'From a Distance'? God looking down, watching us and our lives, and there being harmony and peace and hope deep down in everything. Like the medieval mystic Julian of Norwich: 'All shall be well and all shall be well and all manner of thing shall be well.' Sister Margaret felt a lightening of her own heart as the plane rose. *Italy, here we come!*

Fifteen

After she had successfully sorted out the tray and how it unfolded, and checked where the life jacket was, Sister Bridget felt able to really enjoy the flight. It was a joy to read the in-flight magazine, so gloriously glossy and colourful, and she felt particularly blessed because there was an article on Italian cooking. She wanted above all to learn how to make her own pasta, but she knew that their finances were not up to buying new gadgets for the kitchen. Many years ago, on her cookery course, she had visited a restaurant kitchen and had been thrilled by the drama and pace. Nobody else in her community knew how much she wished she had more people to cook for. Sometimes she had fantasies of becoming a celebrity chef and saving the convent's finances that way. Maybe she could cook with Delia Smith one day. She was a Catholic. Or be interviewed by Terry Wogan! She loved Terry – a voice from home. She and Rose had always been such fans of his – he knew what it was like to be an immigrant and make a go of it in a new country. He was a credit to Ireland, and could hold his head up with the best of them. She was always grateful if she caught a little of his radio programme between Morning Prayer and Mass, and delighted whenever she saw him on TV.

'Well, Terry,' Bridget would say, 'of course, like Delia, I see my cooking as a gift from God. Cooking is my worship – I really believe people can be brought closer to God by a tasty pie or a gorgeous roast dinner.' How much did celebrity cooks earn? Surely it would be enough to pay off the convent's debts? Not that she had had much practice cooking elaborate meals. The convent didn't go in for them, though she was proud that over the years she had cooked meals for her community and for Father Hugh that really deserved prayers of gratitude. Preparing and cooking a simple vegetable soup well, she felt, was a really good use of God's gifts, and could be an act of prayer in itself. But she would love to be able to experiment more. Father Hugh liked things simple. If ever she didn't have time to make a dessert (and that was very rare), she knew he would be perfectly happy with a Kimberley biscuit from Mr Abidi's. They were his secret vice – hers too. She knew Margaret and Cecilia weren't particularly bothered about them, but for her the biscuits were a taste of home, an instant comfort fix. Even with Rose gone, Thomas still liked them with his tea. She always saved him one.

It was a sin, wasn't it, despair? You had to have hope. God was good, and she felt sure He wanted them to go to Italy. She wondered how long the people on the organised pilgrimages were staying. Three nights wasn't that long, but she didn't want to complain. Please God, they would be coming back for a proper pilgrimage once they had sorted things out. Maybe it could be a parish one, and Thomas and his family would be with them. That would be lovely. Please God. She read the article slowly and carefully, her eye lingering on the full-colour photographs of the various Italian dishes described. A contemplative peace settled in her soul. Everything was going to be all right. She gave another sigh of contentment.

It was the rosary beads and the happy sighs that did it for the tired businessman. He remembered his grandmother, and her simplicity. He wanted some of that nun's happiness, her innocent enjoyment of life. He wanted a change. He had to make it. He would go straight home and he would apologise properly this time, let his wife know that things would be different from now on. She was right. They couldn't carry on this way. He had to change, get his priorities right. Unexpectedly, with this decision, he suddenly felt more hopeful than he had for years. He wasn't sure why, but he had the sudden feeling that maybe, after all, everything was going to be all right.

Everything was *not* all right for Sister Cecilia. The couple next to her were shameless. Even when she turned to look out of the window she was still aware of whispering and the sound of furtive, giggly kisses. Had they no shame? Would nobody rescue her? Her body turned slightly away from her disgraceful companions, Sister Cecilia resolutely opened her book of devotional reading. Now, there was a woman who would have known how to deal with those shameless young people. St Anna the Astonishing. It gave Cecilia courage just to read about her. What an inspiration. There was a woman who could actually smell sin. They said that she could sniff the odour of godlessness in the most respectable of companies, and so offensive was it to her delicately attuned nostrils that she would run screaming from the scene. Sister Cecilia wished she could run screaming from her seat. Wasn't there some law against it? Surely it should say on the tickets something about kissing on the journey. Sister Cecilia felt quite faint. She closed her eyes and prayed.

'Are you all right, Sister?' The girl next to her had opened her bag and was offering her a sweet. 'You look very pale.'

Sister Cecilia looked confusedly into the kind blue eyes of a young woman with an open face that seemed a million miles from the sexually depraved person she had been sure she was sitting next to.

'I think I've seen you at Mass at St Philomena's. It's funny we're all on the same flight now, isn't it? Here – take one of these. I find sweets help if you're nervous on a flight. I'm Emily, and this is Chris. He's sitting by the window because I'm too scared.'

'Hello, Sister.' A calloused but scrupulously clean hand was extended by the young man sitting next to the window. Sister Cecilia took it briefly and nodded back, slightly disorientated by all the information thrown at her by this enthusiastic young woman who seemed to know her from Mass, and the friendliness, the ordinariness, of the young man turned towards her.

'We've just got married, Sister.' Emily couldn't resist extending her hand to show her ring. 'Well, yesterday. Father Hugh married us at St Philomena's and it was lovely. It didn't rain at all. We stayed in a hotel last night and had to get up ever so early today. But it's worth it. And look,' she said, grabbing Chris's hand and waving it in the direction of Cecilia, 'I've made Chris wear one too, though he might take it off when he's gardening. I know some men don't, but I think that if you make a commitment, you shouldn't be ashamed of showing it.' That demonstration over, she let go of Chris's hand, much to his and Cecilia's relief. 'I think . . . I think it's great, Sister, that you wear your habit. I think it's very . . . brave.'

'Brave?'

'Well, yes, because you don't see many nuns about normally. I don't know if they're all going about in disguise or something, but I think it's a shame. Though there seem to be ever so many on this flight. I suppose it's because it's to Rome. The Pope lives there, you know. Well, of course you do. Sorry.'

Sister Cecilia did not know how to reply to that.

There was a moment's silence.

'So . . . what do you do, as a nun?' asked Emily. 'Apart from praying, I mean.'

'I'm not technically a nun. I'm a religious Sister,' said Cecilia. 'Nuns are enclosed and never go out.'

'I didn't know that!' said Emily.

'But you can carry on calling me a nun. Everyone does,' said Sister Cecilia, trying to make small talk.

There was another pause.

'I was a teacher,' said Cecilia. But not of anyone like you, she refrained from adding. They were much . . . quieter.

'Really? What subject?' asked Emily.

'History.'

'Oh, I love history. Don't I love history, Chris?'

'Yes, oh yes, she loves history,' Chris agreed obligingly.

'I love watching history programmes on the television. We watched one the other day . . .' Sister Cecilia nodded – she could think of nothing else to do. Her social skills were never very finely tuned and over the next quarter of an hour she reeled under the mixed impressions she was receiving from this young woman who kissed in public, offered sweets to strangers, liked nuns and claimed that she loved 'history' but obviously couldn't remember a single historical fact. And how she talked. Sister Cecilia was treated to Emily's considered opinions on as many historical figures as she could remember, based on impressions gained at school and from books, films and television programmes. Just when it seemed as if she was running out of steam, the blessed silence would be punctured by yet another historical offering. Emily presented the Plague, which was 'very sad', and the Fire of London, which was 'very sad', and all the poor people in Victorian times, and *Oliver Twist*, which was 'very sad' too, but 'ever such a good musical'. Mary Poppins and chimney sweeps were mentioned too, and rich children with nannies and how she and Chris wanted children, but she would stay at home with them. Then they leapt, somewhat bewilderingly, to Henry VIII, who according to Emily had eight wives, Mary, Queen of Scots, who, on the other hand, was 'very beautiful and very sad', and Queen Elizabeth I, who never married, 'but she had such a white face, who would want her?'

Sister Cecilia felt she had fallen down some awful linguistic and historical rabbit hole. It was bad enough sitting next to Sister Bridget when she had news to tell of her family in Ireland. Sister Cecilia had long regarded Sister Bridget's letter-reading sessions as penance for past, present and future sins, and she had learnt the art of tuning out and thinking about other things whilst the interminable lists of births, childhood ailments, exams passed, marriages and deaths went on and on. A couple of times she had inadvertently said 'That's nice' at an inappropriate moment – Sister Margaret had had to nudge her when she had said it after an elderly aunt's death was announced – but Bridget hadn't noticed and Sister Margaret, as Cecilia's Superior, had advised her, for the sake of charity, to make all-encompassing listening sounds and to look as if she was paying attention.

All this was very useful in dealing with this young woman, except that it was so much worse. It was impossible to tune her out when she was absolutely massacring her favourite subject, and she would keep asking her and Chris for responses to her ridiculous statements. She noticed that Chris had had the good sense to fall asleep, or at least to pretend to, but Sister Cecilia couldn't act that well. She just had to get away. She politely excused herself and, unable to follow St Anna the Astonishing's example of running away screaming, walked along the aisle in a controlled fluster, down to the saving space of the loo.

As soon as Sister Cecilia was out of earshot, Emily shook her new husband back to a socially interactive life.

'Chris, Chris. Would you wake up? What are we going to do? It's so hard. I can't think of any more history and there's another hour to go.'

'Why do we have to keep talking about it anyway, Emily? Leave the poor woman alone.'

'I can't not talk to her, Chris, that would be rude. She's all on her own. I don't know why they don't sit all the nuns together. Look, there's two in front, and a normal person beside them. Have you ever seen anything so silly?' Before Chris could stop her, the good-natured Emily was standing up and tapping the businessman on the shoulder.

Cecilia couldn't stay in the cramped little loo any longer. She had read the notice about not smoking at least twenty times, and she was guiltily aware that someone had knocked on the door. It really would be selfish to stay in any longer. How was she going to get through the rest of the flight? If only she could swap with the man ahead, but how could she actually say it? Cecilia wasn't the world's greatest diplomat, but she did realise that to beg a complete stranger to swap with her because she couldn't bear to listen to that young woman for one minute longer was rather rude. Since Sister Frances, years ago, had had to speak to her about her lack of

Christian charity, she had tried to remember to be kind to difficult people, even if it didn't come naturally. She was aware that it wasn't her strong point. Summoning the moral courage of the saints and martyrs to her aid, and after a bit of panic-stricken fumbling with the door, Cecilia sallied forth.

With what astonishment and blessed relief did Sister Cecilia see the businessman in her seat and the girl pointing forward to his empty place beside Bridget and Margaret.

'We thought you'd like to sit next to the other nuns,' the girl said, leaning across and, for some reason, speaking very slowly and exaggeratedly clearly, and beaming. Sister Cecilia felt so grateful that she did not feel as irritated as she might have. And the smartly dressed Italian man beside her smiled at her too. Of course, the Italians were very respectful of nuns.

'Thank you very much,' Sister Cecilia said to them both. 'How very kind.'

What a miracle. Thank you, God, thank you, St Anna the Astonishing, thank you. She walked one row ahead and, smiling at Sister Bridget's welcoming beam, sank down gratefully into the haven of her seat.

Sixteen

Margaret opened her eyes and looked out of the plane window. All she could see were clouds, and all she could feel, after that lovely but all too brief peace at the beginning of the flight, was that familiar anxiety again. What were they doing? Where on earth were they going? To some village an hour or so outside Rome that nobody had heard of, to a convent nobody she knew had visited. Didn't the Bishop have enough saints? He had enough relics, anyway. She remembered, as a novice nun, being shown the diocese's relics by the present Bishop's predecessor. There were so many of them, all in little see-through glass boxes, kept lined up in the drawer of a bureau. Bits of cloth from clothes once worn by a saint, rosaries once prayed with, even slivers of bones. None of them were saints people particularly knew or cared about now. Obscure saints from the seventeenth and eighteenth centuries. There was one relic that, it was claimed, had touched a cloth that had touched a bone of a major saint – it might have even been St Thomas of Canterbury, but the curly handwriting in its faded ink on the label of that box was very hard to read. St Somebody. But all holy relics, nonetheless. Margaret remembered that she had wondered whether it was right to keep so many sources of cures locked up in a drawer, away from the people who might benefit. She hadn't dared to raise that with the severe man who was bishop back then, but she did ask at the convent why more people were not allowed to see the relics. Mother Veronica, the novice mistress, had not allowed any criticism of the Bishop.

'The Bishop is absolutely right. Faith is needed. Relics are not magic. Without God's grace no miracles can happen, and this, I am sad to say, is a godless generation. He obviously does not want them exposed to ridicule or impiety.'

Even to Margaret, a very pious novice back then, it had seemed a somewhat unsatisfactory answer. Nobody from Fairbridge even knew those relics were there in the Bishop's house. And plenty of people went to Sunday Mass back then, so there would have been plenty of takers, plenty of dying and ill people who would have gratefully accepted the help of any saint, however obscure, whether the saint came from Fairbridge or not.

But obviously the present Bishop felt differently about this home-grown saint. She had seen the light in his eyes, the way he sat forward as Cecilia spoke. He saw potential in that photo. He saw holiness. He had hope. But they had so little to go on. The plane was stable in its flight, but the anxiety was still rising.

'This won't do,' she said to herself firmly. 'Remember how you felt at the beginning of the flight. When in desolation, remember consolation. "All shall be well."' The in-flight magazine in front of her would be a distraction. She reached for it and flicked past the cookery section, past a feature on handbags, to a section on Italy. She turned to a piece on Keats's house by the Spanish Steps.

*

The rest of the journey passed uneventfully. The distribution of in-flight meals took up a pleasant amount of time. The businessman, having finished his lunch and had it taken away, folded up his tray and then relieved any social tension by closing his eyes and drifting from feigned into real sleep. Emily, relieved of her religious responsibilities by the seat change, cuddled up to Chris and chattered happily about her favourite type of history – how well the wedding had gone – whilst Chris beamed fondly down at his gorgeous and irrepressibly friendly spouse and looked forward to the rest of the honeymoon. Something of their joy must have been in the air, as the businessman beside them dreamt of his own honeymoon, decades ago, and of his wife's welcoming embrace.

The pilot announced their imminent arrival in Rome, and the plane started its descent.

The Sisters had only hand luggage, and they were soon through passport control. The heat hit them as they left the terminal. The friendly woman taxi driver loaded up their overnight bags and they got in the car and drove out of the airport, under a blue sky, into Rome traffic.

The businessman rang his wife from the airport, and told her he loved her. She cried. She had spent so many years waiting for his love to return, for him to be like the young man who had married her.

She rang her sister. '*È un miracolo!*' she said.

Chris and Emily were still at the luggage carousel, waiting for Emily's suitcase, but passing the time very happily holding hands and looking into each other's eyes.

'It's amazing we're here!' said Emily. 'Thank you so much for selling your motorbike, Chris. You're the best husband ever.'

Her bright pink suitcase arrived at last, and Chris swung it off the conveyor belt, wincing good-humouredly as he did so. 'What have you got in there, Ems?' he said.

'Well, I needed to look nice for you in Rome, Chris, in the hotel and restaurant. I want you to be proud of me.'

'I already couldn't be prouder!' said Chris, smiling down at her, thanking his lucky stars yet again for the travel agent who had found such an amazing deal. He still couldn't quite believe it.

Margaret, in the taxi, found the traffic terrifying. It was fast, and there was so much hooting and gesticulating and weaving in and out. She looked in the mirror and saw both Cecilia and Bridget take out their rosaries. Cecilia's knuckles were white, she was gripping her rosary so tightly, but the taxi driver negotiated her way around Rome's traffic with confidence. Margaret glanced in the mirror and saw the others visibly relax as the driver skilfully negotiated the road. Both Cecilia and Bridget put their rosaries back in their pockets, a sure compliment. It was impossible not to be affected by the bright sunshine and such an ancient, beautiful, famous city. Margaret sat up straighter and smiled at the driver beside her.

'I can see the dome of St Peter's!' cried Bridget. 'I can't wait to get to Mass!'

The taxi driver smiled at her enthusiasm. It was Sunday, of course. She had been working non-stop these last weeks. Perhaps it was time for a day of rest for her too. Her son had complained it would take a miracle to get her to take some time off. Maybe it was time for one now. She would go home as soon as she dropped the Sisters off. Yes, it was a beautiful day. Plinio would be so happy.

'Yes, I can see St Peter's too,' said Margaret, trying not to think wistfully of the Spanish Steps and Keats's house, and wishing she felt more enthusiastic about their mission.

In Fairbridge, Father Hugh had got back in time to relieve Monsignor Wilson and was getting ready for the second morning Mass. He had been out for a meal with some parishioners the night before, and was invited out for lunch with some others that Sunday. Everyone seemed to be very aware that Sister Bridget was away, and had promised her that Father Hugh would not fade away during her absence.

'I don't know if I am managing that well, Lord,' he said to himself ruefully, looking at his tummy as he prayed and knotted his cincture around his alb. 'I seemed to eat as much with the Nowaks last night as I do with Sister Bridget. I know lunch with the Smiths will be delicious and I fear for my self-control. I thought it was just Sister Bridget and her cooking, but it's clear already that the problem lies with me just as much, if not more, than with her. The truth is, I just can't say no when people give me food.'

He had already positioned the buckets around the church. He finished getting ready and rang the entrance bell.

'At least it stayed fine for the wedding,' he thought as he entered the church to a rather odd musical accompaniment of plinking raindrops. He smiled as he thought of the bride and groom. He might not see them at church that often, but they were a couple whose marriage he expected to last. They were sufficiently different to complement each other, but their love was definitely strong. There was a great mutual kindness there. Always a good sign. 'God bless them in Rome,' he prayed. 'God bless their marriage. And God bless the Sisters too — may they find what they are looking for.' It would be exciting if they really had found a new saint and the parish became a new pilgrimage site. The £2,000 the Sisters had given them would barely scratch the surface. He would have to ask the Bishop for help. Hints hadn't helped. Even an outright question. Which reminded him – when would he hear about the curate? 'Please, Lord, send someone. And send some money too,' he added.

'The Mass today will be offered for the intentions of the parish,' Father Hugh announced to the congregation in front of him. He suddenly felt a great fondness for them. What would be their intentions? Would they be for financial or spiritual riches? There was something to be said for both of them. It was hard to pray if you were hungry. Father Hugh prayed that nobody in his congregation was hungry. He feared they would be too proud to tell him if they were. He made a mental note to ask Thomas Amis about what the St Vincent de Paul Society knew of recent needs. Thomas and Rose had started it up twenty years before, and Thomas had kept running it after Rose's death. Thomas always knew where the need was – a child's uniform, a debt unpaid. Funds were found discreetly, taken from the monthly collections after Mass, and unnecessary shame and embarrassment avoided.

Throughout that Mass, Father Hugh felt graced with love. It was a simple love for his congregation, which looped back into love for God, and God's love for him, in a beautiful circle. Father Hugh was by no means a slight man, his frame modelled more on Winnie-the-Pooh than St Francis, but somehow, in spite of his own weaknesses and needs, God's love shone through him that day, and he knew it and was humbly glad.

After Communion, he sat in gratitude and quietly and patiently and trustingly asked God about money again. 'I know we mustn't worry about things like this, but please can you tell me how we can fix the roof? I know the church is your people, not the bricks, but they still need to be warm and sheltered. I can't raise this money on my own. I put it in your hands, Lord. And the curate. Please send me one, and bless him, whoever he is. Send him soon.'

George was sitting in his kitchen, chatting to Sebastian over brunch.

'What am I going to do?' he asked, miserably pouring his coffee. 'I have Sarah and Matthew coming tonight. I think Matthew thinks I'm interested in Sarah now. How could I have made such a mess? Mother is right. I'm hopeless.'

Sebastian leapt decisively up onto George's lap and butted his head against George's chest, purring loudly. He put his front paws on George's chest and, still purring, touched his cold nose against George's and looked into his eyes. Then he bent his head and butted George again, his whole body thrumming with love.

'Thank you, Sebastian,' said George. 'I really needed that today.'

Seventeen

Sister Cecilia was radiant, glorying in the huge Basilica of St Peter's as if she herself had made it. She had been to Rome once before, for her fiftieth year in religious life, and it was an unthought-of blessing that she could be back there again. She knew so much about the history – had taught so much about it. Every saint carved, every Pope commemorated – she knew about. These were her people – this was her church. Mass was over now and they were free to explore. She held her guide-book closely, her excitement even closer, but inside she was ecstatic, and Margaret could tell.

Margaret could also see that Bridget would be relatively quiet in the Basilica, but sooner or later some enthusiastic, if whispered, exclamation would be bound to burst out and ruin Cecilia's experience. In general, Cecilia definitely needed to be more patient with people – Sister Helen had been insistent on that in the community – but Margaret thought that just once, just once, for this chance in a lifetime, she could be excused.

'Cecilia – would you like half an hour on your own before lunch to look around St Peter's?'

Margaret had read her thoughts. Two bright spots of excitement showed in Cecilia's normally pale cheeks.

They had come here for the saint – this stop-off in Rome was an added bonus. Cecilia had been disciplined against Greed all her life, which made this taste of what her heart and soul longed for all the more delicious. She had her guidebook; she would walk around and read as many inscriptions as possible – on her own.

'Thank you. That would be . . . wonderful,' said Cecilia, and the fact that this was not an adjective that she would generally use made it all the more touching.

Margaret felt a rush of love for Cecilia and a flood of shame for her own self.

'Just look at how happy she is, Lord. Really, she doesn't ask for much. This is a highlight for her. At home, all she needs to have a good day is Mass, and a little historical research in the library. What was all that about, Lord, not giving her the winning ticket? I know I've been complaining about her doing the lottery, but if we *had* to win, I know both Bridget and I would much rather it had been with Cecilia's numbers. Poor Cecilia. So thank you that she is in this place anyway, not just doing jigsaws of it, even if it makes me feel . . . I'm not sure what it makes me feel, to be honest . . .'

But all that Margaret said out loud was, 'Go on, Cecilia – don't let us keep you waiting. We'll see you by the *Pietà* in half an hour.'

And off Cecilia flew.

Bridget smiled at Margaret.

'Isn't it absolutely beautiful? Would you just look at the marble! Look at the paintings! The statues! Have you ever seen such a church?'

It slightly appalled and surprised Margaret just how little, in fact, she felt for it. It was big, it was ancient, the columns were huge, it was full of priceless, stunningly beautiful art; she remembered feeling awestruck when she came with the school, but this time, somehow, it left her cold. There was even a group of English pilgrims in one of the side chapels singing 'God Bless Our Pope'. It was so . . . triumphant, and she wasn't in the mood for triumph.

'Margaret – I've just had an idea. I'd love to get confession here. It would set me up for the week.' Bridget was beaming.

Lovely Bridget. She would hardly have any sins to confess.

'Why not? That's a good idea, Bridget. There must be some English-speaking priests on duty.'

Bridget rushed off to accost an elderly priest.

Margaret stood, suddenly tired, watching her friend enthusiastically smiling and waving to her, signalling her success, joining a queue in a pew outside a confessional box.

Margaret sat at a distance, her eyes still on Bridget so they didn't lose each other. Bridget, her luck holding as always, was quickly at the top of the queue. Margaret saw a lady in a black mantilla and swollen ankles come out of the confessional and hold the door open for Bridget, who entered, the door shutting behind her. A tall, pale-looking young man slid along the pew and took his place at the top.

Some self-important priests in black walked swiftly past Margaret. Not that she knew they were self-important, and she couldn't even hear what they were saying, but somehow their very confidence in their surroundings, their sense of purpose, their importance, depressed her. They reminded her of those patronising priests from the diocese who had so casually retired her and handed her beloved school to another. They hadn't listened. They had handed her school to a man, talked over her head, and not even said sorry.

Margaret, the retired headmistress, bastion of calmness and pillar of the Church, felt suddenly hot and tired and . . . to her consternation, angry. Furious. Where on earth was it all coming from? This place was so big, so sure of itself – too sure of itself – too certain. What had it got to do with her? Margaret looked around and felt out of place, out of sorts.

'It's not you, Lord,' she said. 'I do know that. But it's the Church. Not just the building. Mass was tiring and crowded and hard to pray in, and now all I seem to see everywhere is all those men in black. It just suddenly doesn't seem fair. I know it's your Church, so there is a bit of a problem here. I'll have to talk to you later about this. I can't handle it at the moment. I don't know why I am suddenly so very angry, but I am.'

Sister Bridget came out of confession and knelt down in the pew. Margaret checked her watch – five to one – it was reasonable to make an escape now.

The one good thing about St Peter's being so big was that the time it took her to walk a little way ahead of Bridget towards the *Pietà* gave her a chance to hide her feelings. Dear unobservant Cecilia was waiting for them, punctual as usual, even though it must have taken a heroic effort of will to tear herself away.

'Are you feeling well, Margaret?' Cecilia, from the heights of her architectural ecstasy, bathed in the love of her subject, had a sudden rare moment of understanding that all was not well with her Superior. Bridget, surprised, turned to look at Margaret too.

'You're very flushed, Margaret – Cecilia is right.'

'It's nothing. I just need a little sit-down. I'm a bit tired, that's all.' Really, Cecilia was the most awkward person. All those years she could be counted on to not notice any emotion and all of a sudden, at the most inconvenient time, she had to start. She couldn't cope if they began fussing. But she did feel unwell.

'I'm perfectly all right. I just feel a little dizzy. It's probably our early start. Nothing a little sit-down and a bite to eat won't fix.'

At the thought of food, Bridget looked less worried. That was it. Margaret hadn't been eating enough.

Bridget and Cecilia linked arms with Margaret down the steps. The piazza was huge, and it seemed to take ages to get across it, and the restaurants were full of people, but, by a miracle, they found some seats.

'I'm sorry, but that was the most unspiritual Mass I've ever been to,' Margaret declared as they sat at the table. Bridget had managed to get a glass of water brought for her and sipping it was making Margaret feel a bit better, but the bubbling anger still remained. 'Did you see the elbowing and pushing when it came to Communion?'

'Sister Margaret!' said Sister Bridget, a bit shocked. 'A Mass is a Mass! It was crowded, that's all. It's because of Blessed Julia, and all the people who came from Russia to honour her. They were excited, that's all. If we manage to get Sister Angelina and Edward Mortimer made saints, I'll be waving flags, I can tell you!'

'I couldn't agree more,' said Sister Cecilia. 'And the Pope was saying it.'

'That's part of the problem. Did you see those other Sisters?' said Margaret, still grumpy. 'I couldn't believe it. One of them practically pushed poor Sister Bridget over when she saw she was in the queue to get Communion from the Pope. She should have stayed in her own queue. It doesn't matter who said Mass or gave Communion – it's the same Holy Communion.'

'We'll have a nice plate of pasta here – could we have a menu in English, please?' called Bridget loudly and urgently to a waiter, sounding rather like a culinary paramedic summoning backup assistance.

'I'm fine, Bridget, don't fuss,' said Margaret, embarrassed to see everyone turn to look at her.

'You're not yourself,' said Bridget, worriedly.

No, no, you're wrong. I am myself and that's the problem. I suddenly can't stand it. I cannot stand all the clericalism and pomp and power, and I cannot find God anywhere here. What sort of religious Sister am I?

They chose their meals from the menu and ate their delicious lunch, Bridget making sure Margaret had pasta. It did actually make her feel a little better.

'What a lovely morning, thank God,' said Bridget. 'This food is to die for, and St Peter's was out of this world. What a blessing to get confession there,' she continued, 'and didn't I get a grand old Irish priest, Father Donovan I think it said on the sign. He gave a lovely confession. Lovely. And he recognised my accent and it turns out he has a cousin comes from the next parish to mine back at home. Isn't it a small world? I knew his cousin's sister, as it turns out. One of her sons became a priest and conducted his own mother's funeral. Wasn't that a blessing? So it really *is* a small world. Such a lovely way with him. Did you go in the end, Margaret?'

'No, no, I didn't.'

Bridget looked thoughtfully at her.

'Well, we have the taxi booked at five, from the English College. That lovely George from the travel agency gave us this map, and it says it takes twenty minutes to walk from here. So it's two o'clock now. We have about two and a half hours. What shall we do?'

'Why don't we meet up here at half past four?' said Margaret, suddenly decisive.

'I'd like to go back to St Peter's,' said Sister Cecilia.

'I will come with you, but I'd like to do a bit of shopping for cards and souvenirs for parishioners,' said Bridget. 'I think Father Hugh would like a new rosary. I might get that lovely George something. I must get something special for Mr and Mrs Abidi. Some Italian biscuits maybe. So where are you going, Margaret?'

'I don't know,' lied Margaret. 'I think I might stay here for a bit. Have some coffee. I'll be fine. I'd like some quiet time, Sisters. I will see you here later.'

Cecilia was fine with that, but Bridget looked more reluctant to leave Margaret, who stared her out, pretending a serenity she didn't feel.

Back in Fairbridge, George was flapping. He had set the table beautifully, with a white tablecloth and candles. He had put on Spanish music, and he was cooking a paella as Miguel had taught him, and for afterwards, there was a chocolate cake. That had been funny. Father Hugh, the Roman Catholic priest from round the corner, had come in with a cake tin just before the agency closed on Saturday.

'My name is Father Hugh from St Philomena's. I think we have a mutual acquaintance,' the priest had said, his eyes twinkling. 'Sister Bridget is in Rome, but she gave me strict instructions to give this to the nice young travel agent, and I don't want her to get cross with me.'

So George had taken the cake, and it made him happy to think that Sister Bridget and Miguel were both going to be present, in a way, at this strange dinner.

'Why did I say those things about Sarah?' he berated

himself. 'I've somehow got to give a clear message without being crass.' He caught sight of the framed picture of him and Miguel on the window sill, arms across each other's shoulders, laughing. His heart beat harder. He had a photo album from Spain. If Sarah was nice, if she was anything as kind as her brother was, he would show it to them. He would try to show them the truth he had kept hidden for so long. He hoped they would understand.

The doorbell rang.

'Wish me luck, Sebastian,' he said to his cat, then, gently locking him out of the kitchen, he went downstairs to open the door.

Eighteen

As soon as George opened the door to Matthew and Sarah, he realised Sarah was the patient district nurse who came to dress his mother's leg.

'Hello there!' he said, welcoming them in. 'You're the nurse who my mother was so mean to the other day. I'm so sorry about her. She was in pain, but she was awful to you when I was there. I hope she isn't still being difficult.'

'Hello back, and please don't worry,' said Sarah, smiling reassuringly. She looked very different but equally pretty out of uniform. He didn't remember her blonde hair being down before, and she hadn't been wearing make-up. 'I'm used to it. She's in pain. People in pain lash out.'

'Yes, but it's still not very nice for you,' said George, concerned and embarrassed. He took their coats and hung them up.

'What a lovely flat!' said Sarah. Matthew gave George the bottle and chocolates they had brought, and rather shyly sat down.

George brought drinks and nibbles for them, and Sarah and Matthew listened to the Spanish music he had put on whilst he quickly finished cooking the paella in the kitchen and then brought it to the table with a flourish.

Sarah and Matthew together were delightful guests. Sarah chatted about visiting Spain when she was younger and about wanting to travel again. Matthew had brought some very special wine, and looked wonderfully shy and handsome in blue jeans and a blue shirt that brought out the colour of his eyes. After dinner, they went to sit in comfortable armchairs, and Sebastian wandered in and decided to jump onto Matthew's lap, which delighted George.

George decided to get the album out. It was now or never. He had drunk a little too much, to give himself confidence.

'I thought I might show you some photos from Spain,' he said, a little too casually. Nobody ever saw these precious pictures of that most precious man. Now, these people were going to see photographs of him – pictures George's own mother had never seen. There Miguel was, playing guitar, laughing, holding a cat, eating ice cream. There he was teaching, laughing with students. There he was, the best and kindest and most loving human being George had ever known, whose absence was an ever-present hurt in his heart. There were a few after his first diagnosis, when his face was thinner than usual, when the shadow of death was beginning to be thrown. The later photos were in a drawer. George could not bear to look at them even now.

Sarah took the album and knew immediately what she was seeing. It wrung her heart.

'Who is this?' she asked, gently. But George, sensing her kindness, and feeling the tears well up in his eyes, still could not quite dare to overcome the habit of years.

'My . . . partner – that is,' he rushed to say, 'my business partner. We ran a language school together.'

'Where is he now?' asked Sarah again, dreading the answer.

'He. He . . . he, um, died,' said George. 'Excuse me, I think I must sort out pudding. Tea, coffee anyone?' He rushed back into the kitchen, and Sarah and Matthew heard him blow his nose loudly, and the sound of cupboards opening and shutting.

'I think George is gay,' Sarah said quietly to Matthew.

'Sarah! I don't think that is any of our business,' Matthew said back. 'We can't know for sure. He specifically said Miguel was his business partner. He even specifically said he wanted me to bring you tonight. We don't want to make any embarrassing mistakes.'

No. You *don't want to make any embarrassing mistakes, Matthew. I know you are shy, I know you were bullied at school and had your heart broken at university, I know Dad humiliated and frightened you and yet you could never risk losing his approval, but I think you love this man, and I completely understand why. You can't live such a hesitant life. You've got to be a bit more daring, like that artist you love so much.*

But she smiled at her brother. He was not someone who could be rushed. 'I'm sure you're wrong, Matthew,' was all she said. 'He's just grateful to me for looking after his mother. Between you and me, she's a terrible bully, but I didn't want to upset him.'

'Is she?' said Matthew, concerned.

'Yes. I just have to see her every day whilst her wound is a problem, but poor George is stuck with her for life.'

'Right,' said George, bringing in the chocolate cake, sparklers stuck all over it, a resolutely cheerful smile on his face. 'Let's eat this in honour of the cook, the absolutely fabulous Sister Bridget!'

*

As soon as Sister Cecilia and Bridget had gone, Margaret finished the coffee she had ordered and consulted her map and guidebook. She had decided she wasn't going back into St Peter's. She was going to Keats's house by the Spanish Steps, and nobody was going to stop her. It would take her about half an hour to walk there, half an hour back, leaving her just over an hour for her own private pilgrimage.

St Peter's was a basilica full of beautiful art, but it didn't move her, not in the way that simple bedroom where Keats had died had done. She needed to go back there so much, and she couldn't exactly say why. All she knew was that she wasn't leaving Rome – she couldn't leave Rome – without seeing it again.

Margaret walked as fast as she could, focused, past brightly coloured stalls, shaking her head at pushy street sellers, weaving around loving couples, avoiding tourists taking photographs, students chatting. She marched beside the river, the water sparkling in the sunshine, barely registering all the loveliness outside her because of the rising desperation inside. Why this overwhelming need in her? Crossing the Ponte Cavour, her heart beating faster as she knew she was nearing her destination, she refused to be beguiled by the beauty of the scene and pressed on, past the fountain designed like a boat, and arrived at the door of the Keats–Shelley House like some desperate medieval seeker of sanctuary.

It was closed.

She refused to take it in. *Closed on Sundays.* She could not bear it, she absolutely could not bear it. This was the only place she wanted to be, and it was shut to her. She knocked on the door again and again, as if pursued by demons. They had to let her in. She knocked and knocked, like someone shut out from salvation.

And nobody answered.

'So that's it, Lord. What about "knock, and the door shall be opened unto you"?'

Margaret turned and bumped into someone coming in the opposite direction.

'Sister Margaret? Is that you?'

'Katy? Katy Bradshaw?' So she was still working there.

'Come in, Sister! Are you feeling all right? Let me give you a glass of water,' said Katy, and stepping ahead of her, she miraculously unlocked the door of the Keats museum and led her into the cool interior.

Once inside the house, the relief was immense. Margaret at last felt the peace that had eluded her in St Peter's, and a sense of wonder that the door had opened when she had given up all hope.

'It's closed on Sundays. I'm only here to do some tidying up and cleaning for tomorrow. I'm so glad to bump into you like this!'

'We're only here for the day, on our way to somewhere else. I wanted to see it again. The first time I was here – the last time – was with Sister Helen.' Margaret found herself sobbing as Katy found her a chair. 'I am so sorry, Katy. I don't know what is happening.'

'Please don't apologise. I am just so glad to see you again. It was so lovely when you all came on the visit here. I've never forgotten it. I remember you and Sister Helen standing here with us and you sharing what Keats meant to you. I was talking to the girls about how he wrote "Heard melodies are sweet, but those unheard / Are sweeter", and I remember you sharing how that was what you felt like as a religious Sister – that you were following an unheard melody and were straining to hear it, but your longing to hear it, and your belief that it was infinitely sweet, made you carry on.'

'Did I say that?'

'Yes. I don't know if I understood it completely, but it made sense somehow. That your life wasn't so much about lack but about longing – that it was beautiful, in the way that poetry and art are beautiful. I often think about that.'

Tears streamed down Margaret's face. 'Oh, thank you, Katy. I'm afraid I can't quite get in touch with that at the moment. As you know, the school is closed, and Sister Helen is dead, and I can't feel anything and I don't know what is to become of us, the three of us left. I can't hear anything, and sometimes I'm not even sure, to be honest, if there is even anything to be heard. Goodness, what you must think of me talking like this – pounding on your door like that and crying. I'm so, so sorry.'

'Please don't apologise, Sister. I was very sorry when I heard that Sister Helen had died, and I wondered how you would be feeling,' said Katy.

'Did you?' said Margaret, startled by such thoughtfulness.

'Yes, you were such good friends. You loved each other so much. You made me think that religious Sisters really are sisters in a true sense. And then I heard about the Sisters leaving the school and everything changing, and I felt so sad. It was a lovely school.'

'It was, wasn't it?' sniffed Margaret.

'And you were a wonderful teacher. Would you like to come and see Keats's room again?'

'I would, I would. Thank you.'

They stood in the simple room where Keats had lived and died, and Katy opened the window so they could hear the sounds from the square outside, the fountain splashing, the hubbub of people talking, laughing, calling out to each other.

'What a beautiful friendship he and Joseph Severn had,'

said Margaret. 'This is the very fireplace where Severn used to cook meals for Keats. And I remember hearing that he hired a piano and played Keats symphonies by Haydn.'

Margaret stepped forward and looked at the death mask of Keats on the wall.

'He looks so beautiful. So at peace. Severn said that after he died, he thought he might still just be asleep.'

'Do you remember how Sister Helen stood here, and after you quoted those lines about unheard melodies, she said that for her it was death that was a bit like finally hearing an unheard melody?' said Katy.

'I had forgotten that,' said Margaret.

'It helped me when she said it, because my mum had died while I was doing my A levels – I don't know if you remember, Sister?'

'I do, yes. I'm so sorry.'

'Anyway, Sister Helen said that and it comforted me, because Mum had loved music so much. I liked the idea of her finally hearing something she had longed to hear before.'

Margaret blew her nose. 'I wonder if Sister Helen already knew about her own cancer when she was here? I've always worried that she didn't share it with us earlier. She went so quickly at the end.'

'I don't know. I just remember what you said in reply to her then. It made a big impression on me. Do you remember?'

'I don't remember.'

'You said, maybe it wasn't death that was the unheard melody, but eternal life, breaking into ordinary life? I can almost hear it now, here in this room, hearing the sounds from the street and thinking about the dying Keats here. You were talking about all the truth and beauty of Keats's life and poetry, and also about all the love in this room, the love of Joseph

Severn for his friend, and how he nursed him to his death, but that wasn't the end, and the love still remained, somewhere unseen and unheard, but also in the poetry and in the room. She really liked that.'

'Did she?' said Margaret. 'I'm so glad. Thank you, Katy, for telling me.'

'I think you were right. I think that love is still here,' said Katy. 'It feels so special to stand alone in this room and feel it. I've enjoyed working here so much, and I love meeting the visitors, but I like coming in to clean and tidy on Sundays when there is nobody else about, and taking a moment to just "be" in this room.'

'It's lucky for me that you do,' said Margaret.

Margaret went over to the wood and glass case to read the letter by Joseph Severn about Keats's death.

'"He is gone – he died with the most perfect ease – he seemed to go to sleep. On the 23rd, about 4, the approaches of death came on,"' Margaret read out loud. Then, her voice breaking as she said them, Keats's own words, quoted by his friend:

'"'Severn – I – lift me up – I am dying – I shall die easy – don't be frightened – be firm and thank God it has come.'"'

She read on, wiping her eyes as she did so, barely able to get to the end, but forced somehow to carry on.

'"I lifted him up in my arms. The phlegm seemed boiling in his throat, and increased until 11, when he gradually sunk into death – so quiet that I still thought he slept."

'I didn't nurse her, you know,' Margaret wept, suddenly leaning on the case for support, crying harder, more than she had cried for years. 'I didn't nurse her. She went into hospital, and she was gone so quickly. Too quickly. I would have done anything to have looked after her, to have had more time.'

Katy gave her a hug and held her.

'But you know, Sister, I remember she said something about that too, in this very room. I don't know why it stuck in my mind so clearly, but maybe I was meant to remember it so I could say it to you now. She said how she often thought about Keats worrying about how hard it was for Severn, nursing him. Keats did worry about that. I don't know if Sister Helen would have liked you to nurse her and suffer like that. Honestly.'

'I loved her so much,' sobbed Margaret. 'I wish I could have shown her that love at the end like Joseph Severn did. I wasn't even with her in the hospital when she went. None of us expected her to go so quickly. I would have been at her bedside. I wish I could have told her.'

'She knew, Sister. We all knew. You were best friends, soulmates. That's what always struck me about you. That's why you're feeling so awful. You're bereaved, and I think you were in shock and only now is it hitting you. That's what it was like for me, anyway. I had to go to a counsellor at university because it suddenly hit me, long after the funeral and everything, that Mum would never be coming to see me graduate, or marry, or anything. I couldn't see the point of anything for a while.'

'Oh, Katy, you are like an angel from God today. It's a miracle meeting you here like this. I can't thank you enough,' said Sister Margaret, wiping her eyes. Katy found her a tissue and she blew her nose gratefully, then they spontaneously hugged each other.

'It's so lovely to see you again! You know, Sister, you coming here has helped me too,' said Katy, 'so thank you. I've been wondering about it, and now, after our conversation, I've definitely decided that I'm going to apply to do an MA on the Romantics, and do my dissertation on Keats.'

'I'm so pleased to hear that! Sister Helen would have been delighted too.'

'Have you got time for a quick coffee?' asked Katy. 'Then I'll walk you back to where you're meeting the others.'

'That would be lovely,' said Margaret.

'So, you said you were on the way to somewhere else,' said Katy as she locked up. 'Is it a pilgrimage? Where are you going?'

'I'll tell you all about it over coffee,' said Margaret. 'It will be a relief to get it off my chest!'

Nineteen

After coffee and a catch-up with all the convent doings, the lottery win and the Flying Nun, Katy walked back with Margaret to wait outside the English College, and there they were joined first by a quietly ecstatic Cecilia and then, barely minutes later, by a very bubbly Sister Bridget, carrying two bags and with an anecdote about an unlikely (for anyone but her) chat with a Swiss Guard. Cecilia and Bridget were both surprised and absolutely delighted to see Katy in Rome and to hear about her plans, agreeing that meeting a St Philomena's old girl was a very good sign for the Order.

'Aren't we having a day full of blessings?' enthused Bridget, smiling at them all. 'I've been shopping and then I've just had such a lovely chat with a wonderful young man, a Swiss Guard called Dominic. He's just been made a corporal, so he can get married now, but I hadn't realised that normally Swiss Guards have to be celibate. He told me about a woman he has fallen in love with and I said she sounded marvellous, and he should take the fact that corporals can get married as a sign that God approves, and not hesitate to ask her this very day! Dominic said he was glad a nun had said that and I had put his mind at rest, and we have swapped addresses. We're going to keep in touch, and if she says yes I might even be invited to the wedding! Imagine! Provided we have the money, of course, Margaret,' she added hastily.

'I don't know how you do it!' said Margaret, fondly. 'You're amazing, Bridget. I think if you went to the top of Mount Everest you would still make a friend. Did you enjoy St Peter's, Sister Cecilia?'

'It was magnificent, thank you,' said Sister Cecilia, emphasising the adjective in a most un-Cecilia-like way. Her eyes were sparkling, alight with a fervour that took Margaret slightly aback.

A car drove down the road and stopped. A very handsome man in his mid-fifties got out, smiling.

'For Cardellino?' he asked in perfect English, but with a light Italian accent.

'Yes, to Cardellino,' said Cecilia, declaiming it as if it were a call to arms.

He took the Sisters' bags and loaded their luggage in the boot.

'Katy, I can't tell you how much it has helped me to meet you today,' said Margaret, turning and giving her old pupil another hug.

'I'm so glad. You helped me too, you know,' said Katy. 'I really was finding it hard to decide what to do next. I know now, and I also want to come and stay with you all in the convent in Fairbridge when I get back, if that is all right with you?'

'How marvellous!' said Bridget, unashamedly eavesdropping as she got into the car. 'Pray for us on our adventure, Katy.'

'Yes, pray for us,' said Margaret, meeting Katy's eyes, glad that she had shared her worries with Katy in the café. She was such a thoughtful girl.

'Don't worry, I will,' said Katy. 'It all sounds very exciting! I can't wait to hear what you find out!' And she stayed to wave as the Sisters drove off in the car.

'So, Sisters,' said the smiling man. 'Welcome to Italy! My name is Francesco and my wife and I are very happy that you should be coming to Cardellino today. The drive is about forty-five minutes, so relax and enjoy the scenery. Allow me to say that it gets better the nearer we come to Cardellino.'

And it did. After half an hour on the motorway, they turned off onto winding hill roads into a countryside of olive trees and vineyards, fir woods and isolated farms, their terracotta-tiled roofs so different from the roofs of Fairbridge.

'I think I saw scenery like this on that holiday programme,' Bridget exclaimed happily. The car began to wind its way along many twisting roads and up a steep hill. Eventually, it slowed down as they drove through narrow cobbled streets lined with houses with walls of various shades of yellow, pink and cream, blue or brown or yellow shutters, and ornate wrought-iron balconies with hanging baskets of bright geraniums and big terracotta pots of flowers on the doorsteps.

'Oh! How pretty!' exclaimed Sister Bridget, clapping her hands. 'It's just like the brochures for Italy at the travel agency.'

Francesco turned into the main square of Cardellino, with its pink and stone square-porticoed buildings, a fountain in the centre and a church with steps and a bell tower to one side, then drove round, coming to a stop in front of Hotel della Sacra Famiglia.

'That's named for the Holy Family, isn't it?' said Sister Bridget. 'How lovely!'

Francesco opened the car doors and courteously helped the Sisters to get out, then opened the boot and took their bags.

'Come, I will show you to your rooms,' he said, and led them into the hotel.

The salmon-pink paint was slightly peeling, but the walls were covered, unexpectedly, with stunning framed black-and-white photographs of buildings and people from Italy, but also from around the world – Ethiopia, Greece, Ireland, Norway. Many had a beautiful, dark-haired woman laughing into the camera – and in some Francesco was with her, his arm around her. In some of the photographs the couple seemed younger, in some older, but they always looked happy, and were often in little groups of friends.

'What lovely photographs!' said Margaret.

'Thank you. By trade I am – I was – an architect, but photography is my hobby, and Maria and I like to travel. We have visited many places over the years, and actually, many people in these photographs have ended up staying here. We run the hotel and normally go away in the winter, but due to my grandmother's old age our travels have been put on hold. We can't leave her on her own.'

Francesco smiled at them, but Margaret noticed the strain in his voice.

Bridget sniffed appreciatively.

'Now that's a lovely smell,' said Bridget. 'What's cooking?'

'Sauce for the pasta. Made to a family recipe,' said Francesco, proudly.

They followed him up a narrow staircase to a corridor.

'Sister Cecilia is here,' he said, passing the first room and turning back to speak to them. He brought her bag into it and she followed him. 'Sister Bridget here . . .' He did the same for Bridget and the next one. The Sisters took possession of their rooms. At the last one, he opened the door and went into it with Margaret, bringing her bag over to the wooden chest under the window. He opened the windows and a refreshing breeze came in, with a smell of woodsmoke. Margaret was surprised by the loveliness of the view, the lights of the houses below coming on one by one in the dusk. In the warm air, the buzz of scooters, the occasional hoot of a car horn and the sounds of families chatting and laughing took on an intimate, friendly character. Dogs barked in the distance, and a bird was singing in the branches of a nearby tree.

'It's beautiful!' she said, and, embarrassingly, found her voice wobbled a little.

'You like it?'

'I love it. Thank you.' She didn't look directly at him in case he saw the embarrassing tears in her eyes.

'It's a pleasure. We have a meal waiting for you in one hour. That is all right?' Francesco asked.

He looked at her, and Margaret had a sudden impulse to confess to him that nothing had been right since Sister Helen had died, that she was lost and needed help. First Katy, now this man. Once she had started sharing her grief, would she ever be able to stop? She couldn't spend the rest of her life crying.

'Yes, yes, that would be lovely. Thank you.' Then, shyly, '*Grazie.*'

'*Prego,*' he replied, smiling. 'Well, I will tell the other Sisters and see you all later,' he said, and carefully closed the door behind him.

She was relieved to hear him go before she started crying again.

'This won't do, Margaret,' she said, and wiped her eyes.

She kicked off her shoes and took off her veil. Then she lay down on the clean, fresh, comfortable bed, and fell fast asleep.

Margaret was woken by a gentle knocking at the door.

'Sister Margaret. Are you awake? I think we are supposed to go to dinner.'

Margaret opened her eyes. Where was she? It was dark in the room now.

The door opened carefully, and Bridget came in.

'Are you all right? I looked in earlier, but you were so sound asleep I didn't want to wake you.'

Margaret sat up and blinked as she switched on her bedside lamp. She tried to smile.

'I'm fine. Just a little tired. But it is beautiful here, isn't it?'

'Oh yes!' said Bridget. 'Sister Cecilia and I went for a little walk just before dark. We walked up the steps to the church, but it was already closed. And we saw a big house on one side of it, where apparently the priest lives, and a bigger building the other side, set a little way back, which apparently is *the* convent.'

Margaret sat on the edge of her bed and smiled up at Bridget.

'Good. Let's go and eat, then.' Margaret put her veil back on, and they went downstairs.

They sat in the dining room at a table covered with a snowy-white cloth. The table was set for five.

'I hope you will be happy if Maria and I join you?' said Francesco, smiling. 'You are our only guests here tonight.'

'Certainly,' said Margaret in surprise.

Francesco was a handsome man, and he had changed into a crisp clean blue linen shirt, which looked good against his tanned brown skin, teamed with black trousers and well-polished shoes.

'We will eat as a family!' said Maria, entering. She was the tall, tanned, beautiful Italian woman they had seen in the photos, with a wide smile and large brown eyes. She looked a little younger than Francesco, and wore bright red lipstick, a long, colourful, loose-fitting dress and sparkling hooped silver earrings. She embraced each of them before she sat down, and her hug was soft and firm and sweet-scented.

'Tell us all about yourselves!' she urged in English as perfect as her husband's, with that same light Italian lilt, while she ladled out the delicious hot vegetable soup brought in from the kitchen.

And Sister Bridget, at least, did.

Before they had finished the soup, Francesco and Maria knew all about the precarious finances of the convent and the church, having had a dramatic account of Father Hugh's worry over the leaking roof, Sister Margaret's worry over bills, the lottery win and the letter and photograph in the desk. Francesco and Maria were wonderful listeners, and nodded and smiled and laughed at exactly the right points. Sister Bridget was flushed, but with excitement. She accepted the offer of a top-up of her glass of wine from Francesco, and beamed.

'This photograph of the Flying Nun? Do you have it at all?' asked Francesco.

Sister Cecilia took out a leather pouch from her pocket and unzipped it, passing Francesco and Maria the letter and photo. They were fascinated.

'Yes, yes, I see her,' they said to each other.

'Do you know anything about her?' asked Sister Cecilia. 'Was she known outside the convent?'

'She was, Sister, and to be honest that was why we were so keen to meet you. We have some information, but we need to check some things out, and we hope to be a bit clearer about what we can share by tomorrow lunchtime. Sorry to be so slow. I hope you understand. It's a question of getting permission.'

'How exciting!' said a rather tipsy Sister Bridget.

'Thank you,' said Cecilia, bowing her head.

'I am sorry to have to ask you to be patient, but I promise you it will be worth it. In the meantime, it has been very good for us to get to know you. We are so sad to learn about the church and Fairbridge and about your financial problems.'

'I'm so sorry we have burdened you with those,' said Margaret, embarrassed.

'Not at all. It gives us some . . . context,' said Francesco, reassuringly.

Margaret was still tired, but in the cool of the dining room, with a welcome breeze coming through the window from the jasmine-scented night air, she began to feel better. Everything about the meal signified welcome – from the snowy-white napkins and the sparkling crystal glasses to the way that Francesco and Maria were dressed so smartly, as if hosting a special meal. They were treating them as guests of honour, listening to their every word with unfeigned, relaxed appreciation. Sister Cecilia was being cajoled into talking about her favourite subject: the many good deeds of Edward Mortimer. By the second meat course, Sir Edward Mortimer, medal-winning veteran of the First World War, owner of the mill that had given most of Fairbridge its employment, philanthropist and pious Catholic, widowed early with no children, who had spent his life helping others, had been established as the nearest to a saint on earth they would ever hear of.

'He sounds wonderful,' said Francesco, and he and Maria beamed at each other and at Sister Cecilia as if somehow she had complimented them. Cecilia was relaxing, smiling in a way she never usually did. 'Do you have a photograph of him at all?'

Sister Cecilia flushed. 'I do, actually.'

'Do you?' said Margaret, astonished.

'I found one in the archives in the library. I thought it would be nice, as he is interceding for us, to bring it with us on this trip.' She said it defensively, not meeting Margaret's eyes.

She stole it! She didn't ask permission. She took a photograph of her beloved Edward from the archives. Well, well, well. The things we do for love.

'I'm the only one who uses the archives anyway,' Sister Cecilia continued. 'I will replace it as soon as we return.'

She delved into her bag and brought out an envelope. Carefully opening it, she extracted a small black-and-white newspaper cutting, and laid it carefully and a little shyly on the white tablecloth.

It was an original cutting from *The Universe*, the Catholic weekly, dated 1925, and showed a tall, handsome man with a grave face standing with a group of nuns outside St Philomena's Church, and a girl in 1920s dress. The caption was: *Edward Mortimer, generous benefactor of Fairbridge, welcomes a new recruit to the recently established Order of St Philomena.*

'Let me see! Sister Cecilia! Is that you next to him?' said Sister Bridget.

Cecilia flushed a little. 'Yes. He was always keen to meet new entrants to the Order.'

'May I?' said Maria, leaning over. She took it and showed Francesco. 'He was very handsome.'

'And you were very pretty,' said Bridget to Cecilia.

Cecilia pursed her lips.

'Not that that has any relevance at all, Sister,' she reprimanded her, but she reached for the photograph and Margaret saw her look at the photo again before putting it back in the envelope.

'I believe he was a saint,' said Cecilia. 'My greatest desire is to see him canonised, to be at the celebration in Rome. But we will need proof that he has worked miracles, and for some reason there isn't any proof, as yet. I think he is sending us this holy, levitating nun as a saint for Fairbridge first.'

Bridget had been completely unaffected by Cecilia's reprimand. She was in a realm she hardly ever entered. Nobody really cooked for her, and they never went out to restaurants.

'Have you ever tasted such soup?' she said. 'And the meatballs – cooked to perfection. I've never tasted anything like that sauce in my life. Absolutely out of this world. Absolutely. And did you ever eat a dessert like this? Exquisite! What did you say this dessert was called?'

'*Tiramisù*,' said Francesco.

'And what does that mean, exactly?'

'"Pick me up", you could say?'

'Well, it certainly has. Congratulations! You are wonderful cooks!'

Francesco and Maria smiled. 'We didn't cook this.'

'Oh. Well, then, do you think I could go into your kitchen and meet the chef when the meal is finished? Would that be all right?' asked Bridget.

'Certainly. Nonna will be delighted.'

'Your grandmother? Are you saying your grandmother cooked all this meal?'

'Yes. She is a very good cook, an artist. Today she cooked it all. She said she wanted to cook for our English guests. It makes her happy.'

'I don't speak any Italian myself. Would you help me speak to her?'

'That won't be a problem. She will speak in Italian, but I will translate.'

So they finished their meal and Bridget prepared to go back to the kitchen with Francesco, willing to miss out on coffee rather than miss the chance of speaking to Francesco's *nonna*.

'I do love Bridget,' thought Margaret. It was great to see their cook so happy. She so rarely had a chance to talk about food with anyone who loved it as much as she did.

'It's really pearls before swine, cooking for Cecilia and me,' she explained to Maria over coffee. Cecilia had already excused herself and gone to bed, and since – judging from the enthusiastic chatter coming from the kitchen – Bridget would not be emerging for some time, Margaret had decided that the Sisters would each say their Night Prayer on their own in their rooms tonight.

'Really! You are not swine!' remonstrated Maria, throwing her head back and laughing.

Margaret felt oddly touched by this. She had forgotten she could make people laugh. Helen had often laughed.

'Thank you!' she replied. 'No, but Sister Bridget really is a highly trained cook. Father Hugh is lucky to have her. He'll miss her when we leave.'

'Leave? Why would you have to leave?'

Margaret hesitated, but it was a relief to talk about this without the others.

'What we told you . . . We really have no money to carry on. It isn't just about fixing the house.'

'But what about the lottery win? Hasn't that solved your problems?'

'It wasn't that big a win, Maria. It was an answer to a prayer in that it has allowed us to pay for this pilgrimage and to get the repairs done to the house, but really only so that we can sell it. We're not the only ones suffering. Our parish church roof is in a terrible state too – we gave some money towards it, but Father Hugh is in a very difficult position, and the parish is in debt as well. They can't afford to support us. We lost – we lost Sister Helen unexpectedly, the head of the school we ran. I tried to take over Helen's work but we ended up losing the school as well.' Margaret looked stricken for a moment, but recovered herself. 'There are no new vocations into our Order, and there's just not enough of us to justify staying in that big house.'

'But what will you do in another convent?'

'Oh, there's always work for us.' *I hope so, Lord, I hope so.* 'I'm sure God will provide.' *Sorry I am such a hypocrite. I want to believe this – you know I do, Lord. Feelings aren't everything.*

'You don't want to go, do you?' said Maria, looking intently at her. 'As you said, the Sisters of St Philomena have been in Fairbridge for years. Since Edward Mortimer founded the Order.'

'It will be hard to go, but that's part of religious life. We just have to accept that if the Lord wanted us to stay, He would have made it possible,' said Margaret, but she didn't convince either of them.

From the kitchen came the sound of people laughing.

'Sister Bridget and Nonna are getting along like – how do you say it? – a house on fire,' said Maria, smiling.

'Well, goodnight,' said Margaret. 'Thank you and Francesco for a truly wonderful meal and welcome, Maria.'

'I will tell Nonna,' smiled Maria. 'Sleep well. Goodnight. It is so very important for us that you are here.'

Margaret climbed the stairs.

She entered her room, undressed and said Night Prayer sitting up in bed, listening to the breeze in the trees outside her window.

'Hello, Lord,' she said. 'It has been quite a day. I can't quite believe everything that has happened. Thank you. Thank you for my bumping into Katy at the Keats House, thank you for Francesco and Maria – they are such interesting people. I needed all this after St Peter's. I still don't know what we are going to do, and I can't quite talk to you about Helen yet, but I will. I'm just a bit too tired. So I will just do Night Prayer, if that's all right with you.'

She opened her prayer book, and settled comfortably into the rhythm of Night Prayer. Tired as she was, she felt a tiny resetting of the dial, another repositioning, so subtle it could be mistaken as unimportant, and so important that nothing was impossible, nothing unimaginable.

'I'm not sure why we are here, Lord, but I know you know,' said Margaret. 'I trust you will tell me in your own time. Thank you. Thank you even after all my moaning about this trip. I really do mean that.'

She put her Divine Office book back on the table, switched off the lamp and fell deeply asleep.

Twenty

The next morning, the Sisters met in the lounge for prayers, and after they finished there was still half an hour before breakfast.

'Why don't we go for a little walk? I'd like to get our bearings,' said Bridget. 'I think I saw a graveyard – that would be interesting.'

Margaret smiled. Only Bridget could make visiting a foreign graveyard a fun excursion. Although she did know that if she ever visited Rome again, she wanted to see Keats's grave in the Protestant Cemetery. But that was different. She knew Keats. Well, she felt as though she did.

They left the hotel and emerged into a beautiful Italian spring day. The Sisters were delighted by how lovely the countryside was – the colours of the roofs, the honeyed buildings. Birds were singing, a cockerel was crowing, and from somewhere in the distance there was the sound of a moped, and dogs barking.

They walked past the houses with the brightly coloured

geraniums, past the presbytery and church to the outskirts of the village, past the convent, and to the village graveyard beside it.

'Now, it should be open – yes, here it is. Lovely!' said Sister Bridget enthusiastically.

'Look – look over there,' said Cecilia suddenly. On the side of the graveyard bordering the convent grounds, the wall that formed the boundary for the other three sides had been replaced by what looked like fairly new high metal railings, in front of which had been planted some saplings. The young trees had not yet grown enough to hide the fact that behind them, in a corner bordering the convent garden, there seemed to be some sort of improvised shrine, beyond the railings and inaccessible from the cemetery.

The Sisters peered through. They could see simple crosses and, between two trees, a small white marble monument, positioned near the low wall so it was out of reach from the graveyard. Lots of candles, some big, some obviously near the end of their waxy lives, were burning around it, placed on saucers on the ground.

The white monument itself had, as its centrepiece, a marble statue of the Madonna and Child. Radiating out from the top of the monument, like children's play washing lines, were lengths of string, the ends tied to the branches of the trees on either side and what looked like hundreds of tiny babies' booties and hats and the occasional sleepsuit pegged on to them. The effect was as if white, pink and blue petals were cascading down from the trees. In amongst the candles, scattered on the ground before the Madonna and Child like bright, oversized confetti, were babies' rattles, and leaning against the monument, as if waiting for a child to claim it, was a huge teddy, wrapped in cellophane with a label attached to it.

'Look up in that tree.' Margaret pointed.

They looked, and Bridget exclaimed with delight. High above them, hanging in the branches of a large cypress tree planted in the convent garden, were what looked to be at least fifty shining, brightly coloured ornaments.

'How pretty!'

'Have you seen what they are?'

'They are . . . they are cradles. Tiny little cradles. And little feet and hands – how strange. Little feet and hands in something like brass, and look, there's a baby's rattle – quite a few of them. Just hanging, like Christmas decorations. I've seen them in chapels in Spain when thanksgiving prayers have been said,' said Margaret. 'How strange.'

'"Obtaining for them the gift of a child",' quoted Cecilia. 'Isn't that what the priest wrote in his letter? This is obviously a shrine where people pray for a child, and it is clear that these prayers have been answered. There are miracles happening here, I am sure of it. We were right. We are in Cardellino, and I think this is the graveyard of our first Fairbridge saint. We were right. The convent is saved!'

'Thanks be to God!' said Bridget.

'It really is extraordinary,' said Margaret. 'Sister Cecilia, it really does look like you have been right all along. Something important is happening here, that's very clear.'

Sister Cecilia nodded.

So Cecilia was right all along. You really have found a saint for us. I just can't take it in. But why isn't this more famous? How is it that this is such a secret?

Margaret felt flustered and made a show of looking at her watch.

'Well, I suppose we'd better go back for breakfast, before visiting the convent itself,' she said. 'Discovering a saint shouldn't be done on an empty stomach.'

'Amen,' said Sister Bridget.

Maria brought in bread rolls and coffee.

'How are you, Sisters?' she said, smiling. 'Did you sleep well?'

'Wonderfully,' said Bridget. 'And we've had a bit of an adventure here already. We've found the wonderful shrine – we saw it in the convent grounds. So we are going to go and see the nuns this morning.'

'This morning?' said Maria, concerned. 'Please don't.'

'Why?' said Margaret.

'If you will only wait until lunchtime – we have things we want to tell you about the Flying Nun.'

'We have to speak to the Sisters in the convent to get permission to set up the pilgrimage. The Bishop wants us to,' said Sister Cecilia, firmly.

'I know, I know,' said Maria, flustered. 'I just . . . I would ask you to wait, that is all. After we talk to you at lunchtime, then we can arrange a visit to the Sisters. They might not be able to see you when you just turn up. We can ring them. If you want us to.'

Maria looked very anxious, and Margaret suddenly felt uneasy. Something was wrong. It had felt as though Sister Cecilia had found a missing jigsaw piece, but maybe it wasn't for the right picture after all.

'I can give you leaflets about Cardellino. There are lovely little shops, a café for tea. There is a beautiful church, and a small museum. There will be plenty to do this morning while you wait.'

'We'd like to see the leaflets,' said Margaret, if only to make Maria feel better.

'Thank you,' said Maria, looking into her eyes. 'You will have a nice morning. And then I promise you I will ring the convent if you want me to.'

Father Hugh came back from an urgent, very early-morning visit to St Luke's Hospice, said early Mass, and decided to make himself a boiled egg and toast for breakfast. He was no clearer about how to raise the money, or whether he would have a curate, but attending a dying man and comforting his heartbroken widow put things into perspective. The prayers for the dying were so beautiful. He hoped he would be attended by a priest in his last moments too.

He took the top off the egg, and looked with satisfaction at the hard white and the softer yolk. Delia Smith had been right, God bless her. A small saucepan with a lid and a room-temperature egg. Boil the water first, then lower the egg into it, leave it in simmering water for a minute, then take the saucepan with the egg still in it off the heat, keeping the lid on, and seven minutes after the water started boiling, it would be perfect. It felt like another miracle, even though he had merely followed the instructions of a good Catholic cook very closely. He was wishing he could show Sister Bridget that he could, indeed, boil an egg, when the doorbell rang. He sighed, but did not hesitate, pushing his chair back and going to open the door to whoever needed him this time.

But nobody did.

'Parcel to sign for,' said a helmeted motorcyclist. Father Hugh signed, intrigued, and walked back into the presbytery kitchen with a rectangular brown-paper parcel containing something hard.

'What can this be?' he said to himself, tearing off the paper.

He missed Sister Bridget again – this unexpected delivery would have delighted her. She loved mysteries and surprises, however small.

The contents were so unexpected that Father Hugh could not deal with them by himself. He crossed himself and said a quick prayer, then went over to the pile of newspapers he had on the side. He found a recent copy of the *Fairbridge Gazette* and took it over to the table, opening it out beside his forgotten boiled egg and looking through it until he found the article and name he wanted.

He picked up the phone and dialled a number. It was just nine o'clock.

'Could I have the number for the university, please?' he asked. 'The Department of Art History.' He wrote it down, then dialled again. 'Could I speak to a Dr Matthew Woodburn?'

Breakfast was over. Margaret took the leaflets from a relieved Maria and the Sisters set off, but before long Cecilia was taking a left turn when Margaret and Bridget were going right. It was clear that Cecilia had no intention of sightseeing.

'Sister Cecilia. Where are you going?' said Margaret.

'To the convent, of course.'

'But Maria . . .'

'Maria is not a religious Sister. She may have to ring ahead, but I am sure they will speak to us.'

'She said to wait until after lunch.'

'We promised the Bishop. Maria is not in authority over us. We have seen the shrine. We know the saint is there, that there are miracles. There is no reason not to go this morning,' insisted Cecilia, and carried on walking.

Margaret looked at Bridget in desperation. Bridget smiled and shrugged her shoulders.

'Sure, what harm can it do? It's true, Maria has no authority over us, and I would like to know more about that shrine.'

'I just . . . I feel bad.'

'Why? We made no promise. She doesn't need to know. What the eye doesn't see, the heart doesn't grieve over,' said Bridget, setting off after Cecilia.

'I'm not sure if that is true,' said Margaret, but followed them all the same.

As the Sisters walked up the path to the convent, it was obvious that a side path led directly to the white marble shrine.

'Shall we pray there for a moment?' said Cecilia. 'Do we have a minute?'

'She looks so excited,' thought Margaret. 'At least Cecilia's faith is strong.'

'Yes, let's,' said Bridget.

Cecilia led the way to the shrine. They stood in front of the grave, the line of babies' clothes stirring in the breeze like Tibetan prayer flags.

Cecilia prayed fervently. She found the numerous brass booties and small casts of babies' hands and feet rather off-putting and so closed her eyes. The fact that maternity had passed her by was no burden to her at all. Nevertheless, such obvious evidence of successful intercession by the Virgin Saint could only be a positive sign, and she allowed herself to feel proud that her historical research had led them to this point and possibly to the saving of both the convent and the diocese. The others finished their silent prayers before her and waited patiently.

'She looks so happy, bless her,' thought Margaret. 'Italy has . . . transfigured her.'

They continued to the convent building, where an elderly

nun in a black habit and veil answered the door and led them into an attractive front room with comfortable chairs and a simple crucifix on the wall.

The door opened and a small and very pretty nun in her mid-forties came in, also wearing a smart black habit and veil in a good linen material, with a simple silver cross around her neck. She looked poised and elegant, whilst exuding quiet energy. Margaret was aware of her own old habit and felt tired and out of place. Out of place in a convent. What was going on?

The nun spoke in perfect, attractively lilting English.

'Welcome. My name is Sister Gabriella, and I am the Superior here. How can I help?'

'Well, Sister, we are Sisters of St Philomena, from Fairbridge in England, and we are here at the request of our bishop,' explained Margaret. 'We believe that a girl from Fairbridge came here in the 1920s, became a nun and levitated. We have heard about the miracles associated with the Flying Nun and we feel that it would be worth investigating her sanctity. We have funds available to us and we could help start up initial proceedings to begin the canonisation process.'

The Superior seemed less than pleased. She frowned.

'You are aware that any canonisation process must be instigated by the bishop of this diocese?'

'Yes, obviously we are aware of this,' said Margaret, slightly taken aback by this new frostiness. 'This is not, you must understand, an official visit. We just want to talk to you. We would love to know more about her, as in a way, because she came from Fairbridge, she is our local saint too. So we would like to offer our services should you too wish to follow up the cause of your Sister, and make you aware that we can help you financially, because we know that the process can be expensive.'

'That is most kind of you, but it is really not necessary.'

'Surely—'

'The graveyard . . .' interrupted Sister Cecilia. 'It is clear that there are miracles happening there, that childless couples have been given babies.'

The Superior sighed. 'All I can tell you is that this shrine has been associated with miracles, with the gift of children, that is true, but we prefer to not encourage this, as it is not officially recognised by the Church.'

'Why not?' asked Sister Margaret.

'There are procedures, steps we would need to go through in order to have it an official shrine. We choose not to do so.'

'But why not? Is it because of the money? Because as we have just told you, the Bishop has promised financial help if you need it,' said Sister Cecilia.

Sister Gabriella shifted, and Margaret noticed a flash of irritation mar the composure of her face.

What's going on, Lord?

She decided to appeal to her as a fellow religious.

'Sister Gabriella, we are here because Ellen Kerr used to be a parlourmaid in Fairbridge for the family who helped us establish our Order. In England, we are experiencing great difficulty attracting recruits to the religious life. Our bishop believes that if Ellen Kerr, as a local girl, could be found to have then become a holy nun who levitated before her death, and worked miracles after it, and if she could therefore be officially recognised by the Church as a saint, we might have an upsurge in devotion to the church in our diocese. That is why we have come. Surely this could only be a good thing for your convent? For your Order?'

Sister Gabriella spoke slowly, her words measured.

'So, you have heard about the miracles and you believe that

they are being performed by a nun who used to be called Ellen Kerr, a girl who lived in your diocese in England?'

'Yes.'

'And this is the only reason you are here?'

'Yes.'

'So, if I was to tell you that the nun buried in the shrine was never Ellen Kerr, but was in fact a Sister Bernardina, a local girl born and bred here – this would take away the point of your visit?'

'Is that what you are saying? That the levitating nun was not Ellen Kerr?'

'I am saying that the miracles you have heard about are being performed at the shrine built on the grave of a Sister Bernardina, born and bred here.'

'And the Flying Nun?'

'Yes, this shrine is called the shrine of the Flying Nun, yes.'

For a moment there was a stunned and disappointed silence, broken by Sister Cecilia rustling in her bag for the precious evidence.

'What about this?' Sister Cecilia held out the photograph, and they all noticed with concern that her hand was shaking. 'What about this, Sister? This clearly states that the Flying Nun was Ellen Kerr.'

Sister Gabriella sat up straight and stared Sister Cecilia in the eye.

'The nun buried in the shrine of the Flying Nun, where all the miracles are taking place, was not Ellen Kerr. It was Sister Bernardina, born and bred in Italy. You will have to tell your bishop so. I am afraid you have had a wasted visit.'

Twenty-One

Back in Fairbridge, Father Hugh was in an emergency meeting with Dr Matthew Woodburn, who had cycled over as soon as he had put the phone down.

'I must see them,' said Matthew urgently, taking off his cycle helmet as he entered the kitchen.

Father Hugh pointed to the table. There, lying against the brown paper they had been wrapped in, were two exquisite paintings, full of colour and love. One was of a traditional Madonna and Child against an Italian landscape, the other of a laughing young woman and a toddler in a garden, the young woman wearing a dress that placed the painting in the 1920s. The faces of both women were beautiful, and the same.

Dr Woodburn gasped. He went forward and looked closely at them, taking out an eyepiece from his pocket to examine them carefully. He sighed at the end as he put his eyepiece back, a happy, reverent sigh.

'You do know how extraordinary this is, don't you?' he said. 'These are absolutely exquisite, and so rare. You appear to have been sent not one but two original Jack Mortimer paintings, neither of which I have ever seen before. These are previously undiscovered masterpieces!'

'I am beginning to understand, yes,' said Father Hugh, sitting at the table. 'And do you think these paintings are worth a lot of money? Would they raise enough to fix the roof, do you think?'

'Fix the roof? Father, I wouldn't be surprised if you could do that and still have tens of thousands left over!'

Father Hugh felt dizzy and had to grasp the table.

'And you say there was a note with the parcel?' said Matthew.

'It's very short and simple,' said Father Hugh, picking it up with hands that shook a little. 'It says, "We have just heard of the parish's urgent need, and we hope that the sale of these paintings will solve your immediate money problems. If possible, we would like the Madonna to be kept in the church, but the priority is to fix the church roof, so if you need to sell both, please do, and we will send another for the church."

'There is no name, no address, but the courier's note said it was sent from Cardellino in Italy, and the strange thing is that's the very place where our parish Sisters have just gone. I don't know what it all means.'

'And they say they have more – that if you need to sell both they will send you another?' said Dr Woodburn. 'This is beyond my wildest dreams! I have to go to this place, to Cardellino. I have to go immediately.'

'Immediately?' said Father Hugh, rather taken aback by the fervour of the academic.

'Yes. Was there any address at all apart from that?'

'No, but the Sisters told me that it is a very small place, not far from Rome. I have the address of the hotel somewhere – Sister Bridget gave it to me if I needed to contact her. I think she didn't quite believe I could manage without her.'

'I'm going to the travel agency now to see if I can get a flight to Rome today,' said Matthew.

'You go ahead and I'll find the address and join you there. What shall I do with the paintings?'

'Lock them in a safe. Don't tell *anyone* about them. When I get back, I will help you get them valued and put one or other or both in an auction. Father Hugh, you will never have to worry about money again!'

Matthew cycled home and found his passport, then cycled as fast as he could to the travel agent's. George, who had already spent over an hour with a very undecided couple who were thinking of possibly going on a river cruise for their golden wedding next year, but maybe not, caught a glimpse of him through the window before he burst into the shop. Suddenly a difficult morning was irradiated with love.

'I tell you what, Mr and Mrs Lewis,' George said politely but decisively to the dithering couple, 'take these brochures and have a think about it, then get back to me when you are ready. You probably need a bit more time and I don't want to pressure you into anything.'

The couple blinked and nodded, overwhelmed with gratitude towards this wonderful man, who had spent so long with them and yet was releasing them back outside without taking any of their money. They normally dreaded shopping as they could never make up their minds and often ended up buying things they didn't want as an apology for taking up so much of the shop assistant's time.

'Thank you very, *very* much, young man,' said Mr Lewis,

looking more confident than he had all morning. 'This is excellent service.'

'Really excellent,' agreed his wife, grabbing the brochures, relief all over her face.

'I shall recommend you to all our friends!' said Mr Lewis.

George wasn't sure if that would be a blessing, really, imagining hordes of their similarly unassertive friends taking up his mornings, unable to decide what holiday to take, but he smiled and thanked them. They were a lovely old couple, and he was glad he had consciously channelled Sister Bridget's kindness when talking to them. But he would be bankrupt if all his customers were like them.

'I think I *do* want to go on a cruise now, Henry,' he heard the wife say as they left. Maybe he would get a sale after all.

But at this moment he wasn't interested in a sale. At this moment he was only interested in the impossibly handsome man in front of him, who had taken off his helmet and put it on the counter and, uncharacteristically for the patient man George knew, was practically hopping up and down with impatience.

'Something extraordinary has happened. Could you get me a ticket to Rome today, George?' Matthew said urgently. 'As soon as possible?'

Margaret couldn't bear to see the defeat in Cecilia's eyes as she stared disappointedly at the photograph in her hand, all her hopes dashed.

'Help me, Helen,' she prayed. 'What would you have done? You were always so good at getting the truth out of the girls. Sister Gabriella is hiding something, I am sure of it, but I'm not as clever as you were at asking questions.'

A sudden inspiration struck her.

'Sister Gabriella, did a girl from our diocese – a girl called Ellen Kerr – ever become a nun in your convent?'

She noticed the relief in Sister Gabriella's eyes.

'No – a girl called Ellen Kerr never became a nun in our convent.'

This was the truth. Margaret knew that this was the truth, and Sister Gabriella knew that Margaret knew this. The two Superiors stared each other out for a moment, and there was a triumph in Gabriella's gaze that she could not quite hide.

Margaret turned and gently took the photo away from Cecilia.

'Sister Gabriella – do you know who the nun in this picture is?'

There was another silence, but this time they all knew that something had changed. They could feel Gabriella struggling for an answer.

'I suppose that I cannot just ask you to leave us alone?' asked Sister Gabriella, her bluntness softened by a tone of desperation, almost of pleading.

'I am sorry, Sister,' said Margaret. 'We have travelled a long way at some expense, and I have to report back to the Bishop. It's not something we are just going to drop without good reason.'

'But there is good reason.' Gabriella looked around at them all. 'Believe me – there is good reason. There is no hope of a canonisation out of this, and bringing in investigators from the Vatican will all . . . it will all just cause unnecessary scandal and upset.'

'Is this why Maria didn't want us to talk to you directly? Can you tell us what is going on?' asked Sister Bridget. 'What is happening at the shrine, for example? Why isn't this Sister

Bernardina you speak of being investigated? I know her canonisation will not benefit us, but with so many miracles . . .'

'Nobody wanted the miracles.'

'Pardon?'

'Nobody wanted the miracles. Mother Julia thought that burying Bernardina there would put an end to it all . . . Instead, it all started up again. It got even worse, if that were possible.'

'Worse than what?' asked Margaret.

'I wasn't here at the time, of course, but this whole business of the levitation was such a problem. Then, of course, the visitors came, people started asking questions, which was the last thing they wanted, particularly with the child . . .'

'What child?' said Cecilia, looking over at Margaret to see if she understood what the young Superior was saying.

'Apparently, nobody could understand why she levitated like that, not even her. In the chapel in prayers, but, most difficult of all, in the garden. The villagers claimed they had seen her. That's when . . .'

'That's when what?'

Sister Gabriella frowned. 'I . . . I have to think. I have to pray about this. There are more people involved than just the convent. I must ask you to leave.'

'Sister, we have only a couple of days.'

'I have to ask you to leave, I am afraid.'

The Sisters found themselves escorted back to the front door, which was firmly shut behind them.

'This is so exciting! Now, do you want a hire car from Rome to Cardellino?' said George, as he organised Matthew's tickets. He had found a midday flight that he should just about catch.

'No, I can't drive. I'll get a taxi.'

'I'll come with you!' said George suddenly.

'Pardon?' said Matthew.

'I . . . I could come with you and drive you from Rome to Cardellino,' said George. 'I'm used to driving in Italy and Spain.'

'I . . . No, no, thank you. No, that's . . . I can't expect you to close your shop.'

'I'd love to. Honestly. I'd love to help.'

'To help?' Matthew looked uncertain. George couldn't quite work out what Matthew's emotions were. His own heart was thumping.

Matthew shifted from one leg to another and looked down, avoiding George's eyes.

'I . . . Don't worry. I'll get a taxi in Rome. Thank you. How much will that be?'

For a moment, George felt winded with disappointment.

What do I do, Miguel?

Father Hugh rushed, panting, into the shop.

'This is the address where the Sisters are staying.' He gave the paper to Matthew, who gave it to George.

'I'll see you when you get back. I have a hospital visit to get to. God bless the journey!' Father Hugh said, and was gone.

George read the address. 'This is where I booked them in. It's the only hotel in town. The problem is, it was closed for refurbishment and they made a special exception for the Sisters. I can ring them and plead your case, though.'

'Please do. Otherwise I'll stay somewhere else nearby. I just don't want to miss my flight.' Matthew suddenly looked uncharacteristically panicked, and it twisted George's heart. Matthew needed him, whether he knew it or not yet. A new, calm certainty replaced the hurt.

'Go. Go home and pack, and I'll book you a room there, or

somewhere near. You're not going to get your flight if you stay here too long. We can settle up later. I'll drive you to the airport.'

'Are you sure?' said Matthew.

'Of course!' said George decisively. 'Go! I'll be with you in half an hour, maximum. Leave this with me. I've got your address here.'

Sarah was in when Matthew rushed home.

'What's up?' she said.

'Something amazing!' he said, bounding up the stairs two at a time. Sarah followed him.

'Tell me.' She stood at his bedroom door as he rushed around his room.

He opened and shut drawers, hurling clothes into a small carry-on bag.

'The Catholic priest in Fairbridge has just been sent two rare original Jack Mortimers from somewhere in Italy, and whoever sent them says they have more. I think we've stumbled on the lost works, Sarah. George has got me tickets to Rome and I'm going now to find out about it.'

'That's wonderful! You don't speak Italian, though, do you, Matthew? Will that be OK?'

'Well, it should be. Most people speak English. I have some basic . . . Actually, George offered to go with me, and to drive me there from Rome.'

'That's brilliant!'

'I said no.'

'Why on earth did you do that?'

'I just . . . It's too much. He has his business, and there's his cat. He can't just close up and leave.'

'Don't be ridiculous. He offered.'

'He's taking me to the airport anyway. He'll be here soon.'

'Ask him then. Ask him to come with you.'

'I just can't.'

'Matthew! Please – don't let this chance pass you by. You don't want us to be stuck in the same comfortable rut, twins living together, for the rest of our lives, playing it safe? I don't, anyway. Come on, Matthew. Seize the day!'

'Look – I have to phone the department and explain what is happening,' said Matthew, irritably. 'Could you just leave me alone for a moment?'

Sarah shook her head and went downstairs, and then suddenly had an idea. She ran out the door and waited at the end of the drive until George and his Mini turned up.

She ran to the window.

'Go back quickly and get your passport, George. He needs you, whether he knows it or not.'

'You think?' said George.

'He wants you to come but he is too shy. He isn't sure if you're interested. He thinks you might like me that way. You don't, do you?'

'You? God, no! Sorry.'

'I didn't think so. Look, George – have you time? I do think you should go. He can't drive or speak Italian and he has a terrible sense of direction.'

'Um. Yes, of course. But . . . Sebastian!'

'Give me your keys and I'll look after him. I love cats.'

'And Mother?'

'I'll deal with her too. I'm due to do her dressing tomorrow. Don't worry. Go.'

George was back in five minutes, pressing his keys and a piece of paper into Sarah's hands as Matthew climbed into the car. 'Where you can contact me.'

She pressed some paper into his. 'My telephone number,' she said.

Matthew noticed, but said nothing.

The road was clear and they got to the airport in plenty of time. They listened to the radio, and made strangely stilted conversation. They were arriving at the turns to 'Drop-off' or 'Car Park' and George had to make a decision.

'I meant it, Matthew. I'm happy to come with you.'

'No, really, no. I just . . . Thank you. If you could just drop me off here,' said Matthew, pointing left, to the drop-off sign.

And George turned left.

He was watching Matthew walk into the terminal when his mobile rang.

'Well?' It was Sarah's voice.

'He doesn't want me to go with him,' said George.

'*Aaagh!*' came Sarah's reaction down the line. 'George – you strike me as someone who's up for adventures, who isn't afraid to take risks?'

'I used to be, certainly. Miguel said I jumped at life.'

'Do you like my brother?'

'Yes. Yes, I like your brother. I think he is wonderful.'

'Then, please, please don't let him get away. He needs you. I know he does. And you'd be so good together. Our father was very strict when we were growing up, and then when he was only eighteen he was so hurt when he first fell in love. He just doesn't take risks. Please, I'm sure he still thinks you're interested in me. Just go. I'll look after your cat. *Please.*'

Back in Cardellino, the Sisters stood on the road outside the convent.

'Well, she wasn't on the best of form, that's true,' said

Bridget, breaking the silence. 'But she says there are other people involved. I don't think this is over yet.'

'Why does Bridget have to be so relentlessly positive?' prayed Margaret furiously. 'It's unbearable. Why can't she just be normal and admit that it's a disaster?'

'It's a disaster,' said Sister Cecilia. She looked tired and deflated.

'Look, why don't we go back and hear what Maria has to say at lunch? There must have been a reason why she didn't want us to go this morning.'

'That's a good idea, isn't it, Sister Cecilia?' said Bridget, but Cecilia didn't reply.

They walked in silence for a bit until they got to the hotel.

'Lunch is at one, isn't it?' said Cecilia. 'I think I will go to my room for a while.' She went up, an old, tired and dignified nun, unsuccessfully trying to hide her disappointment with the morning's work.

Bridget and Margaret followed her to their rooms.

'Let me show you something, Margaret,' said Bridget cheerfully, opening her door. 'I found such a lovely little Swiss Guard toy in Rome for James, Thomas's great-grandson. He is such a dote.' Bridget went over to the window and rummaged in a bag. 'I got a mug for Thomas and a tea towel for Linda and a key ring for Sophie. I'll show you them too. I'm very pleased. Here's the little soldier.'

Bridget's inappropriate happiness with the ridiculous, kitsch little soft toy was the last straw.

'Why didn't you get a soft toy of the Pope whilst you were at it?' said Margaret.

'They didn't have any,' answered Bridget, taking the question at face value. Then she saw Margaret's face.

'What's the matter, Margaret?'

'Just . . . I just wonder what a religious Sister is doing spending convent money on four generations of a family she isn't related to,' said Margaret.

'We each have a little spending money, Margaret. I didn't know there would be a problem,' said Bridget.

'It's just . . . he's a widower——' said Margaret, hating herself as she said it, but unable to stop the mean words leaving her mouth. Why was she doing this? She had even been to confession about this.

'Oh no, we are not having this again. Stop. Stop that right now,' interrupted Bridget loudly and firmly, a tone in her voice that Margaret had never heard before. She glanced at her and had a shock seeing Bridget gripping the sides of the chair and suddenly looking so furious. It was a new, scary position, being the recipient of Bridget's anger.

'Sorry. I just thought . . . you're a religious Sister . . . You . . . He is a man. You know what I mean.'

'I do know exactly what you mean,' replied Bridget. 'And I knew exactly what you meant back in Fairbridge when you commented about the Amises being around all the time. You upset me very much that day, Margaret. Your attitude made me feel . . . horrible. Ashamed. But I went and had a good chat with Father Hugh and he helped me see you were beside yourself with stress, and I forgave you. But that doesn't mean you can keep going on insinuating things, being nasty. Stop it.'

'I'm your Superior——' began Margaret, but she was ashamed at how petulant the words sounded. She knew she might be Bridget's Superior in the convent, but she definitely wasn't superior to her as a person. This was so horrible. In her misery, she had given in to a moment of meanness and it was all getting out of hand.

'Why didn't you talk to me?' Margaret continued, in a more conciliatory tone.

'About what?' said Bridget. 'About how I was missing Rose? About my feelings for Thomas? About wondering, if my life had been different . . . ?'

The two Sisters stared at each other, shocked. Margaret was ashamed and overcome by the hurt and honesty she saw in Bridget's eyes.

The anger between them ebbed away, leaving only pain.

'You've been so busy coping with the convent and the bills and trying not to murder Cecilia and me – don't deny it,' said Bridget, 'I know we're driving you around the bend – that I asked Our Lord and Our Lady for help, and I went to confession to Father Hugh, and I sorted it all out without bothering you.

'But don't take me for granted, Margaret. I haven't done anything wrong. I know that, and Father Hugh reassured me. I love Thomas because he is a good man, but I haven't endangered my vows. It's just, it has been very difficult in the community these last couple of years, losing so many people, and with you being so angry and stressed and on edge all the time. I've had to pray for patience with you.'

Margaret opened her mouth and then shut it.

'I know you're trying your best, Margaret, but you're not exactly fun to be around, and I know that the accounts are dragging you down, but recently you always rush off to the office and never offer to wash up, and I don't believe you have ironed or taken your turn with the laundry, or offered to cook, or just helped out with the housework, for weeks and weeks. Sister Cecilia and I have taken all that on, because we know you are overwhelmed, but still . . .'

Margaret felt shocked tears fill her eyes.

'And Cecilia, God love her,' continued Bridget, 'isn't the best of company. It was so much easier when there were more of us, when there was a proper community. Father Hugh and Thomas and his family talk to me, and need me, and they aren't constantly irritated with me – don't deny it, Margaret, you are. They seek out my company and they listen to me, which is more than I can say for you and Cecilia.

'I've been very lonely, and, yes, at times I did wonder whether my life would have had more meaning if I had met a man like Thomas instead of joining the convent.'

Margaret felt everything crash about her. She had never, for one moment, believed all her little digs, she realised. They had just been ways to express her own misery, jealous ways to punish Bridget for being happy when she was not.

'I'm so . . . sorry,' she stuttered.

'It's all right. Father Hugh and I had a good chat. I know deep down where God wants me to be, where I feel peace. I am very happy as a religious Sister and I know it was right to join the Sisters of St Philomena, so I know God won't abandon us, and will show us what we will do next.'

Margaret's voice shook. 'I'm so sorry. I will be more aware of sharing the community tasks. I do love you, Bridget.'

Bridget got up, and Margaret felt herself somehow ushered to the still-open door.

'I know you love me, Margaret. And I love you and Cecilia. But it isn't easy for any of us just being the three of us, and you're right, we do need to ask God to show us a reason, some work for our community.'

'I just wish He'd hurry up, that's all,' said Margaret, wearily.

'We need to ask for the grace of patience,' said Bridget. 'I'll see you at lunch.' And for the second time that morning, Margaret found herself ejected, outside a firmly shut door.

Twenty-Two

'Are they having an argument?' asked Francesco. The raised voices upstairs had not gone unnoticed.

'I think they are very stressed. Sister Margaret is, anyway. I think she is at the end of her tether,' said Maria.

'They need our help,' said Nonna, suddenly. 'Jack told me I could decide what to do. What we did last night was a start, but it's not enough to help in secret. I see that now. Now is the time. And now we have the others who rang today coming too. We can tell them all together.'

'Are you sure, Nonna?' asked Maria, looking at Francesco.

'Yes. I am sorry I have held you back so long. I know it has not been easy for you. But somehow, meeting Sister Bridget last night, and knowing what a difference we can make, it feels like time.'

George parked the car and rushed into the terminal. He managed to get a ticket, ran to the gate and boarded the flight at the very last minute. He stowed his bag in the locker and took his seat, panting.

I'm glad I could get on at the back. The thought of walking past Mat-
thew to my seat . . . Miguel, what am I doing? I can see the back of his
head from here, but he has no idea I'm on this plane. At least Jenny was
happy to have an unexpected paid holiday. This is going to cost me a for-
tune if we are away too long, but I don't care. I have to do this. I have
to do this now. Matthew is so special, and he needs me. I can't lose this
chance of love again. I just hope Sarah is right.

The safety announcements over and seatbelts buckled, the plane taxied and then suddenly they were up, flying to Italy, Matthew and George together, though Matthew wasn't aware of it yet.

Maria went up and knocked at Sister Bridget's door.

'Hello, Sister. I'm making fresh pasta and Nonna said she thought you might like to join me.'

'I'd love that!' said Bridget, smiling, immediately following Maria downstairs. If Maria hadn't heard it, she would never have guessed that Bridget had raised her voice to Margaret. Maria gave her a quick tour of the kitchen, the pasta-making machine, the special flour, the stove, the coffee makers, whilst Nonna sat in an old wooden chair in the corner and smiled, and then seemed to fall asleep.

Maria showed Bridget how to make the pasta mixture and roll it through the machine, and then how to use the machine to make spaghetti.

'You were telling us last night about the financial problems the church and the convent are having,' said Maria, as Bridget happily fed the dough into the machine.

'Yes, it's a terrible strain,' said Bridget.

'If you don't mind me saying so, you don't seem under a strain at all, Sister. Sister Margaret seems much more stressed.'

'Well, I suppose it's the way I am. Unlike Sister Margaret,

I'm not a worrier. I just have a feeling everything will be all right. I don't know why, I just feel that Jesus is looking after us. The lottery win, the letter, the photograph of the Flying Nun. I believe God has a plan, that we are meant to be here.'

'How many Sisters are in the convent?' asked Maria.

'Just the three of us.'

'That's very small, isn't it?'

'Well, it was much bigger, much livelier. It got smaller quite suddenly, really. A Sister left to get married, and some older Sisters died, and then a younger Sister died unexpectedly.'

'That would be Sister Helen, wouldn't it?' said Maria.

'Yes,' said Bridget, startled. 'How did you know?'

'Something Margaret said last night when she was telling us about the school closing. She seemed very fond of her. I could see she was still suffering. Still grieving.'

There was a pause as Bridget fed another sheet of pasta dough through the machine. She couldn't enjoy watching the spaghetti quite so much now.

'It must have been very hard for the ones who were left,' continued Maria.

'It was. And my family in Ireland were having a very hard time. My nephew was having problems, so that was very worrying.'

'I'm sorry to hear that,' said Maria.

'We have a great parish priest, thank God. I spoke to him, and friends in the parish. I talked to them. And I was able to help my sister and her husband and my nephew through it, thank God. I prayed so hard.'

'And did Sister Margaret help your family too?'

'I told her my nephew was having a breakdown, and she was very good and insisted I go back to Ireland to help them. But I didn't really talk to her too much about it. Margaret was in bits after Helen died and she was struggling with the school, being made head teacher. I didn't really want to burden her.'

'So after Sister Helen died, Margaret became head teacher, then she lost her job as head teacher, and she suddenly became the Superior of the convent, and took on all the worries and responsibility for the debt?'

'Yes,' said Bridget. An unexpected pang went through her, something like fear. Maria seemed to be telling her something, and she wasn't sure she wanted to hear it.

Maria paused. 'You know, I think that sometimes, when we live together, when we are very close, we still may not know quite how much another person is suffering. When Francesco and I first realised that we weren't ever going to be able to have children—'

'Oh, I'm so sorry to hear that,' said Sister Bridget. Maria waved her hand.

'Thank you, Sister. I'm not bringing this up to talk about us. I say it because when we first were grieving that, we were both so careful of each other, we didn't tell each other what we were feeling. We suffered alone too much. It was Nonna who got us to talk.'

'I didn't want to burden Margaret . . .' Bridget began, but then she saw Maria's face. 'This isn't about me, then, it's about Margaret now?' she asked.

Maria nodded. 'Sister Bridget. I hope you don't mind me saying, but I see a strength, an optimism in you that Sister Margaret doesn't have. You are, if I may say it, tougher than you look. Why aren't you the Superior?'

'But Sister Margaret didn't have a job. I did. I'm the parish Sister, the priest's cook and housekeeper. He needs me.'

'Could he not manage anything without you?' Maria asked, gently but firmly.

'Well, he can't cook. I mean, I don't actually know if he can cook. I've never seen him . . . he has never needed to. He's very busy . . .' Bridget became aware of how defensive she was sounding.

'I do the parish bingo. Margaret would not be able to do the bingo,' Bridget continued. But she met Maria's eyes and found herself blushing.

'So . . . I hope you have enjoyed learning how to make pasta,' said Maria.

'Yes, yes I have,' said Bridget. 'Thank you. I'll . . . Thank you, Maria. I think I may have learnt a little more than I expected. I think I will have a little pray before lunch.'

They looked at each other and gave each other a spontaneous hug.

'You are a strong woman,' said Maria. 'Stronger than maybe you admit.'

'Thank you,' said Bridget, a little ruefully. 'Maybe I need to think about that,' and she left the kitchen.

An exhausted Margaret had gone back to her room. She had closed the shutters, leaving a window open for fresh air, lain on her bed and gone straight to sleep. She slept well, yes, but her dreams were ridiculous. She and Helen going up a hill, and Cecilia and Bridget riding a cow flying over the moon, and Father Hugh up in the sky, flapping his arms like a portly bird, surprisingly graceful in flight.

She woke and blinked, disorientated for a moment in the shuttered room. Some birds were singing outside her window, and for a moment she let herself do nothing else but listen to them, paying attention to the freedom and unselfconsciousness of their calls.

And then she was hit by it.

A grief that winded her in its unexpectedness. Sobs that made her gasp.

She sat up and felt under her pillow for a tissue.

'Oh my goodness, Lord, what is this?' she cried. 'Where has this all come from again? I thought I'd cried it all out in Rome. I feel terrible . . . absolutely terrible.'

She got out of bed and on to her knees, put her head on the white duvet cover and cried and cried as if her heart would break – had broken. The words came from her very depths.

'Why did you take her, Lord?' she cried. 'Why did you take Sister Helen? I miss them all, but Helen was so young. It was terrible when Sister Frances went, but she had been ill for so long, it was a release, and she was so full of faith and peace, it was a happy death. She wanted to meet you. I'd like to go like her. I am very sorry Sister Basil had such a stressful time with the accounts and I didn't notice, but her last months were happy in the hospice. But Helen . . . she had so many more years of service. She must have suffered such a lot, and she hid it from us. I loved her so much and I never got the chance to tell her. Was that wrong? Were you angry with me? I didn't think you were that sort of God, but now I wonder if you are punishing me. It feels like you are punishing me for some-thing, and I don't know what it is. I know that's not true. That's the devil speaking, making me feel like this. But if you aren't punishing me, why do I feel as if you are?

'I spent most of my religious life with her. And I loved it. I loved her. I know some Orders used to say we should not have special friends in religious life, but you know. She was my best friend, my soulmate. Literally. We talked about you so much. I loved you more through knowing her. She was so beautiful, Lord, outside and in. You know. You have her with you now. We laughed so much. It was fun, it was hard work, but she ran our school and our community with such wisdom . . . I have failed since you took her.

'I lost the school and now I don't know what to do about the convent. What are we going to do? Helen said I would manage, but I haven't, Lord. I am useless.'

Sobbing, she patted her pocket for a handkerchief to wipe her eyes and then dried them, child like, with her sleeve instead. She felt unable to rise from her knees to look for one. She had to keep praying, asking the questions in her heart.

'Was it all a big mistake, Lord, me joining the convent in the first place? I thought I was following your call, giving my whole life to you, but was it all a big mistake, my life, one big self-delusion? I don't have a husband, I don't have children. I'm tired and I don't feel well, and what good have I actually done in my life? What good can I do? Without Helen, I don't seem to be able to do anything.

'We don't even have a levitating saint now to bring back to the Bishop. I'm sorry I was so difficult about that – you see, I didn't even have the faith to be enthusiastic about it. Maybe it is my lack of faith which has made it all go wrong?'

She lifted up her head. Her hands were wet with tears, her cheeks were flushed, the tears still pouring, and the pain was searing. She put her hand to her heart.

'Why did you take her, Lord? She was so much better than me. Maybe you wanted her in Heaven to be a saint with you, but couldn't you have left her with us – with me? You have so many angels – I only had one. She was our real saint, and I am so, so tired of just being me now that she has gone, and trying to make sense of life without her.

'What is the point of me? You have to help me, Lord, as I just don't know. Show me why I am still here when Helen is not.'

There was a quiet knock at the door.

'Wait a moment, please,' she called, and catching a glimpse of her tear-blotched reflection in the mirror, splashed her face with water and dried it, hoping it would hide the fact that she had just been weeping from whoever was on the other side of the door.

It didn't.

'Margaret!' exclaimed Bridget with concern. 'What's the matter? I'm sorry I got so cross.'

'No. It's . . . it's about Helen,' Margaret blurted out as Bridget came in and closed the door behind them.

'Helen? Oh, Margaret. I'm sorry. I know you miss her.'

'I do. I miss her so much.' Margaret found herself crying again. She sat back down on the bed, and Bridget sat next to her, and put her arms around her.

'I loved her so much, Bridget. I don't know what to do without her. I made a mess of being head, and I don't know what I'm doing as Superior. I'm hopeless. I miss the others, but I know their time had come. I just don't understand why God took her.'

'It's all right, Margaret,' Bridget soothed.

'I'm so sorry for saying that about Thomas, about Rose, Bridget. That was so awful of me. I didn't mean it. I can't believe I've been so horrible.'

'It's all right, Margaret, I know. But you know, I've just had a little pray, and I think I was so angry with you because I knew you had a point. Not about me and Thomas, but about the community.'

'What do you mean?'

'I think – I know – I've been selfish, Margaret. Something I've just realised when talking with Maria. You know, I missed the big community too. I think, to be honest, that I was frightened of our community getting smaller, and I wanted a big community again. I got that in the parish, so I think I used being a parish Sister and helping others to excuse me neglecting being part of the convent. I find Cecilia difficult at times, and I'm sorry I didn't support you enough, Margaret. You were mad with grief after Helen and stressed by the new job. I should have been home more, I see that now. I hid behind my role in the parish, behind cooking for Father Hugh and bingo and sorting out the Amises, and I should have looked after you more. I'm sorry.

'I think you *have* done a good job, but I have been talking to Maria, and praying, and I know deep down that Jesus wants me to be Superior now. You've done enough these last years, had enough stress. I can lift it off you. I really should have done it from the start. I don't feel daunted. I feel a bit ashamed and cross with myself, but not daunted at all. I think I should take my turn.'

Margaret's tears stopped flowing. She looked at Bridget, stunned.

'But how will Father Hugh manage?'

Sister Bridget got up, pushed open the shutters and looked out of the window. The room filled with light. She turned and smiled at Sister Margaret.

'Ah, Father Hugh will manage. So will Thomas. They'll have to. I'll still cook for them sometimes, and they can come and eat with us in our community, but they are grown men and I have been treating them like children. And you know the person who really needs a bit of mothering?' She smiled at Margaret. 'You.'

And she put her arms out and Margaret, feeling lighter and happier than she had for months and months, gladly rushed into them.

Father Hugh, on impulse, on his way back from a busy morning of hospital and home visits, went to buy some eggs from Mr Abidi. He was tired and hungry and torn between despair about ever getting a curate to help him, and excitement about what the paintings he had been sent could mean. Please God Dr Woodburn was right, and they were truly Jack Mortimer's work. But he couldn't concentrate on anything, good or bad, until he had eaten.

It turned out to be one of those rare times when the shop was quiet, and the only people in it were Mr Abidi and Cuthbert Brown, and this, in turn, gave Father Hugh the courage to ask a very intimate question.

'Could either of you tell me how to fry an egg? I know there's a knack to it,' he said to them as he reached the counter with a basket loaded with a box of eggs, a tin of beans, some bread, and an impulse packet of Kimberleys. 'I'm thinking of having it on top of beans and toast for my lunch.'

'It's got to be a fresh egg,' said Cuthbert, delighted to be asked.

'All my eggs are fresh,' said Mr Abidi.

'Of course. I'm sorry. No question of that,' said Cuthbert, hastily. Mr Abidi nodded, accepting the apology, and leant forward to hear more.

'So, you cook it gently – gas or electric cooker, Father?' said Cuthbert.

'Electric,' said Father Hugh.

'Right, on the electric cooker, not more than three out of ten. Use plenty of oil and that will stop it sticking. Don't rush it, it will cook quickly enough whilst you heat the beans. Flick a little bit of oil across it to cook the top before you serve it.'

'Wait, Father Hugh!' said Mr Abidi. 'All my eggs are fresh, but I do have some which have been delivered from a local farm this morning, and I haven't put them out yet.' He disappeared out the back and returned with them.

'You will get no fresher in Fairbridge,' he said.

Father Hugh thanked them both for their support, paid for his shopping and drove home, muttering the instructions like a mantra under his breath until he could write them down. As soon as he got in, he scribbled: *No. 3, plenty of oil, no rush, heat beans, flick a little bit of oil.* Then he laid the table, put all the ingredients out on the worktop, washed his hands, put on an apron, said a prayer and started to cook.

Father Hugh sat at the table, said grace, took his knife and fork and cut into his lunch. He took a mouthful and closed his eyes in appreciation, shaking his head in wonder. It was perfect. The freshly made, crisp brown buttered toast with the hot baked beans, a fried egg with a deep yellow yolk in the centre of the pure white on top of the beans, the knife cutting into the yellow yolk, which spilled out onto the orange beans and the toast below, the strong, hot, milky mug of tea – all were perfect. All the timings were perfect, the textures were perfect, the taste was out of this world, and the most amazing thing was that he, Father Hugh, and nobody else, had made it.

This lunch was a miracle. A thing of beauty.

He took his time, savouring each bite, each swig of tea. He finished the meal, then brought the crockery over to the sink and washed it all up in hot sudsy water, ending up with the pan. He rinsed and dried everything, and put them away. Still on a higher mystical plane, he went over to the phone.

'Hello. This is Father Hugh from St Philomena's. I have to speak to the Bishop urgently.'

The Bishop put down the phone and stared at it. He had never heard Father Hugh be so decisive and sure of himself.

'I just have to have a curate, John. I can't carry on like this. I'm parish priest, chaplain to the university and the schools, and I've so many visits to the hospital and care homes, and all the Masses on weekdays and Sundays. I don't need money any more – I've just had an extremely large anonymous donation, so I can completely fix the roof and sort out all the other problems – but there is still only one of me, and St Philomena's needs two priests.'

'You have been given an anonymous donation, you say?' said the Bishop. Astonishing. Father Hugh did not strike him as a man who knew very many rich people, or who would be at ease with them if he did.

'Yes. I can't tell you any more details at the moment, because I don't know the exact amount myself. I just need to say, John, that I know I do not need the money I asked for maintaining the church any more, but I *do* still desperately need a curate, and as you know, I have been asking for a long time. I understand that Monsignor Wilson has also been asking . . .'

'Hmm. Monsignor Wilson has, as you say, been asking, but . . .'

Jeremy Wilson was actually irritatingly pushy and far too competitive at golf. The Bishop had not enjoyed his recent rounds. He had also seemed to be taking it for granted lately that he would get the curate from Rome, and that, the Bishop felt, did not show proper deference, proper respect. And Father Hugh had at least got the money together to pay for the roof without the diocese having to help. He had actually said he did not need money any more. Extraordinary. No, let Father Hugh have the bright young priest finishing his studies in Rome, not Monsignor Wilson. He could help with the chaplaincy duties too. The university could use a clever young cleric. Father Hugh and he would make an interesting team.

'Yes, Father Hugh. I am minded to say yes. I believe there is a suitable curate who can join you in a month or so.'

Twenty-Three

Nonna, small and old, came and joined them at the lunch table, smiling shyly at them all, and Maria and Francesco started the meal by serving them all the fresh pasta Sister Bridget had helped to make, covered in a delicious creamy sauce.

Maria spoke to Nonna in Italian, and the old lady nodded.

'I am sorry, Sisters,' said Maria, 'to keep you waiting any longer, but we had a phone call after breakfast and we are being joined by someone else who needs to hear the story this afternoon. He is travelling from Rome to Cardellino today, so if we could just wait until late afternoon, I can call you down and Nonna will be able to tell you what you need to know. It will save her having to tell the story twice.'

'Sure, we can wait a little more!' said Bridget, beaming at Nonna. 'We could get nothing from the nuns this morning.'

'Yes, yes, I heard that,' said Maria, with a note of reprimand in her voice.

'I'm sorry,' said Margaret, calm now, her red eyes barely noticeable. Even if Sister Bridget was going to take over being Superior, she still felt she had to take responsibility. Cecilia was so embarrassing. And Cecilia wasn't volunteering her own part in this, even though she was the one who had insisted on going. It was so unfair.

'I did warn you, Sisters,' said Maria. 'I heard from the nuns you were upset, and I wish you had listened to me.'

'So you do know about the Flying Nun?' said Sister Cecilia.

'Yes. I think we can answer all of your questions, once our additional visitor is here.'

The expected visitor headed towards the taxi rank. George, the unexpected one, who had managed to run and push his way so that he was only a little behind him through passport control, knew it was now or never.

'Matthew!' he shouted.

Matthew turned, incredulous, and stopped, waiting for him to catch up. George noticed, with a sinking heart, that he didn't look that pleased.

'Um. Hello. Fancy meeting you here,' he said, once he had caught up with Matthew, slightly ruining the effect by having to stop and pant a little before speaking. He didn't do much running as a travel agent.

'George? Why are you here? What are you doing?'

'I'm coming with you. I want to.'

'But what about the agency? Your mother? Your cat?'

'Sarah is looking after all of them. Well, Mother and Sebastian, anyway. The agency will cope.'

'Why are you and Sarah getting involved? I said I would be fine on my own,' said Matthew, defensively.

'It's not "me and Sarah",' said George, willing Matthew to understand, but he didn't. 'Anyway, I can drive us there. It will be easier. I can get a discount for a hire car. That's cheaper than a taxi.'

'The university would have paid anyway,' said Matthew, somewhat ungraciously.

Miguel. Can you inspire me here? It's not exactly going well.

'Look. I'm sorry. I realise you don't want me here. But here I am. So why not use me? I can drive and I speak Italian. I feel like a holiday. I'm nosy. I genuinely want to find out about these paintings too. Indulge me,' he found himself saying, and it seemed to work. Matthew smiled, if a bit reluctantly.

'Sorry. I just. I thought Sarah was . . . Never mind. Sorry, George. Thank you. It is nice to have your company.'

'Sure?' said George, though he wasn't sure what he would do if Matthew said he wasn't.

'Yes, I'm sure,' said Matthew, and when he smiled, George felt his heart soar.

'There's a car-rental desk there. I am sure I can get us something, and a map. We'll be there in no time.'

Sarah let herself into George's flat. Sebastian appeared, purring loudly, winding his way in and out of her legs, then jumped up on the work surface and, still purring, pushed his bewhiskered face against hers, briefly touching his small wet cold nose against hers. As she stroked his body from his head down to his tail, he stretched and arched his back in pleasure.

'Thank you,' she said. 'You're glad to see me, at least. I don't know if I am going to be as welcome the next visit I make. *And* it's my day off, too. Wish me luck, Sebastian.'

She stroked him again.

'See you later, Sebastian. I'll be back to feed you,' and reluctantly she set off.

'Yes? What do you want?' said George's mother, opening the door a crack.

'It's Sarah. The district nurse.'

'What are you here for? I've had my visit today from another nurse,' said George's mother ungraciously. 'I don't need you.'

'And I love you too,' Sarah muttered under her breath.

'Pardon?'

'I'm not here about your leg. I'm here about George, your son.'

The door flew open. 'What about George?' said his mother, alarmed.

'No, sorry. Please don't worry. He asked me to check on you because he's gone to Italy.'

'To Italy? No, he hasn't. He's working in his travel agency – his own business. I don't know what sort of game you're playing, young lady, but I wasn't born yesterday. I will be ringing him, and I will be ringing the police, too, if you carry on telling me lies,' and she started to close the door.

'Look, you don't have to believe me, but your son George has gone at very short notice to Italy to help my brother Matthew, Dr Woodburn, a lecturer at the university, track down some paintings by the artist Jack Mortimer. As you will know, George speaks fluent Italian – and before you say it, I know he lived in Spain too and can speak Spanish – and he is going to interpret for my brother. And he gave me the keys to his flat so that I can feed Sebastian, and he asked me to come and check on you.'

Sarah waved the keys at George's mother, who recognised the key fob and was placated.

'Interpreting, you say?' she said, a little proudly. 'You'd better come in, I suppose.'

To be honest, I'd far rather be with Sebastian. Poor George. If ever a man deserved a break . . .

'You can make us tea, then,' said George's mother. 'That's what George would do.'

'Of course,' said Sarah, filling the kettle.

'So where does my George know your brother from?'

'I think it is from the choir here, actually,' said Sarah, finding the cups and the teapot.

'He was a brilliant scholar, you know. Won lots of prizes. His father and I were very proud of him.'

'Still are, I'm sure,' said Sarah.

'His father's dead.'

'Yes, I'm sorry.'

'Of course I'm proud of him,' George's mother continued, highly offended. 'He has his own travel business, you know. He used to have his own language school in Spain before his partner died.'

'I know.' Sarah brought in the tea on a tray. She had found a little jug and filled it with milk, and put a sugar bowl on the tray too.

'And biscuits. There are biscuits in the tin. George always fills it,' his mother directed. 'So, he's helping a professor from the university with his Italian?' she said proudly.

'Something like that,' said Sarah, coming back out. George's mother had somehow found a photo album and opened it.

'You can see George graduate here,' she said. Her hands were shaky as she turned the pages. There were lots of pictures of him.

'He looks very handsome,' said Sarah.

'Oh, you needn't get any ideas,' said George's mother sharply. 'He won't be marrying you, a nurse.'

Sarah gasped, and was about to say exactly what she thought of such rudeness when George's mother continued, 'Not that he'll be marrying anyone. He's not that way inclined.'

'What do you mean?' said Sarah, carefully.

'You know.'

'I don't.'

'He's not interested in women. He doesn't know I know, but I can tell.'

'Why haven't you said anything to him?'

'Me? Why should I? It's none of my business. If he doesn't want to tell me, if he wants to go away for years and live with a Spanish man and not tell me, not even bring him home to introduce him, why should I ask him? Anyway, he's home now.'

What a mess. Poor George.

'Did you not ask him about his partner? About how he felt when he died?'

'I gave him a home when he came back, before he bought the agency and moved out. I could hear him crying in the night, but he never talked to me about it. How do you think I felt?' said George's mother. 'My husband had died and then my son was shutting me out.'

'So . . . would you have liked to have met his partner?' said Sarah.

'Of course I would! But obviously he didn't think I was good enough for him.'

'I'm sure it wasn't that. I think . . . I think he thought you would be upset.'

'Upset? Because he's gay? Maybe his father would have been. He hated homosexuals. So maybe he would have been. But, still, George should have told us. He is our son.'

'It must have been very hard for him.'

'Hard for him? And what about when his father died – why didn't he tell me then? I am not his father.'

'Perhaps he didn't know you felt differently.'

'Well, he should have,' said his mother sulkily. 'You wouldn't know, not being a mother, but a mother's love is like nothing on earth.'

'So if he told you he had met someone – a man – you wouldn't be upset?'

'Has he? Is it this professor, then? Your brother? The one who went to Oxford?'

'Yes. Well, I'm not sure. That is, Matthew is shy. I don't think he knows George likes him that way.'

'But he does?'

'Yes. Yes, I think he does.'

'And your brother Matthew, is he gay?'

'I think so.'

'You think so? You don't know so?'

'Well, he had a relationship at university, but that went wrong and he never talks about it to me.'

'You see, so you know what it is like.'

Sarah looked at her and smiled ruefully. 'I suppose I do.'

'Is your brother a good man? I think I saw him in the newspaper. Very handsome.'

'Yes. Yes, he is a lovely man,' Sarah smiled. 'Very kind.'

'And rich, I imagine, being high up in the university. And very well educated, like George.'

'Well, not very rich, but—'

'So, he is gay, but he doesn't know George likes him? But you do?'

'Yes.'

'Why didn't you tell him?'

'I tried, but . . .'

'And is George going to tell him?'

'I don't know. He has gone to Italy anyway.'

'He needs to tell him. He can't let a good match like that get away, not at his age. I'm not going to be around for ever. A professor. And an English one too. Have you got his number in Italy?'

'Yes. He gave me his contact number,' said Sarah. 'I'm not sure if they'll be there yet.'

'Well, I want you to ring it now.'

Twenty-Four

In Cardellino, the hotel doorbell and the phone rang at the same time – Francesco went for one and Maria the other.

'I wonder if I could speak to George Sanders?' said a woman's voice down the line.

'George Sanders?' repeated Maria. 'No, there is no one of that name here.'

'Or Dr Matthew Woodburn?'

'Dr Woodburn? Yes. We are expecting him any minute. In fact . . .' Francesco was coming in with two men. 'I think . . . Excuse me, are you George Sanders?' she asked the smaller man.

'Yes,' he said, startled.

'A phone call for you,' said Maria, passing him the receiver.

'Hello?' said George.

'Hello, George. It's Sarah.'

'Sarah? Is anything the matter? Is Mother all right? Is Sebastian—?'

'Yes, both are fine. I have your mother on the phone. She wants to speak to you.'

'Mother? All right. Put her on.' He mouthed 'Sorry' at Matthew.

'George?'

'Yes, Mother.'

'I know you're gay. I don't know why you wouldn't tell me yourself, but there you are. You didn't. And I know you're interested in this professor you're with, so I'm just ringing to tell you to stop dithering. Go and tell him. You're not getting any younger, and I won't always be here to look after you.'

'To look after me?' repeated George, removing the phone from his ear and looking at it, as if he couldn't quite believe what he had just heard.

'Yes. So the nurse has been telling me about her gay brother, and apparently he likes you, and he went to Oxford and has a good job, so what are you waiting for?'

'What am I waiting for?' repeated George.

'Why are you repeating everything I say? I don't think he can hear me,' he heard his mother say crossly. 'You talk to him. I can't get any sense out of him,' and the phone was passed back to Sarah.

'I'm sorry, George,' said Sarah.

'What are you saying sorry for?' George heard his mother say in the background. 'Give that phone back to me.' She came back on the line. 'Listen, George. You're my son. I love you. I don't know why you wouldn't tell me you're gay and had to tell a nurse instead, but there you are. Go and ask that professor to be your boyfriend. Apparently, he's gay too, but he won't talk to his sister about it either. And don't let him being a professor put you off. You're more than clever enough for him. I can't do everything for you. I'm ringing off now. Goodbye.'

George stood for a moment, looking bemusedly at the phone in his hand.

'Thank you,' he said to Maria.

Matthew and Francesco were waiting.

'Mr Sanders?' said Francesco. 'I'm afraid we don't have a record of a room booking for you.'

George clapped his hand to his forehead.

'Oh – I forgot. I was so busy booking the Sisters' rooms and Matthew's that I forgot about mine! I'm the travel agent who rang you originally from Fairbridge.'

'Oh, *sì*. You speak very good Italian.'

'Thank you.'

'Well, you are very welcome. The only difficulty is, is that we are decorating some of the rooms at the moment and Dr Woodburn's room is the only one left. But it is a twin, so if Dr Woodburn wouldn't mind sharing?'

Suddenly it was all too much and George began to sob.

'I'm sorry. I'm so sorry. That's unforgivable. What a mess. I'm so sorry, Matthew.'

'George – please don't cry,' said Matthew, shocked by George's grief.

'I invited myself. I forced my company on you. I thought you would like it if I came. Sarah thought you would like it if I came.'

'No – please don't cry. We'll take it. It will be fine to share,' said Matthew to Francesco. 'We've had . . . it's been quite a day. Thank you.'

He held George by the shoulder. 'George. Please don't cry.' He took out a clean handkerchief from his pocket, and passed it to George. George blew his nose gratefully. 'I am so glad you are here. Thank you for coming.'

Francesco took both their bags and led them upstairs.

'Here you are, gentlemen,' he said, smiling, opening the door and letting them in. 'We will have coffee ready downstairs for you in quarter of an hour. I believe you are hoping to get some news about Jack Mortimer's paintings, Dr Woodburn?'

'Yes, how did you know? Thank you,' said Matthew.

'I'll explain very soon.'

The door shut.

'Matthew, I am so embarrassed. I was so focused on the ticket that I completely forgot about the room,' said George.

'Please don't worry, George. It isn't a problem,' said Matthew, turning and putting his bag on a bed.

'Matthew,' said George.

He turned his head.

'Matthew, I need to tell you. I am not interested in Sarah at all. She knows this. Miguel . . . he was my partner. You see, I am gay. Is . . . is that a problem for you?'

Matthew shook his head. His eyes were full of tears.

'No. No, it's not a problem.'

'I'm gay and I'm in love with you. Is that a problem?' asked George, tears rolling down his face.

Matthew shook his head again. George, his heart beating wildly, walked over to him.

'I think you are absolutely the kindest, most gorgeous, most wonderful man in the world. Is that a problem?'

Matthew shook his head a third time.

'I want to put my arms around you, is that a problem?'

Matthew shook his head again, and George flung his arms around him. To his shock, he felt Matthew trembling and stepped back, looking up into Matthew's face.

'Matthew – are you sure it's OK?'

'Yes, yes, it is, George. I . . . I love you too. I am . . . I am in love with you too. But this is all so new and . . . please forgive me. I'm not used to . . .' He took a deep breath and looked at

George's tear-stained face, into George's kind brown eyes. He felt a little sick with fear, but something told him that it was now or never.

'George – I have no experience with these things. I've only ever loved one man before – at university. I loved him so much, and I thought he loved me too. But I mistook his feelings. When he discovered . . . when I told him how I felt . . . it was terrible, George. He humiliated me – he told his friends. They jeered at me in public, laughed at me. It was unbearable. I couldn't stay in college with them, at university. I had . . . I had a breakdown and came home. Sarah helped me pick up my academic career again, but even there I haven't been brave. I've stayed in my comfort zone at Fairbridge, teaching and quietly researching a minor artistic figure, nothing too spectacular, until this recent interest in Jack Mortimer. Suddenly my research has an international importance it hasn't had up until now, my career has new opportunities. But as for relationships . . . I've just been too scared to try again.'

'Sarah told me you were badly hurt, Matthew. I never ever want to hurt you and I cannot imagine you ever hurting me,' said George, taking Matthew's hands in his. 'We don't need to rush anything. We have to go down in a minute anyway. All I need to know right now is that you are happy that I am here and love you, and that you love me too.'

'Oh, I am and I do, George, I do,' said Matthew, laughing and crying at the same time. They fell into each other's arms. George stepped back, looked into Matthew's face and kissed him swiftly, then tenderly wiped a tear from his cheek.

'My dear, dear love,' he said, and kissed him again, beaming at Matthew. 'You have nothing to fear. And we have all the time in the world.'

Matthew looked back, stretching out his hand in wonder, and shyly wiped a tear from George's cheek. His legs felt weak and he sat down suddenly on the bed.

George came and sat down beside him. 'Look at the state of us. Both blubbing,' he said, holding Matthew's hands, lifting one to his lips to kiss it. 'Blubbing but happy. So happy.'

'We'd better wash our faces,' said Matthew, laughing through his tears, and they hugged again.

As soon as they got downstairs, around half past four, it became something of a party.

'George! What are you doing here? How lovely to see you! Who is looking after your cat?' exclaimed Sister Bridget.

'Hello, Sisters,' said Matthew.

'Hello, Dr Woodburn, Mr Sanders,' said Margaret, puzzled. *What is happening, Lord? I can't keep up!*

'Matthew's sister is cat-sitting, actually,' said George, taking his seat next to Sister Bridget. 'It's a long story, but basically, Father Hugh got sent, completely unexpectedly, two incredibly valuable paintings by Jack Mortimer this morning and he showed them to Matthew here, who is the world expert on Jack Mortimer –' George said this very proudly '– and as the postmark was Cardellino, Matthew decided to come here and find out more.'

'It's an incredibly important find, actually,' said Matthew, eyes sparkling, his normal reserve forgotten in the excitement. 'It is incredible because the letter promises more paintings if they are needed, and it has been one of the great mysteries of the art world why Jack Mortimer's output seemed to stop so suddenly. Every decade or so a painting is released and sold from one auction house or another, but it has been a closely guarded secret as to who is releasing them.'

'Up to now,' said Francesco, who had entered the room with Maria and Nonna. 'Could you follow us, please?'

They got up, chairs scraping, and followed him down the corridor towards the garden, stopping at a door to a room they had not been in. Francesco unlocked and opened it, and ushered them inside.

It was absolutely full of paintings. The room radiated colour. Small and large, beautiful framed paintings of English and Italian scenes covered the walls: children and mothers, families, farmers.

'Will you look at all the Madonnas!' said Sister Bridget, as the Sisters saw, in frame after frame, oil paintings of a gentle Mary cradling, playing with, reading to, running with a baby, a toddler, a child Jesus, indoors and outdoors. In some, Mary wore the traditional long blue robes and veil of countless Christmas cards, but in others she was dressed in 1920s fashion, but still with the golden halo and the Holy Child. There was a contemporary flight into Egypt, with a tired-looking Joseph in a suit leading a donkey carrying Mary and Baby Jesus through an Italian vineyard. There was an older Mary, dressed in 1940s clothes, holding her dead son at the foot of the cross, and it brought tears to Margaret's eyes. The artist had shown so clearly that Mary and Joseph were real people, with real worries, desperately loving and looking after their son Jesus, and somehow that made the Holy Family all the more important.

There were so many paintings that some were stacked, enclosed in bubble wrap, against the walls.

'I can't believe it!' said Matthew, his voice breaking with emotion. George, without thinking, came up and put his arm around him.

'I'm so sorry, I will actually have to sit down,' said the tall academic, and a chair was found for him immediately. 'This is astonishing. These are all Jack Mortimers. This surely must be all his lost work! So ... you sent those paintings to Father Hugh, promising more if needed?'

'Yes,' said Maria. 'Thanks to the interview you gave on the radio, which we listened to on the World Service, we have only just realised that after all these years, we are now sitting on a fortune. We heard from the Sisters yesterday all about the problems in Fairbridge parish and we wanted to help. We decided there was no time to waste, and sent them by courier last night.'

'But why? Jack Mortimer wasn't exactly a practising Catholic. What is the link?' said Margaret, puzzled.

'Why have you got all Jack Mortimer's paintings?' said Matthew. 'Are you some sort of relatives?'

'I am,' said Nonna, speaking in English, with no Italian accent. 'I was his wife.'

'She's not Italian!' whispered a shocked Sister Bridget loudly and unnecessarily to Cecilia and Margaret.

'I don't understand,' said Matthew, bemused. 'Why did he keep his identity so secret all these years? Was it some ruse to keep the markets interested in him? If it was, it certainly worked, but it doesn't seem like the man. He was a joyful, sociable man who loved the art world, not a recluse.'

'That was for me,' said Nonna. 'I need to explain a bit more. Maybe we should go back to the dining room.'

'Don't worry, Dr Woodburn, we will let you back in to catalogue it all,' smiled Francesco. 'We don't want to keep his work hidden any more.'

Matthew got up, shaking his head. 'It feels like a dream,' he said to George. 'I cannot tell you how miraculous this is for me. This is the single most marvellous thing that has ever happened in my academic life.'

And George beamed back, and Margaret noticed, and saw how his face was radiant with love and admiration as he looked at Matthew. There was no mistaking the love. It was real, and it was beautiful. She felt a protective pang at their vulnerability at loving in such a way, in such a world, and honoured the tenderness between them.

Ah, now I understand. God bless them.

They all made their way back to the table, their eyes and hearts still full of colour, their minds full of questions.

Francesco brought in coffee.

Nonna spoke.

'I know, Sisters, that you are trying to find out what happened to an English girl called Ellen Kerr, who came here in the 1920s,' she said. 'And the time has come to tell you.' She put both hands on the dining-room table as if to steady herself, and then, standing up, helped by Francesco, said calmly, 'I am Ellen Kerr.'

Twenty-Five

They looked at her with utter amazement.

Cecilia shook her head. 'No, you can't be. You see, you were married to Jack Mortimer. The Ellen Kerr we are looking for was a nun. That's why we are here. For the little Flying Nun.'

'I know,' said Nonna gently. Cecilia had gone very white.

'No, you see,' Cecilia continued, 'we have a photograph. Of Sister Angelina. It says on the back that this is what happened to Ellen Kerr. It is to Edward Mortimer. It tells him to forget her.'

'It tells Edward Mortimer to forget *me*.'

'No, you don't understand. We are looking for Sister Angelina. You are Nonna. You're not a nun.'

'No, I'm not.'

Cecilia searched in her bag for the photograph, and placed it on the table with trembling hands. 'There you are, you see – a young nun, levitating.'

'Yes, I know, that was me,' said Nonna patiently. 'It's all a long time ago now. It was after the war – the First War. I was young and working as a maid in the Mortimers' house. Edward was back, but he was still suffering from shell shock. I recognised that anguish as soon as I saw him. I had helped nurse my father and saw how he had suffered with the same affliction. Such sights break your heart. You don't forget them. He tried to hide his state of mind from his parents, from his fiancée, from everybody, but I could hear him crying in the night – like my father did before he died. I couldn't bear it. He was such a gentle soul. He was so good, so polite to staff, and so handsome, and I thought he was wonderful. He was always kind to me. I had a lot to do with him at first, when he was convalescing from his physical wounds. I cleaned his room, and he was always grateful. I liked to be in his company. I felt he enjoyed mine. We were like each other, I think. We had both suffered. I think we recognised that in each other, but of course, we never talked about it. He was engaged to a beautiful young Catholic woman from his own class, and I had no thoughts that there could ever be anything between us. He got better, was up and about. When I cleaned his room in the day, he was no longer there.

'One night, his parents were away – they and all the rest of the staff had gone up to Scotland for the summer, but Edward had chosen to stay behind for some reason – and I heard him cry out. Cook was away, visiting her sister. I didn't think about it. I was up early, lighting the fires, I heard the scream and I knew, immediately. I went in to comfort him, to do something – anything – to help. I don't know how, but . . . there was so much sadness, so much need, we were both in grief, hurting so badly, needing comfort. We only did it once. Those were innocent times, even for an officer. He was a very religious man. He didn't really know what he was doing – neither did I, come to that. We just knew we were sad, and needed and trusted each other. And I got pregnant.'

'No. No, you didn't do that. Edward didn't do that. He would never ... He was a good Catholic ...' said Cecilia, outraged.

'Yes, yes, he was, Sister. And I was too. I knew the morning after that we had made a big mistake. I didn't even know him. I knew he was engaged to someone he loved. He was about to be married. We met and we both said we would never do it again. He was very apologetic, very concerned, very anguished. I reassured him. We were both shocked. And then we avoided each other. He married and I went to confession. I thought it was all over. So, then, months later, when I discovered I was expecting a child, I knew I could not tell him. Nor could I bring so much trouble to my widowed mother, so I ran away. I went to the only relatives I had in the world – my mother's parents, my grandparents, in Italy. They were very surprised at first, but they were lovely. They listened, they understood, they did not judge, they just wanted to help. We needed time to decide what to do, and they asked the nuns to take me in, so that the town wouldn't find out, and the nuns did. I had come with nothing, so they gave me a novice's habit to wear, and they put me in the kitchens, and I found that I had a gift for cooking. Their old cook had died – influenza, I believe – and I taught myself more Italian from the cookbooks she had left and a dictionary. It kept my mind off things.'

'How did all the levitation start?' asked Sister Bridget.

'I don't know. All I remember is I was so worried about the future – and lonely. My grandparents were so kind, and Mother Superior was a very good, compassionate woman, but some of the other Sisters weren't so kind to me, a single pregnant girl. I felt judged – and I judged myself. I had been to confession. I knew I had received absolution, but somehow, somewhere, I still didn't believe it. But one day when I was feeling particularly desperate, I was in the chapel and I just remember one moment of surrender – and everything changed.'

'What do you mean?' It was Margaret now.

'It's hard to explain. I just had this moment of seeing what a terrible mess it was, and how I couldn't do anything to sort it, and I sort of hurled it at God – and at the same time . . .'

'What?'

'It just happened. I didn't ask for it – I didn't know such things could happen to ordinary people like me. One minute I felt completely alone – the next, it was like someone was hugging me. I can't explain it. I just got overwhelmed with . . . I just felt completely and absolutely and unconditionally understood, forgiven and loved – and the Sisters told me it lifted me off my feet. I was in the chapel at Night Prayer the first time.'

'What happened then?'

'Well, I just wanted to stay in the convent and carry on cooking in the kitchens, and praying every spare moment I had day and night – and of course the Mother Superior, who was a kind and holy woman, knew about the baby and was concerned for my health, and concerned about what the Sisters told her they saw. The trouble was that I didn't understand it myself. It was very . . . embarrassing. There was one nun in particular – Sister Bernardina. She thought I was the lowest of the low. She didn't hide the fact that she thought it was disgusting that I was an unmarried, pregnant girl and she didn't like the attention I was receiving either.

'Part of me agreed with her assessment of my position. I knew I could never go home to my mother – she was a poor war widow with my brothers to look after, but she was young and she still had a chance of a respectable marriage. I wrote to her to tell her I was safe with her parents, but I didn't explain why I had run away. I was too ashamed and I begged them not to tell her either. But the feelings I had, the . . . levitation, it made me think that God maybe didn't think so badly of me. Not only that, I knew that He loved me. That I was worthy of love, and so was the baby growing inside me. And I knew I loved that baby too.

'And then Jack turned up out of the blue. Edward was ill with guilt and anxiety about my disappearance and Jack wanted to put his mind at rest. He found out that I had family in Italy, and tracked down my grandparents, who ran this hotel. They got mixed up and thought he was Edward, the father of my child, so they told him I was now a nun called Sister Angelina, and sent him to the convent. He came to the orchard to find me. I was supposed to be working there, with the others, but I remember the sunshine and the green leaves, the birdsong, and the blue sky, and that feeling of overwhelming love again. Jack took that photo and sent it to Edward. He really thought, at that stage, that I was a holy nun.

'Jack decided he wanted to paint the village, and my grandparents took a liking to him and invited him to stay here with them. They were sorry for him – they still thought he was the father of my child, and they were concerned that they had lied about me being a nun, and they contacted the Mother Superior, and it was arranged that Jack should come to see me. Jack was the last person I expected to see. When he found out I was pregnant with his brother's child, and not a nun at all, he stayed around to help me work out what to do next, and . . . well, the rest is history. We fell in love, he married me, brought up and loved my son, David, as his own. We told my mother and were reconciled. But we made the decision not to tell

Edward as he was so fragile, and married. We worried he would guess that David was his child. It could have destroyed his relationship. But I have always worried that it was the wrong thing to have kept his child from him, that I was selfish. I suppose I was terrified that he would take David from me. I hoped they would have their own family, but in the end they had no children of their own, and then his wife died, and I began to believe that we should contact him, tell David and Edward the truth. Then war came again, and telling Edward did not seem such a priority. My Jack and David were part of the resistance here, and all I cared about was them getting through it.'

'Ah,' said Matthew. 'How interesting!'

'Jack got through, but David and his young wife were killed in the war.'

'Oh no, how sad,' said Sister Bridget, and there was a shocked and empathetic murmur from the others in the room. Nonna nodded, acknowledging the kindness and concern.

'Well, we were left with their child, my grandson, baby Francesco, and after all we had gone through, I couldn't bear to open old wounds. I know I was selfish, but I put off contacting Edward again, and then I heard he had died too, and it was too late. I have always felt sad that he lived and died not knowing he had a son and a beautiful daughter-in-law, as well as a grandson and granddaughter-in-law in Italy.'

'Nonna, you look tired,' said Francesco, as his grandmother seemed to sway with emotion. He stood beside her, his arm protectively out behind her in case she fell. 'Here, sit down.'

'Are you shocked? . . . I am sorry to have caused this . . . upset,' said Nonna Ellen, diffidently, looking anxiously at the rigid figure of Cecilia, eyes closed, seemingly turned to stone by what she had heard.

'Not at all, Nonna,' said Margaret. 'You have done nothing wrong. It is we who have intruded . . . I am sorry. If we had known . . .'

'If we had known, we would *never* have come,' said Cecilia. 'Never. You *did* do wrong. You sinned. What you did to Edward, a good Catholic man – leading him astray, tempting him – was disgusting. It was unforgivable. Unforgivable.' She was standing now, shouting at Nonna Ellen.

'No – that's a terrible thing to say!' said George, shocked.

'Sister Cecilia!' said Margaret, getting up and going over to her.

'Cecilia – you mustn't say these things,' said Bridget, but Cecilia pushed her aside and walked out and up the stairs.

'I am so, so sorry,' said Margaret to Nonna.

Nonna shook her head.

'It's all right. It's a relief, really – I was a little worried I would have that reaction. But I understand where your Sister Cecilia is coming from. I forgive her.'

'I don't,' said Francesco, angrily. 'Nonna does not deserve this.'

'Sister Cecilia was very wrong,' said Maria firmly. 'Nonna was a single mother who married the man who truly loved her. He loved her and he loved David, her baby, Francesco's father, and he was grateful every day of his life that she married him. She is a beautiful, beautiful person.'

'I know, I know,' said Margaret. 'I can only apologise. I . . . She is old, and set in her ways . . . but that's no excuse. For some reason, it seemed as if God was telling us to come here, but . . . I am so sorry – and I want to thank you, Nonna, for sharing this wonderful story. Please believe me, Francesco, we have only respect for your wonderful grandmother, and we are sorry for all she has gone through.'

'We love you,' said Bridget, throwing her arms around Nonna, who hugged her back.

'Help!' prayed Margaret. 'What are you doing to us all, Lord? What do you want now?'

'I can only apologise again. I . . . I'd better go and check on Cecilia . . .' said Margaret.

'Please do,' said Nonna. Francesco and Maria both kissed her cheeks, and she took one of their hands in each of hers and squeezed them gratefully, smiling. She looked very tired, but very relieved.

Cecilia was standing on the landing outside her room, one hand on the wall, her eyes closed.

'Sister Cecilia. Are you feeling quite well?' whispered Margaret. Cecilia did not open her eyes, but Margaret's heart was wrung to see her shake her head and a tear roll slowly down Cecilia's fragile old papery-white cheeks. Suddenly, everything about her seemed fragile. The indomitable spirit, the certainty, even the self-righteous anger, had all suddenly ebbed away. It was almost unbearable to see.

'Do you want to come back and rejoin us?' Margaret said gently.

Again, Cecilia shook her head.

'Would you like me to help you to your room?'

Cecilia nodded, and Margaret linked arms. She was struck again by how light Cecilia seemed, so very old.

'Lord, help her. You have taken away her foundations,' Margaret said silently. 'I know the truth is supposed to set us free, but it feels like it has destroyed Cecilia. That can't be right, can it, Lord? I thought you didn't break the crushed reed or quench the wavering flame? I know she was so wrong to say those cruel words, and she is too judgemental, but still, she doesn't deserve to have everything she loved and hoped for annihilated.'

Margaret opened Cecilia's door.

'Sister, you lie down and rest. You have had a shock. I will come up and check on you later.'

Obediently, like a child, Cecilia kicked off her shoes and lay on her bed, eyes closed. She shifted into a foetal position.

Margaret sat beside her, and tentatively put her hand on Cecilia's shoulder. Cecilia stiffened and opened her eyes. Staring at the wall rather than at Margaret, she said clearly, 'I am quite all right, Sister Margaret. Please rejoin the others. I would like to be alone.'

Margaret hesitated, but Cecilia, regaining some of her stubbornness, closed her eyes determinedly.

Margaret closed the door carefully behind her.

'The trouble is, Cecilia, that you are truly alone, and you won't let anyone near you,' thought Margaret sadly, as she went down the stairs to join the others.

Twenty-Six

When Margaret went back into the dining room, the conversation started up again.

'I don't understand how the shrine fits into all this?' said Sister Bridget. 'It looks like there are miracles being performed there. Who is doing them if it's not you?'

'Well, we had a letter from a cousin of the Mortimers mentioning the levitation, saying that Edward had shown them the photograph and asking if they could come to visit. Apparently, they were living in Rome, had been trying for a baby for years, and they wanted to ask for the Flying Nun's intercession. They thought I must be very holy, you see.

'Well, nobody wanted the scandal. The last thing I wanted was for Edward to be in contact. Everything about the baby would have been in the open and I knew Jack was right – Edward would have been destroyed by it. He was such a serious, pious man, and so fragile after the war, he would never have lived with the shame.'

'So what happened?' said Matthew.

'Mother Julia helped me write a letter to Edward to get him

to leave me alone. Mother Julia dictated the words, writing about my new life in such a way that it might seem I was a nun and about to die, rather than, as it happened, about to leave the convent to marry.

'Then, as if God wanted to support our story, we did have a death – old Sister Bernardina's. She collapsed in the chapel during morning prayers one day and that was the beginning of the end. I left to marry Jack, Sister Bernardina died, the community buried her in a simple grave, and then the English couple living in Rome came – they were desperate for a child and they were willing to try anything. Mother Julia told them a little lie, that Sister Angelina just meant "little angel" and Sister Bernardina had been a little angel – she certainly hadn't! – and had died. Then they asked if they could pray at Sister Bernardina's grave, and Mother Superior couldn't really refuse. So they prayed. And then there was a miracle – after years of trying, the wife became pregnant!'

'Really? After praying at that nun's grave?' said George.

'Yes, really! Sister Bernardina didn't even like children! Can you imagine! So the English couple insisted on paying for a beautiful statue of the Madonna and Child to be put on Sister Bernardina's grave, and word got around and people desperate to start a family began to come. It was lucky that this place is so hard to reach and there was a particularly bad winter, so that slowed the pilgrims down – it was mainly a local affair – but Mother Superior knew we had to do something before the spring. In the end, she had to go to the Bishop and explain it all. The Bishop was furious, especially when he heard that the real person who had levitated was an unmarried mother. He said that devotion to the Flying Nun was to be stamped out immediately and he preached sermons about unsubstantiated miracles and folklore, but of course that wasn't so easy.'

Nonna coughed a little, and Sister Margaret, who was next to the water jug, poured a glass for her and passed it to Matthew, who passed it to Nonna. They watched in concern as she drank it, and then she smiled at them all. It was obvious that telling the story was helping her.

'Thank you, Sister,' said Nonna. 'Well, things did get better . . . Pilgrims to Sister Bernardina's grave still came, but it all trickled away in time. The Sisters kept directing them to praying to St Gerard Majella, patron saint of childbirth – they had prayer cards made up to give them – and talked about Sister Bernardina as having had a great devotion to that saint, which she hadn't. I am afraid the good Sisters told a lot of white lies on my behalf. They talked about praying to St Gerard and visiting Rome, and in the end people just wrote for the prayer cards and visited St Peter's and it seemed to work just as well, babywise, so it never took off nationally. Just locally.

'Then the war came, and we had other things to worry about. But after the war, local people started coming back. They know it is the grave of Sister Bernardina, who didn't even like children, but nevertheless she somehow seems to be good at interceding for them to have babies. Maybe she found her real gift after she died. And Edward – he was a good man. He respected what he thought was my dying wish and we never heard anything more. And he founded a convent in my honour.'

'Yes – you are the reason our Order exists!' said Margaret, looking over at Bridget.

'It's amazing,' said Bridget, shaking her head at the wonder of it.

'Honestly, God,' prayed Margaret. 'What are you like? What can I say?'

And she had a sudden, overwhelming desire to laugh, but managed to suppress it.

'Do you mind if I ask you about the experience of levitation?' said Matthew, shyly. 'Can you remember how you felt?'

'I can never forget. It's hard to explain. Like a . . . it's like a distillation of love – like a concentrate of love. It's tiring – that's all I can say. It is wonderful – you feel so happy, but so exhausted. I don't actually want to feel it again in this life – I don't need to. The memory – the shadow of it – is enough. The feeling stopped coming to me as soon as I married, and I was grateful. I found it in the love of Jack – I recognised it was of the same essence, but human strength. That's strong enough for me.'

Nonna smiled at Matthew, and without realising it, he glanced over at George, who smiled back at him, and a feeling of pure joy filled his heart. Finding George was his own miracle.

'Didn't people want to tell the press? These days – with the telephone – I would have thought . . .' said Sister Margaret.

'You forget about our village,' said Francesco proudly. 'We are family. People here know what happened in the past. They may talk amongst themselves, yes, it is true – but they would never want to hurt Nonna Ellen.'

They were quiet for a moment.

'So what does it all mean?' said Margaret, half to herself.

'I don't know,' said Nonna.

'Were we meant to come here anyway, I wonder?' said Sister Bridget. 'We wouldn't have come here without the photograph.'

'I don't know. I am so sorry to disappoint you. I know for you to make Fairbridge a site of pilgrimage you needed Ellen Kerr to be a dead saint – but as you see, here I am, old but still alive, and no saint, dead or alive, yet still God and my family love me. That's all. And I hope Edward forgives me in Heaven for keeping his son from him. That's all I want. At least David is with him in Heaven now, and his wife, Francesco's mother, and my Jack. Brothers together again.'

'Still, I feel sure there is a meaning to us finding the photograph and coming here,' Sister Bridget said firmly.

'Thank you so much for sharing your story,' said Margaret, struck not just by the remarkable nature of the levitation, or by Ellen's love for Jack and Jack's for Ellen, but by all the love in all the intertwining relationships – imperfect, fragile, wounded people but each trying their best and so each caught up in something so true and beautiful.

'It's a pleasure, dear,' said Nonna. 'But I do hope we can share more. We want to give you some paintings. We know that the market has changed and suddenly we are sitting on a fortune, and we want to use it in the best way possible.'

'Really?' said Margaret, astonished.

'Yes. I can't think of anything that I would like more than to help the convent Edward founded. We can give you as many paintings as you need to solve all your money problems.'

'But then what shall we do?' said Margaret worriedly, out loud. 'There are still only three of us.'

'Thank you so much, Nonna,' said Sister Bridget. 'As Superior, I can say that we will certainly take the money from the paintings, and I think I know exactly what we shall do.'

'Do you?' said Margaret, and the sense of relief was overpowering. She was no longer Superior, and Sister Bridget knew what they were going to do.

'I had a dream last night. It was amazing,' said Sister Bridget.

Oh no, not one of Sister Bridget's dreams. They're longer than her letters from her sister.

'It isn't long, Margaret, before you worry,' said Bridget, mind-reading. 'I was cooking pasta. Pasta of all shapes and sizes, sauces all the colours of the rainbow, biscotti, cappuccinos with chocolate sprinkles. Wonderful. But the thing is, I wasn't here – I was in the convent kitchen and Terry Wogan, Daniel O'Donnell, Delia Smith, the Pope himself, were all there, and the Pope said, "Forget about the Flying Nun! Give me more of that tiramisu!"'

Bridget paused, expectantly, beaming around at everyone.

'And that means what exactly?' said Margaret, bewildered.

'I know!' said George, excitedly. 'You are meant to cook, aren't you, Sister Bridget?'

'I don't exactly know how we'll do it – but I know if it is God's will, it will all fall into place. I think I know how to bring money and faith back to the diocese, even without a new saint!'

'How?' said Margaret.

'We'll turn the convent into a hotel like this one, but it'll be a type of retreat house – food for body and soul. We'll spend the money doing up the bedrooms, and start by giving people bed and breakfast, but then we'll move on to evening meals. We can do Italian cooking, like in the dream. There are no Italian restaurants in Fairbridge. We can have residential retreats too. You could train to be a spiritual director, Margaret. You'd be good at that. I know I could do the cooking, and train up some younger people. There's always a need for places to stay with visitors to the university. We'll be self-sufficient with the garden and then we can use the big rooms for prayer groups and suchlike – the building is perfect for it! We can keep the chapel and everything!'

'Bridget! But how could we run it? You couldn't do it all on your own. And this is a new venture. We know nothing about the hospitality and retreat business!'

'We could help,' said Francesco. 'We could help you have it up and running. We don't need the money now, so we can close the hotel for a bit. We would love to live in Fairbridge for a while – Nonna has been saying that she wants to see it again and visit the family graves. I would love to visit where my family is from.'

'I knew God would sort it all out,' said Bridget.

'I have another idea too,' said Nonna. 'Jack painted the Stations of the Cross and so many of the scenes are set in Fairbridge. I think, if we donated them to the church, that people would come to see them.'

'Definitely,' said Matthew. 'An artistic pilgrimage.'

'And if we also donated the rest of the paintings to the university to make a dedicated gallery – would you curate it for us?' said Nonna to Matthew. 'Jack hid away because of me – now I want his reputation known worldwide. We would make it a condition that they could not be sold, that they are a permanent bequest. And you could be its custodian.'

'I would be honoured!' said Matthew, tears springing to his eyes so that he had to take his glasses off and wipe them. George leant over and squeezed his hand.

'And Sister Cecilia could open a sort of museum of Catholic life in the diocese,' said Sister Bridget. 'She has all those papers and letters. We could be like the Bar Convent in York. The IBVM Sisters have got a museum of the history of their Order there – and they do bed and breakfast. I've seen it on a programme on telly and it's all working perfectly.'

Bridget leapt up and gave Francesco and Maria and Nonna a big hug. 'Thanks be to God – it's all coming together. Our prayers are being answered. Won't Cecilia be made up with it all!'

'How is Sister Cecilia?' asked Nonna, concerned. They all thought of her, white and shocked and angry.

*

Cecilia woke up out of a deep sleep. The misery hit her like a wave.

'I must get out. I must pull myself together before I see the others again – before I see . . . her,' she said. Opening the pouch, and deliberately ignoring the papery deceit of the pictures within, she brought out her rosary beads and, clutching them in her hand for protection, went downstairs, into the deserted lobby and straight out of the hotel without looking left or right.

The others heard her go.

As if on automatic pilot, she walked to the convent, up the drive and to the shrine.

Cecilia stood and pleaded for Sister Bernardina's intercession.

'Oh, Sister Bernardina, by whose intercession so many miracles have happened, help me to understand.'

Cecilia felt unaccustomed tears rise in her eyes. The shrine in front of her seemed to mock her with its excess of miracles, and her own meanness of spirit, her own lack of experience of God, hurt her as she had never been hurt before.

'I only wanted to do something to help the Order. Sisters Frances and Basil and I – we had such hope when we joined. We believed Edward Mortimer when he said we had some great calling, and it turns out he was no better than any other man. And now we don't have a saint at all. Sister Margaret was right. We are useless. We are finished.'

'Cecilia.' Margaret touched her on the shoulder, and Cecilia turned to find them all there, Bridget and Margaret, Francesco and Maria, Dr Woodburn and the travel agent, and . . . her.

'What's it like?' Cecilia said abruptly and hungrily to Ellen Kerr, lover of Edward and Jack, mother to David, grandmother to Francesco. She ignored the others' greetings, waiting for the answer to her question.

Ellen turned and looked into her eyes.

'It's not the levitation that's important – it's the love. The unconditional love.'

Cecilia sank down onto the ground and wept. She was filled only with her emptiness, her aching longing for something that, after ninety years of life, she felt she had only just discovered existed and which she knew that she, Cecilia, could never have.

Margaret and Bridget rushed to put their arms around her.

'I've never – I've never . . . All this love – all this love from God people keep talking about – I've never felt it. I've never felt it. Not even in prayer, to tell the truth. I'm all dried up – I'm nothing . . . nothing. Nobody has ever loved me like that – not God, not my mother, not my father, not Edward Mortimer. How could anyone love me?'

'That's not true, Cecilia,' said Margaret. 'God loves you.'

'We love you,' said Bridget. 'We need you. God loves us all.'

And then Sister Cecilia feels it. Something steals up on her and hugs her tight, inside. Something – someone – puts their arms around her and hugs her inside until she feels she cannot stand it, loves her until she is breathless.

And as Maria and Francesco and George and Matthew watched, they agreed later that they could each have sworn that for a moment they saw the Sisters, as they hugged, rise a little from the ground.

And it felt like flying, soaring, being held in an almost unbearable tenderness. Green leaves and sunshine, birdsong and blue sky, until they felt they would burst with love, until they could bear no more.

Twenty-Seven

George and Matthew knew they would not have seats next to each other going back, but they had the journey home from the airport to look forward to. George, his heart singing at the new love of his life, watched with proud longing as Matthew moved away from him down the plane to take his seat, and was touched and happy to turn to find his own and discover that he was seated next to Emily and Chris.

'Mr Sanders! I didn't know you had gone to Rome, too!' exclaimed Emily, absolutely delighted.

'It was a last-minute thing,' he said. 'I actually went to a place called Cardellino, outside Rome, and met up with my friends there.' He nodded towards the row of nuns in front of them.

'You're friends with the nuns!' said Emily, a little too loudly, her smile lighting up her face. 'That's brilliant!'

George smiled back. 'I hope Rome went well?'

'It was wonderful, thank you,' said Chris. 'I can't thank you enough.'

'Only trouble is, I didn't want to come back,' sighed Emily.

'I've *got* to get a new job. I want to work in a hotel or some-where with people, not just an office. I loved that hotel so much. They made us feel so important, so welcome. It was just the perfect honeymoon, it really was. I want to make people feel as special as they made us feel.'

'Hold that thought,' said George, looking at the Sisters in front and wondering if they could hear. 'I have some friends who are thinking of opening a guest house very soon, and they will need help. I think you might be the perfect person.'

'Ooh – maybe we could live in!' said Emily, excitedly. 'Chris could do the garden! Would they let us bring a cat?'

'Emily! We haven't got the job or the kitten yet!' said Chris.

'I know – but sometimes miracles happen!' retorted Emily. 'Like Mr Sanders finding us that honeymoon deal. I believe in miracles – do you, Mr Sanders?'

George thought of all that had happened, and of the good man in seat 33A, the man he had met when he thought he would never fall in love again.

'I do,' he said.

'Of course, I won't be able to cook for Father Hugh any more. I don't know how he will manage. If he only knew a few basics, I could relax,' said Sister Bridget to Sister Margaret. Sister Bridget was now totally committed to her new role as Superior and head of setting up the new guest house. 'I don't even have time to teach him. I have to get those rooms ready for our Italian guests as soon as we get home, and start the ball rolling for the new kitchen. It has to pass all the health and safety regulations.' She sighed happily, letting her mind think of the pasta maker and the new pans she could buy with a completely good conscience now. This new guest house would provide food for body and soul. They would have to get someone for the garden so that they could grow all the food they needed – Thomas would not be able to do all that work himself. And they would need a receptionist – they would need to say prayers to find just the right people.

'Francesco says he will advise us about the building work we can do, about creating staff accommodation, and everything a good guest house will need,' said Margaret. 'And I am going to contact the Bar Convent in York and go up there with Cecilia. I thought we could ask them about their guest house and how they set up their museum.'

'Do. That's a very good idea. Do it sooner rather than later. Go this week. Poor Sister Cecilia needs a holiday,' said Sister Bridget. They looked over at Cecilia, asleep by the window. 'And you need a break too, Margaret. I don't want you to worry about any of the running of this. I'll take care of that, and getting the right people to help. I just want you to find out about courses. We have the money for you to train to be a spiritual director and study some more theology. I think you'd be great at the retreat side when that part opens.'

'Thank you,' said Margaret. She found it very restful being organised by such benign and confident authority. It suited Sister Bridget to be in charge.

She looked out at the white clouds and blue sky. They were up in the air, flying towards their new life, and she felt utterly supported by Love.

Twenty-Eight

Three months later

It was a warm and sunny Saturday afternoon in July when the Bishop decided to bless the completion of the first stage of the setting up of St Philomena's Guest and Retreat House. The official paperwork wasn't through yet, but the new sign was up, all the rooms were newly decorated and nobody could quite believe the speed with which Sister Bridget had managed to organise so much. There had been an extraordinary outpouring of love for the Sisters when their new enterprise had been shared, and whilst the money from the paintings had covered materials, much of the painting and decorating had been done by volunteers, many of them students from the school (organised by the new head, who was eager to show Sister Margaret and the Sisters support), and also through the university Catholic chaplaincy, encouraged by Father Hugh and his new curate, Father Stephen, who was already proving to be a great help. The kitchen, to Sister Bridget's joy, was now guest-house suitable, upgraded for free by a local tradesman whose daughters had gone to the school. Bishop John, who was very impressed, thought it would be a good photo opportunity for the local news, a good way to stir up interest, and a good witness to the community.

Children from St Philomena's Primary School, which had not yet broken up for the summer, had made bunting for the occasion, and the colourful triangular flags moved in the light breeze. From the road and pavement outside, drivers and pedestrians passing the convent could see strings of bright paper pictures of hearts or crosses or doves of peace, little figures of nuns or praying hands or even cakes or cups of tea. All enthusiastically hand-painted by the children, they were strung across the wall, around bushes and the trunks of trees. They might not have been the baby booties of Cardellino, but Sister Margaret liked how they reminded her of the shrine.

The Bishop stood by the newly painted front door, on the newly tarmacked drive, his golden mitre on his head, shepherd's crozier in his hand, his official vestments adding gravity to the occasion. The student folk group from St Philomena's Secondary School played their guitars and flutes and sang 'Give Me Joy in My Heart' while, flanked by Father Hugh and Father Stephen, with Cuthbert Brown as server, Bishop John blessed the front of the house, solemnly sprinkling it with holy water.

Many members of St Philomena's congregation were there, and other friends of the community, like Mr and Mrs Abidi, Dr Matthew Woodburn with his sister, Sarah, and George, were standing on the drive, joining the celebration. Miss Taylor, convalescing from her operation, was sitting on a chair at the side, next to George's mother and Nonna Ellen. Thomas and Linda, the latter of whom had already had an interview and been accepted to study for a degree in art and architectural history at the University of Fairbridge, were standing with Sophie and her husband Ben. Linda was hand in hand with her grandson James, whose other hand was holding a large and rather alarmingly blue plastic diplodocus, a present from his proud grandmother. Chris and Emily were there, about to move into a newly adapted staff flat, with one of Miss Taylor's kittens joining her brother, Pangur, who was already ensconced in the convent. Chris was to be the guest house's official gardener and handyman, trained by Thomas, and Emily the receptionist, trained by Sister Bridget.

Nonna, Maria and Francesco had come to spend the summer with the Sisters, to help them get the guest house up and running. Sister Margaret looked over at Nonna Ellen. She knew that she had gone to lay flowers on Edward's grave, and her expression of peace showed that she had finally found closure.

Francesco took Maria's hand and kissed it.

'It's a miracle,' he whispered. 'Nonna will stay here with the Sisters over the winter and see the art gallery take shape, and we can travel again and have time together at last. I can take you back to Paris, treat you the way you deserve.'

'You are the miracle, my love,' said Maria, smiling into his face, and kissing him.

George and Matthew overheard, and smiled at each other. They too had learnt what small and big miracles unexpected love could bring about, how loneliness could be transformed, old and painful wounds healed.

'Join us for a photograph, Sister Margaret!' called Sister Bridget, who was standing with the Bishop, Sister Cecilia and Katy, who had come over from Italy, having finished her year at the Keats–Shelley House, and was staying with the nuns, deciding whether she should become their newest recruit. She was going to study for an MA at Fairbridge University, and help Sister Cecilia get together a little museum of religious life. It felt as though she had always been there, and already her cheerful, youthful presence and her tactful working relationship with Sister Cecilia made Sister Margaret feel more hopeful about the future of the Order. If Katy could join the three of them, and be happy, maybe more would follow. The university students who had come to help paint the rooms were a lovely bunch. Maybe there would be more vocations to the Sisters from there. Maybe the Sisters of St Philomena weren't finished yet. Margaret smiled at the thought as the photograph was taken, ready to be framed and put in the hall.

Emily and Chris helped Francesco, Maria and Katy hand around champagne, and the guests wandered through the convent, exclaiming at the changes and improvements.

Sister Margaret stole away from the cheerful crowd for a moment, and found a quiet part of the garden to pray. She sat in front of the newly cleaned-up statue of Our Lady, near the rose bushes. Little Pangur, their white kitten, followed her and jumped up on her lap, then curled up and fell asleep. The leaves in the garden trees and bushes rustled and turned bright sides out in the light breeze. She looked up at the blue sky and watched the clouds move across it, then down at the kitten.

'I'm just having a little break, Lord. I just want to thank you for all the new friends and new directions this year, and for new hope for the future. Bless this new retreat and guest house, and bless the new gallery Matthew is opening.'

Suddenly, she heard a robin sing. It flew down in front of her, cocked its head, looking at her with bright eyes, and then flew away, bringing tears to her eyes and a smile to her face.

'Thank you for that, Lord. I don't know if Sister Bridget's mother was right about robins being souls checking up on us, but thank you for Helen – and thank you, Helen, if you *are* checking up on us, for the prayers! I love and miss you so much, but I know you are in the right place, supporting us from Heaven, and I know that for now, I am in the right place too.'

She picked up the little white kitten who had come to them from Miss Taylor's the last one to be placed, and kissed the top of his head.

'And thank you, Lord, for little Pangur. Thank you for everything! You have filled our lives, and those of our friends, with big and small miracles, and I can't wait to see what you will do next!'

Acknowledgements

I started this book back in 2003, when I was studying part-time, one evening a week for two years, for an MA in Creative Writing at Canterbury Christ Church University, so the first people to acknowledge are my tutors, Dr Andrew Palmer and, very sadly, the late Sarah Grazebrook and the late Michael Baldwin. I also want to thank my fellow students there, who were inspiring to work with, and who gave me confidence.

After my MA I lost my direction and confidence a bit, but a commercial fiction Arvon course with Katie Fforde and Judy Astley was particularly life-changing. Not only were Katie and Judy so encouraging, and I rediscovered my voice, but one of my fellow students on the course was the writer AJ Pearce, who became my friend. For years afterwards AJ kept encouraging me to finish my 'nuns book', and eventually, seeing me draft and re-draft, dither and procrastinate, AJ and Katie Fforde could stand it no longer, and got together and secretly booked the amazing novelist Julie Cohen to mentor me and help me finish the novel. All I knew was that an anonymous person had paid for Julie to do some free mentoring – I had no idea that I had two fairy godmothers, or, in effect, three, as Julie went on to put in many more hours than she originally was booked for, just to get me to the end!

This book would never have been finished or reached an agent without them, and I can never thank them enough!

I have worked on and off on various versions of this novel for literally decades, and I am worried now that if I try to mention all the people I talked to about it, or showed bits to, over this long period of time, I will end up missing someone out, so I would like to say a general big and heartfelt 'thank you' to everyone, friends and family, who encouraged me over the years to keep on with my 'nuns book', who read earlier versions, and who listened to my ideas. You know who you are and I will do my best to thank you in person! I must, however, thank my husband and children, my friend Ruth Washington, who has listened to me talk about the nuns for years, Shelley Harris and Stephanie Butland for their teaching on a weekend course at Gladstone's Library, and my friends Fiona McCarthy, Kate Wilson, Virginia Moffatt, Katherine Mezzacappa, Janie Millman and Mickey Wilson for their feedback on the latest versions, and their encouragement not to give up!

Thank you to my agent for my children's books, Anne Clark, as towards the end of writing this book I have had less time for my children's writing, and she has been so patient and encouraging about this other commitment, and supportive of me as a person.

Thank you so much to Jo Unwin, my agent for my books for adults, for loving *Small Miracles* and for taking it on, and to all her staff, and to the team at C & W, for their hard work and enthusiastic support.

Thank you to Jade Chandler, who, while commissioning editor at Harvill Secker, took *Small Miracles* on, and did so much work with me on it, and then to Elizabeth Foley and Dredheza Maloku who carried on the work, looking after it and me when Jade left. Thank you to everyone who worked on it, and those who are selling it, and thanks for the absolutely beautiful cover (which made me cry when I saw it) designed by Dan Mogford, with the wonderful illustrations by Harriet Seed.

Importantly, I want to acknowledge Sister Margaret, an Irish religious sister I met when I was 15, and with whom I went to stay in the summer of my sixteenth year, over forty years ago now. When I was a six-year-old child growing up in a devout Irish Catholic home on a council estate in Hemel Hempstead, I wanted to be a priest. When told Roman Catholic girls could not be ordained, I decided I wanted to be a nun, and consistently stuck to that right up until my late teens, and then again for a brief time in my twenties. I went to a state-maintained convent school when I was 11 and loved the beautiful chapel, grounds and statues. I met my friend Katy there, the artist Kate Wilson, who has encouraged me to write for over forty years, and I so enjoyed writing that my fictional Bishop has a painting by her! As a student I was too in awe of the few nuns who were still teaching at my school to ever tell them about what I thought was my vocation, but I met my Sister Margaret, who was from a different Order, on a pilgrimage when I was fifteen, and she invited me to come and stay with her community in Scotland. I went and I had such a lovely time.

Before visiting Sister Margaret I had never lived in a convent. I met an elderly nun whose false teeth whistled when we prayed in chapel, and who had been a choir sister, and was rather bossy to another, very patient elderly nun who had been a lay sister. I met a nun who cooked for a bishop, and I even met the Bishop himself, and was shown his collection of relics, a memory I have given my fictional Sister Margaret. The main things I remember about the community, however, are the kindness, fun and laughter. I remember being surprised how they sat down and watched *Dynasty* together, a programme that was banned in my strict Irish Catholic home. I met a nun who was a nurse, more who were teachers, and I was struck by how different they all were, and how they lived, prayed and laughed together, and tried to love each other.

My Sister Margaret was already a retired teacher when I met her forty years ago, and though we exchanged Christmas cards, and she sent me a card and present for my wedding, over the years we somehow lost touch. Writing this makes me feel both very grateful I met her, and very sad that I lost touch and can't hug and thank her in person now. I have absolutely no doubt that she is in heaven, and, I am sure, having fun. In character she was very like Sister Bridget in this book – full of enthusiasm and kindness. She taught me to look for joy in vocation, and that, funnily enough, helped me realise my own joy lay in marriage and family life.

Sister Margaret and the other sisters that summer also gave me an insight into how living in community with women can be, and so I want to thank all the wonderful women I ended up sharing houses with in the years between university and marriage aged 30. We may not have worn habits, or taken religious vows, but we still had to live with and to try to love each other and make allowances for our differences, and we also had lots of fun! I am so glad you are my friends and 'sisters'.

Sisters Margaret, Bridget and Cecilia are imaginary, and their Order is fictional. I was lucky enough, however, to get feedback as to whether their community life was believable from some real-life nuns and religious sisters, so I want to thank various #nunsoftwitter I contacted. It is important to say they are not responsible for the plot or anything else – I just asked them to read my book and confirm the community was believable. Thank you to Sister Walburga (@SisterWalburga), Sister Miriam McNulty of Turvey Abbey (@BirgitteUna), Sister Cathy Edge rsm (@KnittingNun), and Sister Silvana Dallanegra rscj, (@Silvanarscj). Silvana not only advised me on how convent communities work, but also on Italian cooking and customs! Thank you also to Franciscan Sister Clare, who I know 'offline', for her feedback on, and enthusiastic support of, my fictional sisters, and for her prayers!

I got the idea for nuns playing the lottery from a fascinating documentary I watched years ago on TV, and later found again on YouTube, which was about the Sisters of the Bar Convent in York. The Sisters there turned their convent into a wonderful B&B, which I have been to, and recommend.

The method Sister Cecilia used to choose the lottery numbers was the method my lovely dad used. He never won, but he never gave up hope, and I am sure he and my mum have won the ultimate prize and are up in heaven with the original Sister Margaret now, having 'the craic', as Dad would say! Mum died in 2014, Dad in 2017. When Dad was dying he told me he was looking forward to seeing Mum again and said 'sure everyone

I know is up there – and some of them were wild!' I know this book would not have been written without the faith they passed on to me, and their humorous takes on parish life, and I hope they can see it now and are glad!

Lastly, I am not a nun or religious sister, but lucky enough to be married to Graeme, my soulmate, and to have our four beautiful children together. This has ended up being the community I have happily spent the last twenty-six years in, praying and laughing (sometimes crying), learning to love, and making mistakes and asking for forgiveness, and having lots of fun, so this book is dedicated to religious sisters and nuns, to my friends and relations, but most of all to my family – the existence of which feels like a miracle to me! I dedicate this book to them.

Return to the joyful company of the Sisters of
Saint Philomena in

SWEET MERCIES

Coming October 2023

An uplifting adventure about family, friendship
and forgiveness

Pre-order your copy now